BROMBURY

By the same author

The Briarmen

BROMBURY

JOSEPH A. CHADWICK

Crescent Swan
Publishing

First published in Great Britain in 2025
by Crescent Swan Publishing.

ISBN 978-1-8383084-5-2

Crescent Swan Publishing
www.crescentswan.com

For Liz & Josh

Contents

To have another language is to possess a second soul.

Charlemagne

And those things do best please me
That befall prepost'rously.

A Midsummer Night's Dream, William Shakespeare

PART I

The Squire

Chapter 1
Crécy

August, 1346

'**B**rombury! Are you trying to get yourself killed?'

Sir Leland Lockwood's jibe bellowed amidst clashings of steel and sheddings of blood, as if he had, indeed, intended for men on both sides of the battlefield to hear him belittle his squire.

'Apologies, Sir,' Hugh's voice, however, was drowned out by the ongoing battle. 'T'was a mistake. It shan't happen again.'

Whether or not Sir Leland had heard his grovel, Hugh couldn't say, though he was sure the knight would not have bothered to humour him with a response if he had. It had been a foolish mistake, there was no doubt about it. To drop one's sword was, at the best of times, embarrassing, let alone whilst on the field of battle. Despite the much-trodden mud, it had still *clanged* as it hit the ground, a sound which had caused the passing Sir Leland to turn his head, slowing his horse's gallop, it seemed, for no reason other than to reprimand his squire. *Of course, it had to have been as he rode by,* Hugh now found himself thinking, having scrambled to his knees, muddying his gambeson in an effort to retrieve the blade. It was lucky that the enemy was not all too near when Hugh had decided to draw his weapon and charge towards the fray, not actually managing to successfully draw it, let alone charge. It would only have taken one opportunistic Frenchman, after all, to have seen the young squire's grip falter, and then he would have been not so much a young squire, but a dead one.

But luckily Hugh was atop the hill, along with a great many more of his countrymen, and as such, the chances of an opportunistic Frenchman actually making it that far were considerably low. Not only would his would-be-foe have had to ascend the recently rain-sodden slope to have landed the circumstantial blow, but he would also have had to pass the English's far-stretching makeshift barrier; hedgerows and trenches and stakes driven deep in the ground. And it was, in all honesty, highly unlikely that this Frenchman would have made it that far, what with the English's densely deployed longbowmen picking the enemy off from a distance, their devastating volleys raining down onto French cavalry from above.

It had, so far, been a relentless onslaught from the longbowmen, the likes of which Hugh had never seen. That was due in part, perhaps, to the fact that, until that very morning, he'd never before stepped foot on a battlefield. That wasn't to say, having been educated in the ways of chivalry, courtly manners and (perhaps not so successfully) combat since becoming a page at seven years young, Hugh hadn't witnessed his fair share of danger. For those first five years as a page, and his subsequent years squiring – albeit for another knight, whose company he'd far preferred to Sir Leland's – he'd stood by and watched a great many tourneys and brawls, not to mention the occasional duel and even one small-scale siege. Now a man of seventeen, Hugh had been in many a scrape whilst squiring for that very knight, and seen more than his fair share of—

Blood.

Blood was pouring out of the tunic of the man who stumbled towards him. He was using his longbow to help him walk, or try to walk, but after a couple of laboured strides he let it fall to the ground, his hand shooting to cover where the blood was gushing from.

Hugh could see now, as the man fell to his knees, that *he* was a longbowman, one of theirs, only, he was no longer shooting arrows at the French, on account of having been pierced by one just beneath his right shoulder.

'Steady, friend,' Hugh called, approaching the wounded man. 'I've got you.' He knelt down next to the longbowman and assessed the wound. The blood was spilling ceaselessly, the bleeder groaning and grimacing as the colour rapidly drained from his face. Rolling up the sleeve of his own gambeson and taking hold of the sleeve of the tunic beneath it, Hugh unsheathed a small dagger from the scabbard hanging from his belt and began to saw away at it. The linen was sweat-soaked, but between that and the thicker, quilted gambeson he wore over it, only one would make a workable bandage.

Within moments, he'd managed to cut a strip of linen with the blade, but once the sleeve was free, sweat and blood and dirt made securing the makeshift dressing less straightforward a task than he had anticipated. That, and the surrounding skirmish.

'God's mercy!' cried the archer as Hugh struggled to secure the dressing. The cries of battle now seemed to ever-louden as Hugh fumbled to tighten the torn sleeve around the man's wound.

'Forgive me,' Hugh stuttered. 'The arrow has pierced deep.'

'The pain from your fumbling cuts deeper than the arrow, boy!' the longbowman snapped.

'I... I've seen it done before,' Hugh responded, a meagre attempt to reassure the man. He thought back to his time with Sir Guilliam. Dressing wounds had indeed been a skill that his old mentor had insisted he practise on more than one occasion, but now Hugh was growing unsure of himself, his hands suddenly halting. 'I... I think this is how it's done,' he mumbled.

'Less thinking,' the longbowman responded through gritted teeth. 'More *doing*.'

Hugh shook his head, regaining focus on the task at hand, finding his fingers beginning to work again. With a deep breath he pulled the bandage around the wound, once, twice, three times, but the edges caught and tangled, causing him to tug at it awkwardly. The archer winced again, his jaw clenching.

'Sorry,' Hugh's cheeks reddened. 'I should've paid better attention, I've seen it done...' hesitantly, he began to adjust the dressing.

The longbowman managed a weak smile. 'Courage, lad,' he spoke through strained breath. 'My first time on the receiving end. I should've paid better attention too.' He offered a reassuring nod, and Hugh couldn't help but let out a faint laugh at his comment.

Finally managing to secure the dressing – albeit somewhat unevenly – Hugh sighed and sat back. 'It's... well, it's applied,' he said with a hint of tentative pride.

'It'll do,' the longbowman nodded, though clearly still in a great deal of pain.

Nearby, French crossbow bolts fell from above, piercing the ground and perhaps another poor longbowman or two. 'We must back away,' the wounded man said. He attempted to stand, but could barely lift himself from the ground.

'Allow me to aid you,' Hugh said.

'Get yourself to safety, boy.'

'Lean on me,' Hugh ignored the longbowman's protests, helping him into a sitting position. Taking the man's arm on the unwounded side of his body, Hugh propped him up, using his shoulder to take the weight. Rising, he began to inch away. With each small step Hugh could hear the falling swoosh of arrows and clashing steel of swords, cries and cursing from knights and men-at-arms lingering in the air, above the thundering hoof-fall of charging French cavalry.

And now, suddenly, there was a great, glaring ray of light. It blinded him momentarily. Then he realised just how it had found its way into his eyes. It was bouncing off steel plate.

Steel plate worn by a French knight, riding straight for him.

Hugh's heart quickened. His sword was... where was his sword? He must have placed it down whilst assisting the man he now held, or... had he even picked it up after dropping it? He scrambled for his dagger and... no. It was gone too, also left aside during his efforts to give aid. Hugh looked up, meeting the gaze of the charging Frenchman. He frantically glanced around, a desperate search for a means to defend himself. His eyes landed on the longbow, the very longbow the man half-slumped over his shoulder had dropped moments before. His pupils darted between the man atop his horse, which seemed to be growing larger and faster and nearer, and the weapon on the floor. And then time seemed to slow as Hugh made his move. He crouched, carefully but quickly laying the wounded longbowman down on the ground, sliding free one of the arrows kept in the man's quiver as he did so. And then Hugh turned, making to seize the longbow.

He heard the gallops grow louder and closer as he reached the bow. The French knight was full clad in shimmering steel, from great helm to gauntlets, his plate armour glimmering and clanking as he charged atop his similarly adorned steed, plate armour also protecting its head and neck. Both the knight and his beast's metal were decorated with the colourful plumage of their country, an unmistakable sign of the lone warrior's allegiance as the pounding of hoof and clanging of plate grew nearer and nearer.

Hugh gripped the bow tightly in his right hand and brought arrow to bowstring with his left. As he nocked, he couldn't help but dwell, in that moment, on the last time he had held a longbow. It had been in the early days of his apprenticeship to Sir Leland, almost two years before.

'Focus, boy!' his then newly appointed mentor had barked at him as the arrow slipped from his hand and fell to his feet. 'Are you aiming for those targets yonder,' he'd gestured to the row of straw circles set up in the distance, 'or your own feet, Brombury?' Fellow squires, also lined up, longbows in hand, chuckled mockingly at this.

'My grip slipped, Sir,' Hugh had offered his excuse. 'My apologies.'

'You think the enemy will wait for you to pick up your arrow? They'd have cut you down by now.' Sir Leland had then glanced at the arrow on the ground. 'Again.'

Attempting once again (and with reddening cheeks) Hugh had then managed to properly nock his arrow. But as he pulled the string back, his arm had quivered under the tension. Thus, he sent the arrow into a shaky flight, striking the ground short of the target.

'Pathetic,' Sir Leland had uttered, shaking his head as he moved on to scrutinise the next lad's effort.

And now on a field in Ponthieu, Hugh once again found his hand quivering as he drew back the arrow. His aim was crooked, faltering, as he pointed the bow and the arrow it held at the charging knight. He could see now that the Frenchman wielded a warhammer; one side a solid, heavy metal block, the other an unforgiving spike. He was readying the swing now, his horse's gallop only furthering the momentum of the weapon. The knight gripped the weapon with both hands, effortlessly balanced atop his mount despite having no hold of the reins. One hand held near the head of the hammer, and the other further down the handle. The spike of the weapon was aimed at Hugh.

He released the arrow.

Pathetic.

In his mind he heard Sir Leland's words again as it missed the knight. Now upon the squire, the Frenchman swung the warhammer, and Hugh was all but frozen, his body unmoving, except for his still quivering bow hand.

But then he did move, though not of his own accord. He had *been* moved. Shoved aside. He hit the trodden grass beneath him with a thud, turning instinctively to witness the final moments of his saviour's life.

The longbowman fell, parallel to where he had pushed Hugh. His eyes met Hugh's – or what remained of them. His skull had been crushed.

Hugh lay there, unable to get up. The Frenchman was gone, the ferocity with which his horse rode taking him further into the fray which had now made its way behind English lines.

Hugh wasn't sure how long he lay there, staring at the longbowman's broken face. Then he noticed the bandage, his own torn tunic sleeve, still wrapped around the man's wound. It had loosened. He didn't quite know why, but for some reason, Hugh found himself reaching for it, redressing it.

'It's ok, Sir,' he was saying, not quite realising the words he spoke. 'I've… I've done this before…'

And then:

'Brombury.'

The bellowing voice was unmistakable. Hugh turned to see Sir Leland Lockwood, towering over him. His helmet was removed, revealing a mane of silky dark hair, matching that of the dark coated steed he mounted.

'What are you doing, boy?' The knight's manner was accusatory.

'I… I…' Hugh looked from the body of the longbowman to Sir Leland. He wasn't sure how to answer, because he wasn't quite sure what he was, in fact, doing.

'Get up,' Sir Leland commanded, sitting tall atop his horse, seemingly oblivious to the mayhem and violence unfolding all around them.

But Hugh was either unresponsive or unable to obey, as he simply stared at the makeshift bandage he had applied to the man's arm not moments ago, gripping the blood-soaked linen tightly in his hand.

Sir Leland tutted and dismounted. A steel hand at the end of a long armoured arm landed firmly on Hugh's shoulder, pulling him to his feet. As he unintentionally rose, Hugh's own hand remained around his torn-sleeve-turned-bandage, stripping it from the dead man's wound. He held it tightly, eyes fixed on the now bare wound and the arrow that stuck in it.

'It seems I was right,' Sir Leland spoke coldly. 'You are trying to get yourself killed.' He looked at the mangled face of the dead longbowman before them. 'Though it would appear you can't even do that properly.'

Chapter 2
The Stream

It felt, to Hugh, as though a very different sun was setting than had risen that day. Though they had died out hours ago, he swore he could still hear the echoes of the battle – the day itself had been etched by them. They had settled in a clearing not too far from a riverbank, with Sir Leland commanding his retinue to set up camp for the evening. A night of rest was in order, and come morning the long trek back to England was to commence.

Hugh, alongside Sir Leland's two other accompanying squires – Gilbert Giffard and Henry Somerset (two boys of similar age to Hugh, they had been apprentices to Sir Leland before he had begun his tenure under the knight; Gilbert was a blonde, lanky lad, whereas Henry was dark-haired and remarkably dense for his age) – were sat outside of the knight's tent. Two sturdy wooden poles formed the tent's simple frame, meeting at a peak, with a battered canvas draped over them and secured down by the retinue's tent-mender, a man name Peter, who, despite his perpetual limp and crooked stature, had erected the tent in no time at all. Of course, it was not the spacious pavilion that Sir Leland Lockwood was used to, nor was it adorned with the richly coloured silks and wools that you might expect such a pavilion to be prettified with, but he had travelled to Crécy with a retinue of only thirty-two, making such an elaborate set-up neither possible nor necessary (and had their stop-gap camp been finely furnished, they likely would have stood out amongst the many other English camps nearby, which in turn might have led fellow knights and their retinues to speculate that Sir Leland was, perhaps, not battle-hardened – neither good for his reputation or ego).

Of those thirty-two that had accompanied Sir Leland, there now stood twenty-seven, with five of his men-at-arms seemingly having succumbed to the French efforts earlier that day. Not that Sir Leland was bothered by this. None of those presumed to be perished soldiers had been loyal retainers, but rather a mix of paid mercenaries and professional soldiers, whose names, as far as Hugh knew, Sir Leland had not even sought to learn.

Presently, as the daylight diminished, Hugh and Henry sat outside Sir Leland's humble quarters polishing his armour, whilst Gilbert tended to his horse. It had been Gilbert who had removed the knight's armour, almost an hour prior now, and since then Sir Leland had not left his tent. The cook, an inconspicuous, elderly man by the name of Abbott, had been preparing a stew for most of that time, and by now Hugh and Henry and Gilbert, and likely all twenty-seven men who made up the remaining retinue, were beginning to salivate as their hunger grew, the aroma of days old venison, garlic and root vegetables lingering throughout the camp.

'Tell me, Brombury,' Henry said, shooting Hugh a sidelong glance as they polished steel and awaited Sir Leland's emergence, so they might tuck into a bowl of Abbott's stew. 'Did you really reckon that you could take that charging Frenchman, what with *your* bow-shooting?'

'You saw that?' Hugh spat out the words in reflex, the question causing him to suddenly feel somewhat flushed.

'So it's true then,' Henry smirked. 'You did try to shoot a knight?'

'I… I…' Hugh tripped over his words. 'Where did you hear this?'

'Gilbert told me,' Henry nodded to their fellow squire, occupied with his task of taming the mane of Sir Leland's horse.

'Oh, I didn't *see* it,' Gilbert offered an answer, his attention remaining on the brushing. He continued to groom the animal for a moment, before turning to Hugh and Henry, his voice notably quieter as he spoke. 'Was Sir Leland who told me. Said you were all but dead, if not for that longbowman.'

Hugh's head dropped slightly at the mention of the man who had saved him, the image of shattered skull still fresh in his mind.

'Good thing the Frenchman didn't turn back for you, Hugh,' Gilbert went on. 'Likely thought a squire with a weak bow-arm wasn't worth bloodying his blade.'

'Hammer,' Hugh said softly, amidst the snickering of his fellow squires.

'What's that?' Gilbert turned now to Hugh.

'It was a warhammer he wielded.'

'Perhaps he didn't see you at all, Hugh,' Henry added. 'Perhaps it was the Blind King of Bohemia. I heard talk of him charging into the fray.'

'Aye,' replied Gilbert. 'I heard talk too. Heard he met his end today.'

'John of Bohemia is dead?' Hugh's curiosity piqued. He, like many a knight, noble and squire, was more than familiar with tall tales of John the Blind King of Bohemia. It could quite rightly be assumed that every man in camp knew of his exploits across Europe, in fact. From campaigns in Italy to Hungary and crusading alongside the Teutonic Order against Lithuanian pagans – where he would indeed become *the Blind* – the King of Bohemia was revered as a most formidable knight errant. It was more recently that he had lent his support to the French, and thus had found his way to the very same field in Crécy by which the three young squires were now discussing his even more recent demise.

'So they say,' Gilbert answered.

'And what of his end?' Hugh asked, intrigued. 'Did you hear how it happened?'

'I know not,' Gilbert shrugged. 'There were simply rumours of his body.'

'With sword in hand,' came the halting, deep voice of Sir Leland as he abruptly stepped out of his tent. Henry and Gilbert promptly returned their focus to their respective polishing and brushing, whilst Sir Leland's piercing green eyes met Hugh's and lingered. His words were clearly intended as a reminder of the squire's clumsiness that afternoon. 'Chivalrous to the very end. Though, of course,' Sir Leland strode past his three squires, his voice commanding the attention of his entire retinue, until he was stood in the centre of the camp. 'His loyalties were misaligned.'

Within moments, the camp had fallen completely silent. Sir Leland looked around, examining all with a cold demeanour.

'Listen well,' he said, his voice steady and words firm. 'On this day the English triumphed over French folly. They charged us believing themselves lions. But they were lambs, headed to slaughter,' he gazed now, out into the field of the day's battle of which their campsite overlooked. The deep crimson of the blood-soaked soil and the countless bodies that had spilled it, and now littered the land, were still visible, just about, as the sun set ever-lower. 'Quite something, isn't it? Our arrows darkened their skies on this day. The French outnumbered us five to one, and yet still they fell in their thousands to the English longbow.'

Cries of "Aye!" came in response, predominantly amongst the ten or so longbowmen in the camp. Sir Leland walked towards them, at which their cheers subsided.

'It's quite alright,' he assured them, now speaking with a grin. It was the first time Hugh could recall actually seeing the knight smile. It looked out-of-place on his face. 'You longbowmen have earned your merriment.' Sir Leland then glanced at one of the weapons of which they shared their name with. It had been placed, alongside various discarded bows and pouches, by the foot of a beech tree. 'May I?' he nodded to the bow.

'By all means, Sir,' replied the burliest looking and most bearded of the longbowmen.

Sir Leland brushed past the ten or so men, and picked up the bow before returning to the centre of the camp.

'Quite remarkable, isn't it?' he continued, examining the weapon. 'That so simple a weapon would prove the undoing of our enemy.

And to think there are those who believe that English might lies with the use of black powder and blast barrels,' he laughed mockingly. 'No, it is skilled marksmanship that won us the day!' More cheers, louder cheers. 'Oh, the terror they must have felt when our arrows rained down from above. Let the French know that terror next time they think to stand against us, I say. Let them never forget it!'

Sir Leland held the longbow high and further cheers followed, louder still. Hugh noticed that two of these cheers belonged to his fellow squires, as now Gilbert and Henry had been captivated by the knight's rousing.

'Today I witnessed mastery,' as Sir Leland spoke, all of the camp, aside from Hugh, were cheering and clapping and throwing fists in the air. 'Mastery of the longbow, and with it the might of our great England!' The cheering reached its loudest. 'And yet,' Sir Leland said as the applause faded. He turned now to Hugh, and his stern gaze brought with it the gaze of each and every man in the camp. 'I also witnessed incompetence.'

The camp fell completely silent.

It lingered.

'From one of my own squires, no less.' Sir Leland's voice was measured.

Hugh bowed his head.

'You are lucky, boy, that shame is all you left that battlefield with. It may well have been one less limb. Or *head*.' He sighed and once again looked at the bow in his hand. 'Tell me, Brombury, have I not endeavoured to train you to master such a weapon?'

'You have, Sir Lockwood,' replied Hugh, his voice cracking.

'After all, it is only right that a squire masters the longbow. As we witnessed today, it is a vital weapon in any English knight – neigh, any *Englishman's* – arsenal.' He looked about the camp. 'Wouldn't we all agree?'

Nodding and answers of "yes" promptly followed.

'One might even go so far as to say,' Sir Leland continued. 'That it is an Englishman's duty to have himself a good bow-arm.'

Further murmurs of agreement amongst the retinue followed. Sir Leland approached Hugh now, each step slower than the last, as if he were moving to some unheard, foreboding rhythm.

'Is it that you see yourself exempt from duty, Brombury?' he posed to Hugh.

'I… no, of course not—'

'Curious, that a *squire* of all people should resent his duty. It is, after all, expected that you will one day become a knight,' he was getting closer now. 'Do you *actually* want to be a knight?'

'Of course, Sir Lockwood.'

'Then why do you have such disregard for your duty?'

'I don't, Sir.'

'So you're just inept, are you?'

'No, Sir.'

'It can't be *both*, Brombury. Either you are inept, or you simply don't care for your duty.'

Hugh stuttered, unable to form words as the knight grew nearer still.

'Well, which is it?' Lockwood asked, commanded even, now mere steps away from his squire, towering over him, intimidating even without his armour. 'Are you lazy, or are you witless?'

'Forgive me, Sir!' Hugh cried out, slipping from his seated position to his knees, bowing his head at the knight's feet. 'It was a mistake, is all. A blunder, born in the bedlam of battle.'

Sir Leland stood tall over his squire, his chin raised and eyes looking down on the lad. His gaze lingered for a long, silent moment, the surrounding crowd enamoured by the accusations.

'I must train harder,' Brombury uttered, unsure of himself, but knowing it was down to him to end the quiet. 'I must strengthen my bow-arm.'

Sir Leland remained steadfast in his soundlessness. Moments passed. Then: 'Quite right.' He examined the longbow which he still held. Then he looked to Hugh. 'And what better time to start than this very evening.'

Another moment of uncomfortable quiet passed, so, with trepidation, Hugh reached his hand out, expecting to receive the longbow from Sir Leland.

The knight sniggered, snatching it away from Hugh. 'You shan't be practising with this, Brombury. We must start more simply.'

He turned his gaze to the edge of the camp, past Abbot the stew-cooker and his stew-pot and past Peter the tent-mender and the tent he had mended. His eyes landed on a great garment pile; a mound of grime-soaked gambesons, bloodstained tunics and all the muddied and soiled and torn and tattered fabrics that had been worn by the men of Sir Lockwood's retinue during the battle.

'Sir?' Hugh responded.

'What better way to strengthen your arm than to scrub and soak and rinse away the stains of today's skirmishes.' The knight spoke through a sardonic smirk. 'As for the rest of you,' he suddenly turned his attention to the onlookers. 'Time to eat.' He looked to Hugh.

'You can join us when the clothes are clean, Brombury. Though, I can't promise there'll be much in the way of leftovers. Nothing builds up an appetite quite like killing Frenchmen.'

Sir Leland sniggered as he walked past his squire with disregard, the twenty-six other men in his retinue sniggering in-turn, sniggers which quickly became mocking, lasting laughs.

There was a stream not a stone's throw away from where the men had set up camp. Not a stone's throw, that is, if all you happened to be doing was simply throwing stones. To lug great loads of what the men had that day been garbed in – to and from the water (and weighed down by wetness on its return journey) – made the stream seem not so close at all, at least to Hugh. In fact, by his fifth trip, and what with the air accented with the smell of freshly served stew (seconds, or even thirds, by that point) the stroll from the camp, down the hill and to the water was becoming arduous, and Hugh's appetite grew with each shame-wrought step and every sordid scrub.

His hands, by this point, were dyed red with the blood of men he had never met. Hugh didn't mind the blood too much, however. It was the darker stains, the ones that still stunk, that he found somewhat nauseating and were causing him to dry-heave. Perhaps Sir Leland had been doing him a kindness by not letting him eat, he thought, for if he had, it would surely have proven a waste.

The stream in which Hugh now sat by had been, until his arrival, rather tranquil, and the water in which his hands scrubbed and rung out all manner of filth into had been almost pristine. It was cold but refreshing against his skin and he wished, now having worked up a sweat, that he had taken a quick bath in it himself, before muddying it with the stains and blood and shit of the day's struggle.

And yet, despite the dirt which now drifted from the impromptu wash station, the fading light of the evening sky meandered gently upon the rippling surface of the stream as Hugh toiled; a contrasting backdrop to his own dour reflection. With a heavy sigh, he looked into the water; into his own eyes. He examined his tired and weary face, and the flop of greasy, unwashed ginger hair that sat atop it. He looked as gaunt as he now felt, and the only thing he wished for more than a bowl of Abott's stew was to be rid of the stench of the soiled garments surrounding him, which was, he worried, quickly becoming perpetual. His face, he could see amidst the gentle ripples of the stream, bore the marks of the day, a bruise from his brush with death visible beneath his right eye. Staring into the blue of his pupils, he fished out and rang a bloodied coif which had been soaking, and the reflection of his weathered face in the water dissipated with a sudden swash of red.

Chapter 3
The Missing Medallion

June, 1343
Smithfield

Still staring into the blue of his pupils, Hugh rang out the wet cloth into the bucket below, his fresh-faced reflection now clear as day across the surface of the breastplate before him. He wiped the armour dry before taking a strip of linen and beginning to buff, and before long the chest piece had a smooth shine to it.

He could hear the anticipation mounting amongst the crowds outside. Nobles and peasants alike had gathered, the latter demographic likely mingling with locals, discussing with great excitement the grand procession that all eagerly awaited. Amidst the masses, vendors sold their wares, with stalls lining every street surrounding the arena, offering no end of refreshments, from roasted meats, pies, pastries, fruits and cheese, to flagons full of ale and tankards spilling with mead. Others offered vibrant jewellery pieces and trinkets, with all manner of metals on display; some peddled pewter plates and silver spoons, whilst others flogged amulets adorned with semi-precious stones. In the distance, Hugh could hear the trumpets heralding the coming event, followed by the clashing melodies of the many minstrels who'd made the journey to the market, no doubt with hopes of replenishing their repertoires with fresh ballads by day's end.

'As pristine a polish as ever,' Hugh heard the sportive, though ever sincere, voice of Sir Guilliam without so much as hearing a footstep first. Though, upon turning around, the knight stood before him, arms crossed, wearing a warm expression.

'I learnt from the best,' Hugh replied, returning the compliment.

'Really?' Guilliam queried. 'You shall have to let me know their name.'

It took a second for Hugh to pick up on the knight's playful tone, though Guilliam confirmed his jest with a chuckle, stepping forwards to examine his own reflection in the breastplate.

'Cleaning armour was never one of my talents, back in my squiring days.'

'Much better at bloodying it, Sir.'

Guilliam shot Hugh a look. For a second, the squire was worried he had spoken out of turn, but yet another chuckle from the knight reassured him.

'Quite right, Hugh. As long as it's not my blood, of course,' he ran a hand through the white hair atop his head as he studied his reflection. 'Especially not today.'

'You've nothing to worry about, Sir.'

'And what makes you so confident of that?'

'Why, of all the knights competing, you're surely the most...'

Hugh paused as he pondered the right word. 'Seasoned,' he settled with.

'I was worried there that you were going to accuse me of being chivalrous,' Sir Guilliam replied, a grin forming on his face. 'And seasoned a knight as I might be, I still need help getting my armour on.'

Hugh obliged his mentor and began the all too familiar process of assisting Sir Guilliam into the freshly polished steel suit. By the time the knight was almost fully adorned, the spectators, by the sound of it, had multiplied, as had the trumpeting and the heralding. It was no doubt due to the fact, Hugh thought, that by now a great many other steel suited knights were likely making their way into the arena atop similarly suited steeds, squires in tow, bearing their mentor's banners behind them (and likely all their other worldly goods). Huxley, the steed on which Sir Guilliam made to mount momentarily, was a dark spotted destrier, as formidable as his rider once was, though as aloof about displaying the trait as Sir Guilliam himself. Competing in a tournament, however, was not the time to maintain such aloofness. It was at such events, after all, that Guilliam had made his name as one of England's great knights, albeit a great many years prior. Hugh had, mind you, only ever seen his mentor compete in one tournament, not long after beginning his tutelage. Of course, he had heard of the knight and his noble exploits far before that, as had all boys Hugh's age from families who worked noble estates. Sir Guilliam the Great, they'd called him, at one time thought to be the finest tourney knight in all of England. It was undoubtedly why he'd been invited to the impending affair (as he'd made sure to mention to Hugh on multiple occasions since having received the request) by none other than King Edward himself.

'I'm far too old to be jousting,' Guilliam had stated frequently during the weeks preceding the tournament. 'It's an empty gesture, nothing more.'

Hugh had responded, on one particular occasion, something to the tune of: 'But you've been invited by the King, Sir. You can't refuse.'

'Can't I now, young Master Brombury?' Guilliam had answered with a smirk. 'As you yourself say, I've merely been *invited*. Not commanded, nor ordered. Why, I should think that leaves me perfectly entitled to refuse.'

The last tournament that Sir Guilliam had partaken in, the one that Hugh had seen, had been nowhere near the scale that today's promised to be. The reason behind such a turnout was simple: the tournament was to mark the jousting debut of the King's eldest son. The prince, named after his father, was thirteen years of age – only one year younger than Hugh – and had apparently received his first suit of armour at seven years young. It was said that the steel was as black as night, with a lion adorning the helmet.

As Hugh now stood behind Guilliam, he began to tighten the final straps, securing his mentor's breastplate. And then he stopped quite suddenly.

'Hugh?' Guilliam said as the pause lingered. 'What is it?'

Hugh loosened the already in-place straps.

'What are you doing?' Guilliam asked, turning now to face his squire.

'Are you not wearing it for the tournament, Sir?' Hugh queried, directing his eyes towards Guilliam's mail covered chest.

Guilliam looked down, lifted off his mail and now Hugh noticed a look of mild concern quickly becoming an unquestionably troubled expression, as the knight's hand shot to his bare chest.

'My medallion,' Guilliam uttered, frisking the rest of his body now, though shy of pouches or pockets. 'It's gone.'

'You mean to say it's…' Hugh paused. 'Lost?'

'It can't be,' Guilliam began to frantically search the tent. 'It never leaves my neck.'

That was, as far as Hugh knew, quite true. In all the time that he had served Sir Guilliam, Hugh had never seen the knight without the golden oval – attached to a chain of metal far less precious – around his neck.

'Did it fall as you armoured me?' Guilliam asked, now rummaging around in a chest of (less valuable) valuables.

'No, Sir. I only now noticed it wasn't there.'

'Don't just stand there, boy!' Guilliam barked, knocking over a table, sending its contents to the ground, spilling a jug of good wine and an assortment of bread and cheese that Hugh had been quite looking forward to sampling. 'Help me find it.'

Hugh was jarred by Guilliam's tone, if only for a moment. He had never spoken so sternly to his squire. Nonetheless, he obeyed the order, and started to search the areas un-rummaged by Guilliam.

Then the knight sighed and stopped his searching. 'Forgive me, Hugh,' he said, softly. 'To address you so fiercely is improper of me.'

'There is nothing to forgive, Sir. I am your squire, and yours to command.'

'That does not excuse my short temper.'

'I understand, Sir. I know what it means to you.' Hugh knew this because he had asked as much, on one occasion. The pendant had been handed down to Sir Guilliam by his mother, when he was a boy. He had told Hugh little of his life before knighthood, but in telling him why the medallion was so precious to him, Guilliam had revealed that he was the firstborn to a mother who had borne many children, the last of which she would not live to know. It was as his youngest sibling entered the world, and his mother slipped from it, that she passed on to Guilliam the medallion bearing the heraldry of her house. Her own mother had produced no male heirs for her father, and thus the house and the coat of arms would be forgotten, save for the medallion on which it had been engraved.

Hugh had seen it so many times, too many to count, and he could picture that very coat of arms in his mind as he too began unpacking chests, all the while casting a sweeping gaze over the inner furnishings of the tent. The pendant bore an engraving of three geese, wings spread, and a long faded Latin inscription around its edge.

After no more than a minute of the two of them searching, Guilliam glanced around the tent at the unpacked chests and overturned table. His medallion was nowhere to be seen. 'It is not here, damn it. It was around my neck this morning,' the knight looked pained as he spoke, as if he were indeed missing a part of himself. 'Yet now it is gone.'

'Might it have fallen off somewhere?' Hugh asked.

Guilliam chuckled in something of a hapless manner. 'I've no doubt it did. And I've no doubt it is *somewhere*, Hugh. Only I have no idea where that *some* is.'

'The inn, perhaps?'

'Maybe,' Guilliam pondered. 'Though I know for certain it was on my person when I woke this morning.'

'Is it not worth checking the room you bed in, Sir?'

'I… I would say yes, Hugh. It's just,' Guilliam cleared his throat.

'Well, the reason I know for certain it was on my person when I woke, is because it was the *only* thing on my person.'

It took Hugh a moment to comprehend what the knight was getting at. 'Ah,' he said once he did, subtly bowing his head.

'The… um… serving girl,' Guilliam continued. 'She remarked on my state of undress as I made to leave. I know for certain that I had the medallion on then, as I recall informing her that I was not, in fact, undressed, whilst gesturing to it.'

'The serving girl?' Hugh remarked.

Guilliam nodded, a bashful expression on his face.

'Was she not the innkeep's wife?'

'I was leaving through the window, when she said this,' Sir Guilliam cleared his throat once more.

'I recall you dressed when we met at the stable this morning,' Hugh said.

'She was kind enough to toss my shirt and hose out the window too. Though I suppose as much for her benefit as mine.'

Hugh smirked. 'So that's why you didn't take breakfast this morning.'

'I'll have you know she also stuffed a generous wedge of cheese into my left boot before sending it out the window. Alas, I am almost certain it's not at the inn. As you say, we met at the stables this morning.'

'You think the medallion fell off there?'

'It's possible, yes. And after, we came here and erected the tent. Though we know it's not here.'

'So between the stables and now, where else have you ventured?'

'I was wandering the streets, perusing peddlers and their wares, whilst you polished my armour,' Guilliam looked deep in thought, as if he were retracing his steps. 'The perks of being a knight,' he uttered with a healthy hint of self-deprecation.

'So we check the market square then.' Hugh said. 'It's bound to be there.'

'God willing, Hugh.'

On account of the impending tourney, the market that day was bigger than most and more well-attended than usual. Which, of course, only made the knight and his squire's search all the more tricky. In an effort to cover as much ground as possible – before the bustling centre inevitably grew even more bustling – they had split up upon reaching the stall-ladened square.

As Guilliam tried his best to retread the precise path he had walked earlier that morning, Hugh contemplated where to begin, overwhelmed by the sheer amount of people and the ever-loudening haggling of hagglers. Eventually, he settled on what seemed to be the only sensible route to take, and began making his way around the square stall by stall. Every which way Hugh looked he would meet a vendor's eye, inevitably offering himself up as their next potential buyer, be it men selling meats and bread or women offering eggs or cheese or poultry (or even all three). Amidst the many merchants of dairy and wines and spices and baked goods, there were those who sold silks and bartered over boiled leathers, and to add to the already over-packed area, sellers of livestock had started to set up shop, the cries of their cramped cattle worsening an already raucous racket. Though he politely declined each and every merchant and the goods they bid him buy, Hugh made sure to examine all the stalls he saw, paying particular attention to the much trodden ground beneath the feet of preoccupied patrons and passing purchasers.

Twenty minutes or so went by, but still there was no sign of the medallion, though there had been at least a couple of instances where Hugh had mistakenly thought he'd spotted his masters heirloom; first on display at a trinket stall and then amidst a medley of medallions belonging to a purveyor of precious metals, though upon closer inspection it was clear that neither resembled Sir Guilliam's, save for possessing a similar circular shape and golden shimmer. To make matters worse, with so many now making their way through the market, Hugh had lost sight of Sir Guilliam too. Every other step someone seemed to barge into the squire, as people became increasingly packed into the square, eager to acquire mementos of their attendance at the momentous and quickly approaching tourney. And quickly approaching it was, which was not lost on Hugh. He had walked the entirety of the market square two and a half times now, and decided he would wait for his mentor where they had left each other after completing his current lap. If Guilliam had not found his medallion already, then it would be down to Hugh to convince him to ride without it.

But then, as he approached where they had entered the square, Hugh saw it.

Well, not *it*, per say. More, something that stirred suspicion. The small boy with long fingers was a stone's throw away from him, though obscured by the plenty of peasants weaving past and barging into one another. But the woman that he had chosen was neither a peasant nor obscured. Hugh had no doubt this was precisely why the boy had chosen her. She wore a mix of silks and velvet lined linens embellished with intricate embroidery, and a tall, decorative fillet sat atop her head, draped with a white veil, the top of the headpiece making her ever-visible amidst the teeming market square. It was likely this inadvertent beacon that had drawn the small boy to her; a moth to a flame. Following the headdress himself now, Hugh had no choice but to barge his way past the gathering peasantry, all the while trying his utmost to keep one eye on the boy who stalked the woman. As he closed in on the two of them, Hugh could now make out more of the woman's finery. A gem-studded gold necklace hung from her neck, with similarly adorned silver earrings dangling from her ears almost meeting it. But these were not what the small boy's long fingers reached for. From the woman's girdle there hung a leather pouch, dyed bright blue; a contrast to the rich redness of her gown. A floral embroidery of gold and silver thread spoke not only to the preciousness of the pouch, but also the worth of its contents. And even if there was nothing of value inside, the metal clasps that fastened it had been impressed with tiny, glimmering gemstones, which would no doubt fetch a fair price in a market not dissimilar from the one the woman now naively walked.

Stalking his way within arms length of the boy who was stalking the woman, Hugh waited for his moment to act. The boy was perhaps half his age, nimble and dirty, though not too dirty that he particularly stood out amongst the many peasants. Roughly-woven patches of mismatching fabrics made up the oversized tunic and tattered cloak that covered the young urchin, a frayed rope belt seemingly keeping his clothes from slipping off. The sandals he wore were little more than scraps of old leather, though he managed to step silently in them; silently enough to make his way, unnoticed, close behind the decoratively dressed woman (moving slowly as she browsed her way along the stalls), who was quite clearly none the wiser to his fingers as they all but grasped her pouch.

Hugh waited until the boy's forefinger brushed the tiny gemstones. It was then he placed a hand on the oversized tunic draping the boy's bony shoulder. The boy startled, his long fingers withdrawing suddenly from their prize as his scrawny legs instinctively lurched to carry him away. The gaunt shoulder blade slipped from Hugh's grasp; evasiveness was clearly one benefit of undernourishment. But just as instinctively as the boy had made to dash, Hugh clenched his fingers tightly, securing a fistful of the baggy tunic. The already torn garment tore even more, allowing the urchin to almost break free of his clothing-turned-restraints. Almost.

Hugh tightened his grasp and contracted his bicep, realising now just how light the boy was, as his hurrying feet were lifted from muddied ground beneath them, left simply treading air.

'Ged offa me!' the boy yapped, wriggling and writhing, plainly flummoxed. At this, the noblewoman he had been stalking turned suddenly and gasped at the sight of the squire holding the swaying vagrant, her hands shooting to the nearly stolen pouch, checking it was still on her person, before swiftly making away from the unsightly pauper struggling, suspended in the air.

'Easy there,' Hugh said calmly, his grip remaining tight, the boy dangling from his tunic as if he were a carcass stuck up on a meat hook. Though he would be the first to admit that he was not notably strong for a young man of his calling (at least, not compared to some of the squires he had known), it perhaps spoke to just how underfed the boy was that Hugh managed to maintain him mid-air with such ease.

'Calm yourself,' Hugh said after the boy spent a further few seconds fruitlessly squirming. 'I mean you no harm. If you stop struggling I'll put you down, but I'm going to keep hold of your tunic here.'

The boy lurched at Hugh, his uncut, filthy nails near clawing the squire's face, avoiding it only narrowly.

'I said calm yourself,' Hugh spoke sternly this time. 'I have a question for you. If you answer me truthfully, I'll set you down.'

By now the commotion had drawn the attention of passers-by, albeit with only those in more finely fitted attire turning their heads; the mid-air urchin going largely ignored by the peasantry, who were presumably more accustomed to the sight of robbers getting caught mid-robbing. With Hugh standing firm and the boy's efforts to break free proving pointless, eventually he did – reluctantly – calm himself.

'Before I take it upon myself to hold you by your feet and shake you, so I might see precisely how many precious goods you've helped yourself to thus far this day,' Hugh looked into the boy's brown eyes as he spoke, one of which appeared to twitch every few seconds. 'I am going to give you a chance to keep most of your pilfered spoils. I only ask that you give one of them up.'

'I thieved nothing,' the boy said, though he spoke so unconvincingly that even if Hugh hadn't caught him in the act he would not have been convinced.

'A gold medallion,' Hugh ignored the protests. 'With three geese impressed upon it. It belongs to a knight, he walked this market square this morning. Now is your chance to return it. Then I will set you free.'

The boy didn't respond, but he did look away, his twitching eye twitching even faster now.

Hugh gave him a moment.

'So be it,' he said when the moment had passed. Hugh grabbed the boy's twig of an ankle with his left hand and swung him upside down, grabbing the other ankle as he did so. Stolen goods met cobblestone before the squire even started shaking the boy; a block of cheese, loose coins, scraps of fancy fabrics. But no medallion, not yet. So Hugh began to shake the lad, with little else leaving the oversized tunic – now completely concealing the boy's face and somewhat muffling his increasingly agitated cries to be let go – as he did so.

'Where is it?' Hugh asked, as still no medallion fell. 'Give it up!' He shook the boy more vigorously, and now even the heads of the peasants accustomed to pickpockets and paupers being punished had turned to watch the commotion. But Hugh was unaware of his growing audience, his sole focus on retrieving his mentor's medallion.

'You don't understand,' Hugh said, as if he were now speaking to someone who wasn't really there (although if his words were indeed intended for the boy, they surely went unheard, what with the shaking and the tunic covering his face). 'He *needs* it to ride. I must return it to him. It's my duty.'

A clear crowd had formed now, a circle of spectators surrounding the commotion, though not a single one deciding to intervene, it seemed, with the audience allowing the undernourished urchin to be shaken with increasing intensity. Hugh only noticed that a silence had befallen the market – at least in his immediate surroundings – when finally someone did speak.

'Hugh?'

It was a familiar voice. The squire turned to the knight looking at him, amidst the gathered crowd of onlookers. Hugh stopped shaking the boy, slowly setting him firmly on the ground, though keeping a grasp of his tunic. Sir Guilliam raised his arm towards them. He held his medallion in his hand.

'It seems you were right,' the knight said. 'It was in the stables, after all.'

A great wave of embarrassment washed over Hugh, not least because of the crowd, but only now did it dawn on him that his handling of the boy had been perhaps a *little* too firm. He turned to the urchin, who was still gathering himself on the cobblestone, letting go of the fistful of fabric he'd held on to.

'Forgive me,' Hugh said, offering the boy a hand.

But the boy scurried away, pulling his tunic over his body as he made to escape into the crowd. He didn't get far, though. Two loosely armoured men pushed their way through the front of the circle of spectators, and one of them grabbed the boy. It was not armour of fine and polished steel – like that of the kind Hugh had spent his morning readying – rather ill-fitting chainmail beneath vests of boiled leather. They had the look of the local watch.

'What's all this ruckus here then?' the one who hadn't caught the boy barked, almost as grubby looking as the urchin himself, though certainly more well fed.

'That boy is a thief,' came another voice – a woman's voice. Hugh turned and saw the top of a fine fillet bobbing above the crowd. The peasants parted to reveal the woman who the boy had tried to steal from. 'This young man apprehended him, thankfully.'

The watchman grunted. 'Upholding the law's our business, not yours,' he said, his eyes darting to Hugh, a browbeaten look on his face. 'I should snatch you both for disrupting the peace.'

'You'll do no such thing,' Sir Guilliam stepped forwards, into the centre of the circle that had formed around Hugh.

'I'll do what I please in my jurisdiction,' the watchman released a thick pellet of spit as he finished his sentence.

'This lad is my squire, and as my squire it falls well within his chivalrous duty to upkeep the laws of the land, especially when it seems local authorities are unable to.' As soon as the words left Sir Guilliam's mouth, it was apparent there was no need for him to prove his knightly credentials. Even without his armour, he spoke with such self-assuredness and held himself in such a way that it was quite clear he was who he claimed to be, causing the abrasive watchman to shuffle back a step or two. 'Now, I suggest you retract your threat of punishment, unless you wish to explain to the King that the greatest tourney knight in all of England was unable to ride for him today, because *you* took it upon yourself to make a prisoner of his squire. And for doing *your* job, no less.'

A silence befell seemingly the entire market square now, as the watchman who had growled at Hugh cleared his throat, his partner eyeing him nervously.

'Right you are, Sir,' he half-spoke, half-mumbled. 'I weren't aware he was your squire. Meant no offence. We'll take this little thief and be on our way,' he gestured to the urchin held by his partner before addressing the crowd. 'Show's over you lot. Get back to your buying and selling.'

The onlookers gradually began to do just that, and as the circle formed by the crowd dispersed, the watchmen turned away, dragging the cutpurse behind them.

'Wait,' Hugh beckoned the men as they grew obscured amongst the now disinterested market-goers.

'Best not to goad them now, Hugh,' Sir Guilliam placed a reassuring hand on his squire's shoulder. 'Come, I've got my medallion. No harm's been done.'

'The boy—'

'Would have got himself caught eventually.'

Hugh sighed. He supposed Sir Guilliam was right. He turned to follow his mentor, though couldn't help but take one more look over his shoulder at the watchmen.

'No,' he said to himself. And then he marched towards them.

'Hugh—'

But Hugh didn't hear the rest of what Sir Guilliam said, as he had pushed his way through the crowd and fast approached the watchmen. 'The boy is not to be punished,' he declared, once in earshot of them.

A look of surprise came over the urchin's face as the watchman who had addressed Hugh only moments ago turned.

'The boy is a thief,' he said, beneath an expression that suggested he would have said something far less polite, had he not so recently been informed of Hugh's vocation. 'Thieves get punished here.'

'And what evidence do you have of him thieving?' Hugh asked.

At this, both of the watchmen turned to each other, baffled. The look of surprise on the boy's face was slowly becoming one of hopeful anticipation, as he realised that Hugh was now trying to aid him.

'Why, you yourself caught him,' said the other watchman – the one who had first grabbed the boy and was yet to speak.

'Alas, I believe I was mistaken. This boy is no thief,' Hugh turned slightly, noticing Guilliam in the corner of his eye. The knight stood back ,watching with one brow raised.

'What of these, then,' the other watchman, the one who did the talking, stated more so than asked, revealing, in the palm of his hand, the coins that had fallen from the boy when Hugh had shaken him.

Hugh said nothing in response, merely staring at the coins.

The watchman chuckled. 'As I thought,' he said, making to turn away. 'Or are you to tell me the little cutpurse *earned* this?'

'Not yet,' Hugh said. The watchmen faced him once again. 'But he will. I gave him the coin. It's his payment in advance.'

'In advance for what?'

'Helping me prepare Sir Guilliam's steed for the tourney.'

The watchman gawped, and then looked at the knight looming behind Hugh. Guilliam, with a smirk, simply shrugged.

'You're lying, lad,' the watchman snarled.

'Maybe I am,' Hugh said. And then, mimicking his mentor, 'Or, maybe, you wish to explain to the King why the greatest tourney knight in all of England was unable to ride for him today.'

The talking watchman gritted his teeth as a look of confusion washed over the other one. After a moment, he harrumphed. 'Ave it your way, squire,' he said, shoving the boy towards Hugh. 'Though I'll be holding on to this,' he gestured to the handful of coin. 'For wasting our time.'

'By all means,' Hugh said, courteously bowing his head as the two watchmen ambled off. He watched them until they were too difficult to spot amongst the crowd. 'As for you—' Hugh began, though as his eyes shifted to where the boy had been standing, he saw that he was speaking to no one. The boy was gone.

'Not bad, Hugh, not bad,' Sir Guilliam chuckled as he walked over to his squire, giving him a pat on the back. 'Very noble of you indeed. Now, seeing as you've lost your young assistant, you'd best get to the stables. As you said, there's a steed needs readying.'

Chapter 4
Ragstone

September, 1346

The stink never quite left Hugh.

During the return journey, that is. Lugging great loads of soiled, sweat-soaked clothes had imparted upon him a certain scent, and not even a stern sea air had stripped the stench from his person. Even now, as Sir Leland's estate grew faintly visible in the distance, Hugh could feel the lingering remnants of the once pungent potion of odours clinging to him. Thankfully the journey home had passed fairly fast, all things considered. Many of the retinue who had accompanied Sir Leland had parted upon stepping foot on English soil, or – in the case of the mercenaries – had stayed put in France, hoping that they might find an English garrison or two in need of their services.

Those who had returned had headed for the coast of the English Channel on horseback, riding until they found a merchant vessel that might take them. As luck would have it, the first they came across was set to depart the very same afternoon they found it. It was not an English ship, but an Italian one (trade between England and France was, as it stood, somewhat turbulent), which was set to dock at an English port as part of its route.

Hugh found no sympathy aboard the ship, least of all from Sir Leland, who had not afforded his squire so much as a glance since the public reprimanding in camp. He had almost been grateful for the smell which hung to him during the return journey, in so much that it, for the most part, meant that none of the men from the retinue bothered to belittle him further, the stink proving to be quite the deterrent. The only members of their company he did exchange with during their time at sea were his fellow squires – Gilbert and Henry – Sir Leland having made them his emissaries for relaying commands to Hugh.

'Heavens above!' Gilbert had proclaimed on one such occasion as he made his way down into the lower decks and traversed through the cargo that filled Hugh's "quarters" – crates full of sought after spices and other such commodities. 'Reeks rank enough to curl the hair on a donkey's back down here, Brombury.'

'I seem to recall some of your garments in the pile,' Hugh had replied. 'Quite unpleasantly stained, if I remember rightly.'

Gilbert half-scowled in response to this accusation, though rather than openly deny it, was quick to relay the message from above.

'I'm to let you know that we expect to dock the day after next,' he said. 'Then we ride for Ragstone. You're to ride as if there are ten horses between us, so not to blight us with stink, and bathe upon arrival, *before* "insulting Lady Lockwood with your foul stench." Sir Leland told me to tell you those words precisely.'

Though, by rights, the name of Sir Leland's manor house, when most mentioned Ragstone they were referring to the estate as a whole, including the mill and the chapel and the village, and homes within, inhabited by a peasant tenantry that worked the agricultural acreage (roughly three-and-a-half-thousand acres, much of which remained uncultivated woodland). The village itself was modest, and sat south of Sir Leland's manor house, a house built atop a hill, allowing him to overlook the entirety of his estate, the chapel to the west and the water mill to the east. Hugh's quarters were in the courtyard – as were Henry's and Gilbert's – adjacent to the stables and armoury, in which, when at Ragstone, much of the three squire's time was mostly spent. It was a life of tending to the Lockwood's many mares, punctuated with polishing steel plate. It was fair to say that more horses than one might expect to find in a knight's stables could be found at Ragstone, on account of Sir Leland's wife – Lady Mabel Lockwood – being a keen rider; not the most conventional of pastimes for a woman of Lady Mabel's standing. No doubt Sir Leland would much have preferred his wife to engage in pursuits more suitable – embroidery, for instance. But she had, as Hugh understood it, been riding since she was a young girl, and Sir Leland had not always been a man of such noble standing, having acquired his knightly status, and in turn his estate, solely through his marriage to Lady Mabel. Hugh didn't know much about her father, other than he held an important station in King Edward's court, and had allowed a man of much less importance to marry his daughter, that man being Sir Leland. All things considered, tolerating Lady Mabel's love of horseback riding, untoward as it was, was a small price to pay for Sir Leland, what with the land his marriage had afforded him.

* * *

A fair few nostrils flared as he rode through Ragstone's village. He had ridden as far as he thought ten horses might be behind the returning retinue, as instructed, with Gilbert Giffard having begrudgingly lent his horse to Hugh, at Sir Leland's command (forcing him to share with Henry, straddling what little saddle-space remained).

'Master Brombury!' Old Hattie had called out, beating a rug as Hugh's horse trotted past her cottage. 'Was worried we'd lost you in France when I didn't see you riding with Sir Lockwood's—' a whiff struck her as Hugh drew nearer. 'Heavens lad, don't tell me that's you carrying that stink.'

'Forgive me, Hattie,' Hugh said with reddening cheeks.

'No wonder they left you trailing behind,' she'd half chuckled, pinching her nostrils.

He received similar sentiments from the residents of Ragstone unfortunate enough to catch a whiff, but soon enough he was through the village and up the hill. After seeing his borrowed steed to the stables – which for once smelt better than him – he made sure, as per Sir Leland's orders, to head straight to the bathing chamber, as not to "insult" Lady Lockwood with his stink. Thankfully, upon entering, the coals beneath the cauldron were burning and the water in the half-full tub was on its way to being warm. What's more, sat keeping an eye on the cauldron was the welcome sight of Sybil.

'They told me you carried quite the stench,' she said as Hugh walked into the bathing chamber, her hand covering her nose. 'Thought it best I warm the water for you. And good thing I did.'

'Thank you, Sybil,' Hugh smiled.

'You can thank me by getting in, lad,' Sybil said, with a playful wince. She was a woman of later years compared to Lady Lockwood's other handmaidens, though that wasn't to say she was particularly old, not like Old Hattie. Sybil did, however, possess an almost entirely grey head of hair, despite having a relatively unwrinkled face, and Hugh had heard it said that she was actually no older than thirty years of age, though he thought it improper to ask. Of all the handmaidens who worked at Ragstone, he assumed that Sybil had worked there the longest. He also found her to be his favourite, for the simple fact that she was the only one who ever spoke with him on matters other than attending to the Lockwood's needs.

'Should be nice and hot by now,' Sybil said, lifting the cauldron by its handle and carrying it carefully over to the tub, filling it enough for a person to bathe. 'Now in with you,' she said to Hugh, placing the cauldron down. 'And don't be getting out until you've scrubbed that stink clean off.'

'That I can do,' Hugh said with a smile. Sybil left the chamber, closing the door behind her, leaving Hugh to undress. Finally rid of his reeking clothes, he stepped into the tub, dipping his toes into the steaming water first, before slowly submerging the rest of his torso, settling into a warm, rising mist.

By the time Hugh had finished bathing, his fingers and toes resembled dried plums and his skin was scrubbed redder than the hair on his head. But the stink was gone. It wasn't the water induced wrinkles that brought an end to his bath, however. There had been a knock at the door to the chamber followed by a voice.

'Forgive the interruption,' Sybil said as Hugh opened the door to her, half-dry and draped in a fresh knee-length tunic that she had kindly left out for him. She was holding what appeared to be a roll of parchment, sealed with wax.

'Is everything ok?' Hugh asked.

'I… I should have given this to you right away.'

'What is it, Sybil?'

'A messenger came. Two days passed. A fleeting visit, he left no sooner than he arrived. And he… he was looking for you. He delivered this,' she held out the parchment for him to see. He immediately recognised the seal. Three geese, their wings spread.

'Guilliam,' Hugh said.

'Your former teacher?'

'Yes,' Hugh found himself smiling. Since he had left Guilliam two summers ago, he had received no word from the knight. It had, in truth, been a sudden parting of ways, and to Hugh it came as quite the shock. He had since pondered whether or not Guilliam had ended his tutelage, sending him to seek servitude elsewhere, because of something he did. Perhaps the parchment would finally give him an answer, he thought, and then he found that his smile was gone, now worried that it might, in fact, not be such a welcome message after all.

'Forgive me for not telling you earlier,' Sybil said. 'Sir Lockwood prefers to be the first to look upon messages sent to the estate. I was going to pass it on to him. But, knowing it is meant for you… He has no knowledge of it. Still, I should have brought it to you straight away…'

'There is nothing to forgive, Sybil. Thank you.'

She smiled softly and handed him the parchment.

'What do you think it might concern?' he found himself asking her, knowing full well she wouldn't have an answer.

'Good news?' she said. 'At least I hope.'

'Me too, Sybil,' Hugh stared at the wax seal, its three geese staring back at him. 'Me too.'

Chapter 5
A Piece of Parchment Presents a Pressing Predicament

Hugh,

I would pray that these words reach you, were I still a praying man. Instead all I might do is hope that you yet remain in the service of Sir Leland Lockwood, and reside at the Ragstone estate. If you do not, and still this message does somehow eventually find you, then I would ask you burn it now. For it will, by then, be too late.

I doubt very much that you'll have heard what's become of me since you left my service. I never divulged to you, then, the truth of why I abandoned my knightly duties, and for this I am sorry. Believe me when I tell you that my reasons for concealing this from you were justified.

As you well know, those open about their waning faith tend not to fare favourably. And yet, with the passing of years, I found I was increasingly unable to devote myself and my sword to the God that I had always served. A God in whose name I had driven that very same sword through the flesh of countless men. These deeds, I both told myself and was told, were deeds of honour and righteousness, carried out in His name.

But I began to struggle to see the righteousness in bloodshed. This feeling weighed heavy on my soul for many months. Perhaps even years, without my immediate knowing. And over those months, or years, I began to see things not as they are said to be, but as they are. The Church, I now believe, is tainted by the very sin that it had, many times, bid me cut down with my blade. And so I put down that blade, turned my back on the God in whose name I had wielded it, and I wandered into the wilderness. That, Hugh, is why I sent you to seek another to serve. It was not my age catching up with me, as I had you believe. But my conscience.

You are likely wondering what has become of me since abandoning the life of a knight. For many months I journeyed, not knowing quite what I was looking for, though I knew I was looking for something. Not answers, at least I think not. Just something else, something different. And I found a great many different things on my travels, many of them in alehouses, many more than I care to admit. Though I knew that none of these things were what I was looking for either. Until I stumbled across a village, that is. A village of two names.

The first name of this village is Crooklingsham. Tired from my travels, I stayed three nights in the inn, The Unpleasant Pheasant, a welcome establishment for a weatherbeaten wanderer, such as I was. Even more welcoming was the proprietor's daughter and serving girl. Ethel. Her's was the first smile I had seen on my travels that made me forget, if only for a moment, my worries and lift the weight from my weary soul.

As every village does, Crooklingsham has a priest. Father Roger Dobbe is theirs. When this priest learnt of my former profession (I fear I revealed it to a drinking den full of villagers over three nights of appreciating the local ale), he approached me with an offer of work. Before the priest had the chance to tell me what this would entail, I made it quite clear that I no longer undertook work which required me wield a sword. He assured me I would not need a blade, just a persuasive manner, which he, despite our recent acquaintance, felt sure I possessed. Low on coin and, in all honesty, hoping to stay another three nights at the inn, I accepted. This is when I learnt of the village's second name.

Ealdgeat.

Dobbe told me of a community living in the woods beyond the pasture. Pagans, he said. Heretics and heathens. I chose not to tell the good father of my own recent doubts, you'll not be surprised to learn. He said they'd settled in the woods the summer before last, keeping to themselves, but in recent months had begun to build homes on the outskirts of the village. And not just homes, but a signpost too. One that read Ealdgeat. With the outskirts in which they'd built this sign very much being within the boundaries of the village, and the village very much being called Crooklingsham, you can imagine that the villagers, with whom I'd enjoyed sharing ale, were not best pleased with these pagans.

And so, Dobbe said, it was fortuitous that God had sent a knight to Crooklingsham to dispel these pagans, to send them back deep into the woods, not with a sword, but with words, where they were welcome to return to keeping to themselves.

The next morning I set about making my way to the outskirts. Upon arriving at the settlement, I saw a sign that read Ealdgeat, just as Dobbe had told me. And beyond that sign were the heathens he'd told me about.

As I approached, their elder introduced himself to me as Eotenfrēond, a pagan name he'd given himself, no doubt. I explained to him that the priest had sent me to help resolve the grievances that the villagers had with their house building and sign writing, and asked if they'd mind returning to the woods. Eotenfrēond asked what I would do if they refused, to which I answered "tell the priest that you refused." He asked why they had sent me, and so I told him too how I was once a knight, so they must have thought me qualified. He asked what a knight was doing without a sword, and so I told him, and then he asked me a great many more questions, and before long I had told him near enough everything I have told you in my writing thus far.

After some time, Eotenfrēond had one final question for me. He asked if I would join them to eat that evening. And who was I to turn down a charitable offer? The whole reason for my being there, after all, was on account of my dwindling coin. He handed me a bow and said I was to join them on a hunt, and before I could ask where, or when, Eotenfrēond and a group of pagans set off into the woods. So, I followed. Amongst the group was Eotenfrēond, three men, and Eotenfrēond's daughter, Beorhtwyn, a girl not much older than you must be now. Curiously, it was her who led the way. It wasn't long before each of the three pagan men had shot rabbits, though still we ventured further into the woods. I assumed Eotenfrēond sought a beast with meat enough to feed more mouths, a deer or boar, and I suggested we split up to increase the chances of us finding one. But he simply bid me keep quiet and follow his daughter's lead. And so I did. For how long, I still cannot say, though as we ventured deeper, the passing of time began to feel peculiar. Before long I could not tell if I had been following for mere minutes, or if I had been in those woods for days.

What I saw next, I cannot put down in ink, for I simply do not possess the words to do so. And even if I did, I dare not, for fear that these words end up in the wrong hands. All I can say is that I knew, when I saw it, I had found what I was looking for.

Eventually Beorhtwyn led us out of the woods and back to Ealdgeat. To my surprise, it was only early evening by the time we'd returned, yet it had felt as though days had passed. We skinned and cooked and ate the rabbits and afterwards Eotenfrēond told me I was free to return to Crooklingsham. Instead, I asked him if I might stay a while.

I remained with the people of Ealdgeat for four nights before Father Dobbe and some men from the village came to find me. They were more shocked, it seemed, to discover me alive and well, and not carved up as part of a ritualistic sacrifice. Dobbe was less than pleased, to say the least, when I told him of my decision to stay with the pagans. But stay with them I did. Days became weeks and weeks became months. And oh, the things I have seen, Hugh. It was enough to make me renounce my old life altogether. All titles and worldly possessions, everything but my mother's pendant, which I have, as you know, always held dear. Ealdgeat was my home now, and I had no need for knightly riches.

Two days prior to my writing this, they found her. My heart broke when I heard. She was discovered by her betrothed no less, the blacksmith's boy, Hammond. Ethel, with the smile that made me forget all my worries, if only for a moment. Sweet and innocent Ethel.

He'd found her by the outskirts of the woods. Her body was bloodied, scratched and cut as if dragged through thorns. Whichever savage did this showed her no mercy. Yet to the people of Crooklingsham, there was no question who was responsible. It was by pagan hands she had perished. A ritualistic sacrifice, an offering to a false god. We knew this was not true, of course. Still, they came to us, led by Dobbe, parading poor Ethel's body, her father sobbing behind them, and Hammond behind him, demanding whoever responsible step forward and answer for their unholy crime.

What happened next, Hugh, is why I write to you. Not one of us in Ealdgeat stepped forward, because it was not one of us who had committed this heinous act. As we stood in solemn silence, Dobbe revealed that Ethel had been found clutching something. The priest held it high for all to see. A pendant. My pendant. There were few who knew it belonged to me amongst the people of Ealdgeat, but those who did couldn't help but turn to me. Their glances, brief as they were, were enough to attract Dobbe's own. And I could not deny to Dobbe and the band of vengeful villagers before me, that the pendant had indeed belonged to me. They asked me how it was that it came to be in Ethel's possession, but I could not tell them. It is not for them to know. My silence sealed my fate. I was shackled and taken back to Crooklingsham by the villagers and Dobbe, and thrown in the gaol.

My trial took place that very afternoon, overseen by Dobbe. It was a brief affair, with my pendant and lack of any reasonable explanation as to why poor Ethel held it all the evidence the priest needed to condemn me to death. Fortunately, I have been able to appeal to Dobbe's supposed Christian sensibilities. He has agreed to postpone my execution for one month, and granted me a chance to clear my name. Whilst I am to remain imprisoned, he has allowed me to employ a man of good standing and the Christian faith to investigate the matter further, on my behalf.

I have known many a good man during my life, Hugh, though none so good as you. And of all of them, it is you that I know will believe me when

I say that Ethel did not die by my hand. I am counting on it.

I hope you can forgive me for asking this of you, but I fear my life now depends on you making it to Crooklingsham before month's end and clearing my name. I trust this message has been delivered alongside a map, which will guide you to the village. You will have many questions, and upon your arrival I will tell you with words what I cannot in ink. Until then, I wish you a safe and hasty journey. I look forward to seeing you again.

Your friend, always,

Guilliam

Chapter 6
The Plea

Sir Leland remained stern as he read the words, the flickering candle flame illuminating his unmoving expression. Despite the soft silk of his loose tunic, he appeared to have grown irritable, shifting in his seat as his eyes looked over the parchment.

'You wish for me to grant you leave from my service?' The knight finally spoke upon finishing reading, tossing the message onto the table he was sitting at the head of, the parchment sliding past the golden goblet of wine he had been enjoying before Hugh had disturbed him.

'I do, Sir,' Hugh replied.

Sir Leland's eyes met Hugh's, affording him a lingering leer. 'And if I refuse. What would you do then?'

'I would beg you give me the chance to clear Sir Guilliam's name,' Hugh responded, forcing himself to meet the gaze.

'*Guilliam*,' Leland responded sharply. 'Just Guilliam, now. By his own admission, he has renounced all titles. He's nothing more than a pagan.'

'He is an honourable man, Sir.'

'He stands accused of murder, Brombury. And from what I've just read, there's a compelling case against him.'

'He claims he is innocent, and I believe him.'

'And *you*,' Sir Leland half-sneered, 'you truly think you can prove that? Even if you were to aid this man, it would seem to me that his fate is sealed.' Sir Leland stood. 'I cannot see one good reason to grant you leave. It would be a fruitless endeavour, at best. At worst, me allowing you to defend this man could sully *my* name. Though I don't suppose you had considered that.'

Hugh stood silently, still holding his gaze.

'That is all,' Sir Leland said. 'You may leave.'

Hugh remained standing.

'You may leave, Brombury,' Sir Leland repeated, an order this time.

'I believe he is innocent, Sir,' Hugh said. 'I am not yet a knight, and I know you think I never will be. Perhaps you are right. But I am your squire, as I was Sir Guilliam's squire. A squire serves his master, and in return he learns what it means to be a knight. I may not be a fast learner when it comes to jousting or archery, Sir, but I believe I have learnt a great many things about what it means to be a knight. A knight defends the innocent, where no other will,' Hugh paused, his mouth drying up, expecting Sir Leland to shoot him down with harsh words, or even the back of his hand, rather surprised, in fact, that he hadn't already. But he remained silent. So, Hugh went on. 'I believe Guilliam is innocent. And I wish to try my best to defend him. And so I ask again, Sir Lockwood. Please, grant me leave, so that I might travel to Crooklingsham before month's end.'

A quiet lingered. Sir Leland seemed to meander, leaving Hugh unsure whether or not he had even listened to his plea. The knight picked up his golden goblet and sipped, the subtle sound of fine wine being savoured filling the silence.

'I must say, Brombury, I'm almost impressed by your dedication.' Sir Leland placed down the goblet and picked up the parchment he had tossed to the side, glancing over it once more. After a moment, he nonchalantly handed it back to Hugh. 'Fine,' he said.

'Fine?' Hugh uttered, unsure if he had heard Sir Leland correctly.

'I grant you leave. Embark on this errand, if you so desire.'

'I— thank you, Sir Lockwood. Your generosity means—'

'Do not mistake me, Brombury,' Sir Leland cut in. 'Your speech caused me no change of heart. It merely occurred to me, as you rambled, that you are quite right. You will never be a knight. You're too weak. I'd be surprised if you survive the road. And if you do, you won't clear this pagan's name. So go, I have little use for you as it is. In fact, you've done more to sully my name by being in my service than you could ever do on this foolhardy venture. Guilliam's bad fortune is my good fortune, I suppose. It will finally rid me of you.' Sir Leland stood and walked past Hugh. Before leaving the hall, he spoke again, without turning. 'You were your parents' only child, correct?'

'I am the middle of five boys, Sir,' Hugh responded with a hint of hesitation, unsure why he had asked. 'Three died as babes. Pox took my older brother when I was six.'

'So you're the last to carry your father's name,' he looked over his shoulder, affording Hugh a parting half-glance. 'Just know that when you fail, and you will fail, the name Brombury will be forgotten.'

As the door closed behind Sir Leland, Hugh let out a sigh. His hand was shaking, just as it had when he'd held the bow on a field in France. It took a moment to steady.

Chapter 7
A Mount for a Matter of Much Import

To make it to Crooklingsham before the month was through, he would have to travel light – and fast. Travelling light was no issue, he had already packed the few possessions he owned into a satchel. To his waist was tied a half-full coin purse and a sword (not the blade he had carelessly fumbled on the field in Crécy, that had never been retrieved, rather a training sword in dire need of a good whetstone).

Travelling fast was where the challenge lay. He meant to leave before noon (having received Guilliam's message mid-morning, and speaking with Sir Lockwood straight after), and would have to in order to reach the village, which by his best guess would take five or six days to reach on foot, if resting was kept to a minimum. It would, of course, make for a much easier journey if he had a horse; the problem was, however, that all twelve of the mares and stallions at

Ragstone belonged to the Lockwoods, including the rouncey he had ridden back to the estate. But these were for the use of Sir Leland's retinue, and now that Hugh had taken leave of his service, he dared not ask the knight to lend him one, for he knew already what the answer would be. Of the twelve horses, Sir Leland owned four; his own black-furred battlemount and three smaller rounceys (ridden by his squires on occasion), with the remaining eight being the property of Lady Lockwood. Perhaps it was worth attempting to appeal to her better nature, Hugh thought – if she indeed possessed one.

So, he made his way to the manor house, and walked the halls towards Lady Lockwood's chambers, his head down and stride keen. He was wary of running into Sir Leland; after their conversation Hugh knew better than to linger on the estate. Fortunately, the halls were quiet, save for one of the young handmaidens, whose eyes Hugh avoided. Approaching the doors to Lady Lockwood's chamber, he took a deep breath, forming a fist to knock.

But before his knuckles met the wood, the door opened.

'Hugh?' Sybil said, surprised to see him outside. 'What are you doing here?'

He smiled. 'Is Lady Lockwood in her chamber?'

'Not presently,' Sybil raised an eyebrow. 'You wish to speak with her?'

'I… I am leaving Ragstone.'

'Leaving? When?'

'Soon. No later than noon.'

'Sir Leland is sending you away?'

'I am no longer in the service of Sir Leland.'

At this, Sybil's face dropped. 'This is because of the message.'

'Aye.'

'You have been summoned?'

'Yes. My mentor, the knight I squired for before Sir Leland, requires my aid. In offering it, I have forgone my tutelage here.'

'Oh,' Sybil did not try to hide her frown. 'Then I shall be sad to see you go,' she looked over her shoulder, into the chamber. 'Yet… you wish to speak with Lady Lockwood?'

'I was hoping she might allow me to take a horse. The journey to my former mentor calls for haste.'

'I should save you the time in asking then, Hugh. Lady Lockwood was unwilling to spare a single one of her horses even for her husband during your recent travels to France. I would be much astonished if she were to afford one to you.'

Hugh lowered his head. 'Then I best set off at once. The road is long. Farewell.' He turned and began back down the corridor.

'A moment,' Sybil called after him. Hugh stopped and turned his head. 'There might be one beast that the Lockwoods won't miss.'

It was hard to tell just how old the donkey was. Its legs were tucked beneath its stout body as it nibbled lazily on a tuft of grass, apparently unbothered by the two people staring at it.

'Lady Lockwood won't notice him gone?' Hugh asked.

'Oh, I shouldn't think so,' Sybil said. 'She may have to wait a while longer for me to carry the water from the well to fill her bath. This old ass does all the hard work for me.'

'Sybil, if it would burden you—'

'I will be fine, Hugh. I do not imagine he's many seasons left, in all truth. Better he serves you in your business than be spent fetching

Lady Lockwood's bathwater. Here, there's an old pack saddle in the barn. I hope it'll do.'

'It will, thank you Sybil.'

As Hugh set about saddling the ass, the sun nearing its midday summit, Sybil said, 'This old mentor of yours. What is it that he asks of you? If you don't mind my prying.'

'I… he has been accused of… a terrible thing. A thing which he has not done. And has asked for my aid in proving as much.'

'So you are to embark on a quest to save him?'

'Quest,' Hugh laughed. 'You have a fanciful mind, sweet Sybil. This is no quest.'

'No?'

'Quests are for knights. As of earlier today, I am not even a squire. No, this is but a matter of much import, to which I have opted to attend. Nothing more.'

'If you say so, young master,' Sybil smiled teasingly, and Hugh mounted the now saddled donkey. 'Though answer me this, if you will. This matter you have opted to attend. Will it be dangerous?'

Hugh did not reply right away. He sat atop the donkey and thought on Sir Leland's stark assumptions on how he would fare. Yet, with a smile he said, 'No more dangerous than wherefrom I have recently returned.'

'There are few places more dangerous than a battlefield.'

'And yet, I did return.'

With that, Hugh kicked his heel into the side of the donkey and bid it forth. It was surely no steed.

PART II

The Journey

Chapter 8
A Reluctant Wager

There remained perhaps an hour more sunlight when he happened across the inn. Having made better distance than anticipated – once the ass found its stride – and not knowing when next he might near such an establishment, Hugh decided that it was as good a place as any to stop for the night.

Upon entering, he immediately saw why the inn was named The Fighting Cock. In the middle of the alehouse was a large circle of boisterous bodies – rowdy men and even rowdier boys – jeering and cheering and cursing, ale splashing and spilling from their tankards, and in the middle of them the inn's namesake was playing out. Two large roosters reared their wings and frantically jabbed their heads, crowing as if trying to one up the other, or perhaps just in response to the surrounding frenzy.

Hugh thought better than to join the spectators, affording the poor animals no more than a glance before making his way towards whom he presumed to be the custodian of the establishment; an unclean looking man with brisk, greying mutton chops and stains of various shades and textures decorating his shirt. Much like his many customers, the inkeep's attention was fixed on the unfolding bloodsport.

Hugh stood for a moment, waiting on the innkeep, before making an *ahem* sound to gain his attention. Despite hearing him, the innkeep momentarily kept his eyes on the frantic fowls, before affording him a begrudged glance. But as his eyes met Hugh's they widened, as if he were quite astonished to see the squire standing before him.

'I'm after a hot meal and a room, if you've one spare,' Hugh said.

'Right,' the innkeep bumbled, an air of scrutiny about him now.

He eyed Hugh up and down, and it was only then that Hugh noticed how he may seem somewhat out of place amongst the regulars of such a haunt. He was dressed in fabrics far finer than anyone around – in clothes that were, to him, simply fit for riding. He hadn't given it much thought when he'd set off from Ragstone, but now he realised that such squirely attire might, perhaps, draw unwanted attention, in more remote regions.

'You lost, little lord?' the innkeep asked.

Hugh almost laughed at being called "little lord", though it quickly occurred to him that it was a reasonable assumption for the innkeep to come to. Though he carried a sword at his waist, he no longer wore the heraldry of Sir Leland, and with no overt indication of his being a knight-in-training, he most likely did resemble a "little lord", at least amongst present company.

And it was as the innkeep uttered those words that the circle of rowdy men and even rowdier boys' rowdiness diminished, a good few of them having heard the innkeep, and heads began to turn and jeers began to quiet, and before long all that could be heard were the vicious caws of clashing cockerels, and in that moment Hugh thought a better name for the inn might in fact be *The Uneasy Squire*, as all eyes in the alehouse were focused firmly on him.

'No, not lost,' Hugh spoke amidst the sudden air of tension. 'And not a lord,' he made sure to speak up, so that all could hear (for all the good it would do him). 'Just a traveller, weary from the road, looking to fill his belly and for a place to lay his head tonight.'

'Right,' the innkeep said once more, though the word was more drawn out this time.

At this moment one of the men from the crowd stepped into the makeshift arena and picked up one of the roosters, followed by another man picking up its opponent, and after a moment more, their fervent clucking and cawing had all but ceased.

'Here,' came a voice from the onlookers. 'It's custom to wager on one of these here cocks before filling your belly at these tables.'

Rather than turn to face the patrons, Hugh looked to the innkeep in the hope that he would dismiss this notion, though the man simply raised an eyebrow.

'That's right,' came another voice. 'What'll it be?'

Clenching his jaw, Hugh turned, acknowledging the crowd with the briefest of glances. 'That's quite alright. Like I say, I'm simply after some food and a room for the night.'

'Bollocks to that,' another voice now. 'Look at all those pretty clothes of his. Boy dressed like that must be able to afford a handsome wager.'

Hugh looked to the innkeep in the knowingly naive hope he might intervene on his behalf. But the man stood back now, and even appeared to be smirking, condemning Hugh to interact with the crowd.

'I think,' Hugh began, turning slowly, facing the rugged rabble (all of a sudden there seemed to be far more of them than he'd noticed upon entering the inn). 'I shall take my leave now. I'll seek accommodation elsewhere.'

A good many men slipped away from the herd and positioned themselves firmly between the door and Hugh.

'Not so fast, boy,' the innkeep finally spoke. 'We've a room here, alright.'

Hugh almost breathed a sigh of relief, but then the man continued.

'But like the lads say, we've a custom here. Little lords such as yourself surely know it's ill-mannered to disregard the customs of your host.'

With the unease that had been building since he'd stepped foot in the inn suddenly beginning to give way to panic, Hugh looked about the room in an effort to find any alternate means of leaving, other than through the door he had walked in. He could see nothing of the sort, but if there was one, then it too was likely blocked by one of the locals, most of whom now encircled him as if he were one of their roosters.

'I suppose,' Hugh began, attempting to address the room without allowing the pitch of his voice to falter and give away the distress that had come over him. 'If it is after all a custom… then I can spare a penny.'

'A penny!' came a cry from the crowd, followed by an unsettling chorus of cackles and heckles, all of which made clear they thought him to be taking them for fools. 'Such a finely dressed boy can spare more'an a penny.'

'Please, I'm not a lord—' Hugh began, but his words were at once drowned out by harsher heckling, and jeering, and even (he could have sworn) one man growling.

'You've at least a groat, boy,' the innkeep joined in. 'What, with you being after a room and a meal.'

'How about his fancy cloak?' came a voice from the crowd.

'What about that horse he rode in on?' Another voice. 'Saw him stable it outside, fine looking saddle it had.'

Unless he was as stupid as his appearance suggested, the oaf who had uttered those words had clearly not seen Hugh ride in. But he had given Hugh an idea. 'I rode in on a donkey,' he declared.

Around him, the rabble raised eyebrows and looked at one another, unable to make sense of why he would announce such a thing.

'Which proves,' Hugh continued. 'That I am not a lord. A lord would not ride a donkey.'

This seemed to at least momentarily stump the crowd. But they didn't care much for logic, as the chorus of demands that he place his wager picked up again. And not just a groat now, but calls that he bet the donkey itself.

'I… please,' Hugh protested. 'I've a long journey ahead of me. A penny is all—'

'What say this,' the innkeep spoke up, and all the men about him quietened down. 'Wager on the winning cock, and a meal and a bed is yours, free of charge.'

Hugh had expected him to go on, but he didn't, so he asked, 'And if I pick the losing cock?'

'Well,' the innkeep smirked. 'The lads here can have the pick of your purse and divide it amongst themselves as they see fit,' there was a roaring cheer, cut short by the innkeep once again speaking up. '*After* I've taken my cut, 'course, being the proprietor of this cockpit.'

This was met with a far less rambunctious response, though nothing in the way of an objection. The innkeep stepped forwards, looked Hugh square in the eyes and spat in the palm of his own hand, then held it out before him. Hugh looked at the hand, and then about the alehouse once more. It seemed he had little choice. He imitated the gesture – albeit reluctantly and with a little less phlegm – and shook the innkeep's hand. Once more the patrons cheered, though they were not cheers that brought Hugh much comfort, and he swiftly found himself jostled into their ranks, as they reformed a circle, recreating the aforementioned cockpit.

'Ich is it ta be 'en?' a man stood across the pit, opposite Hugh, asked, his lack of teeth quite apparent. He gestured to the respective roosters, each one held by a different man. 'Lef er ry?'

Hugh did wonder whether the man actually knew his left from his right (for he assumed that was what he had asked) and so made sure to point to his choice, though not before taking a moment to examine each animal.

The rooster to the left of him had white and black feathers, many of which had been torn out, and a number of scars and scratches, some fresher than others, no doubt from the bout his entrance had interrupted. It appeared to be not only smaller, but in slightly worse shape than the rooster to the right of him, which had a reddish brown plumage. It seemed an obvious choice.

Hugh pointed to the larger, less wounded of the two.

There was some chatter amongst the men, and after the requisite meanders, murmurs and nods, the two who bore the roosters placed them in the centre of the pit, though kept a hold of the birds.

'Now just one moment,' the voice of the innkeep again. 'A fine choice you've made, little lord, but I'm afraid that cock's no longer fighting fit.'

'It was, not a moment ago,' Hugh said, looking between the birds and the innkeep, who had now pushed his way to the inner ring of the circle.

'Aye, well that was a moment ago. But don't worry, we've plenty of others out back,' he nodded to a man off in a far corner of the room, and Hugh heard a door open. 'We like a fair fight here, after all, don't we lads.'

The men cheered in agreement. And then the door opened again and the man who had gone outside returned, holding a different rooster. He placed it in the pit as the man holding the larger rooster Hugh had bet on picked it back up. The new one had greyish brown feathers, and it stood at half the size of its opponent, the red comb across the top of its head hardly visible, and its beak but a tiny tip protruding from its meagre skull.

'That's barely a rooster,' Hugh protested.

'And you're barely a man,' replied the innkeep. 'Seems fitting.' He nodded to the men in the pit, and not a moment later the roosters were released.

Once more the room erupted into a chorus of cursing and grunting cheers, as the men watched the unfolding fray. The rooster that had been thrust upon Hugh was, unsurprisingly, immediately on the back foot, its larger and clearly more seasoned opponent unleashing a volley of vicious jabs at it, standing tall and spreading its wings, taunting it with high-pitched crows, almost mocking the inferior fowl. But the smaller one had heart, if that's what you could call it. Drawing its head back like a bowstring, it leaped and launched its little beak towards its tormentor, its wings making a slapping sound as it was momentarily suspended a few inches above ground. Not that this did much in the way of deterring the larger one; it simply puffed up its breast and stood tall in defiance of its – if you'll pardon the pun – plucky opponent's attempted assault.

And then, with one of its talons, the larger one clawed the little rooster across the face. Not merely once, but three consecutive strikes, the third of which swatted the malnourished, meagre cock to the ground.

The onlookers let out an almighty jeer in unison, many of them shooting cocksure smirks at Hugh. But he avoided their gazes, focusing his attention on, what looked to be, the last moments of his champion in the cockpit. His rooster was down, but still struggling, crowing and flapping its tattered wings in a desperate effort to get up. But the larger rooster loomed menacingly over it, readying itself to unleash a flurry of finishing blows. The spectators, it seemed, had written it off, many of them clanking mugs and taking hefty sips of ale now, eagerly awaiting the spoils of Hugh's purse. But as they revelled in their soon-to-be victory, Hugh noticed the larger rooster stumble back suddenly.

It was bothered by something; and it was only as the thin membrane of the bird's inner eyelid shuttered, closing for a split second, that Hugh noticed what it was. The rooster's face was in the path of a sliver of sunlight, its eye exposed to a glare of some kind. Behind the rowdy patrons, he could see the sun spilling in through the window, but that alone hadn't caused the rooster to stumble back. Then he looked down, and saw what had happened. The base of the blade which hung from his belt peeked out of its sheath and had caught the light, and the precise spot in which Hugh was standing had caused it to reflect into the cockpit. More precisely, into the eye of the larger rooster.

It had only stunned the cock for a split-second, but that had given Hugh's rooster a chance to find its feet, albeit through a burst of frantic, frightened flaps. As the larger rooster advanced once again towards its opponent, Hugh shifted his stance ever so slightly and the glare from the exposed steel of his sword found the eye of the aggressor again. The cock staggered back a second time. Now the smaller one was not only up, but advancing. So Hugh barely turned again, using the blade on his waist to steer the glare so that it was constantly shining into the larger rooster's eye. He did this subtly, with the crowd still too busy drinking and revelling in their presumed win to notice. Then the smaller one began to unleash its own attacks. They were, naturally, nowhere near as powerful as the ones it had been on the receiving end of, but the glare kept the larger one from retaliating effectively. With each little lunge, Hugh's rooster's jabs and scratches began to wear down its rival.

But the premature celebrations were beginning to die down as some amongst the crowd were noticing that it was *their* rooster on the back foot now. Suddenly they began to boo and hiss (at a rooster, no less, for all the good it did) and Hugh readied himself to conceal the exposed steel of his blade with his cloak. But the men's attention was very much on the cockpit, not him, and fortuitously they didn't seem to notice his interference. And so he continued to subtly reflect the glare into the eye of the larger rooster. All the while, the famished fowl that had been thrust upon him was fast becoming the favourite to win. Not only had it found its feet, but also its aggression. It was on the offensive now, landing jab after jab with its tiny beak, scratching its opponent, spreading out its own wings. Hugh had given the cock a fighting chance and it had taken it. It was wearing its rival down with every jab of its beak and scratch of its talon, causing increasing outbursts of frustration and fury from the onlookers. Hugh didn't need the glare anymore, either (and good thing too, as it would no doubt have been noticed had he kept it up), his rooster was well and truly winning. The jeers of the crowd died down as they begrudgingly began to resign themselves to the outcome, and before long the only sound in the inn was the shrill crowing of their bested fighter, an undeniably unpleasant sound, accompanied by the even more unpleasant sight of the smaller rooster finishing off its opponent.

Once the crowing had ceased, silence fell over the inn. Hugh looked about the place; now a room full of scowling, glaring men, with all eyes on him. Part of him, in that moment, thought it probably wise to make haste and find another inn in which to stay. Instead, he turned to the innkeep.

'One hot meal, if you'd please,' he said, matter-of-factly. 'And a room for the night.'

Chapter 9
The Sack

Hugh thought it best to leave the inn at sunrise, and not push his luck by breakfasting beside the men who were likely still irked at his rooster's victory. It seemed dark – despite the morning sun's ascent in a largely cloudless sky – as he made for the stables, with shadows cast by surrounding, overhanging trees sprawling across the courtyard. He was approaching his donkey when, between them, strutted his greyish-brown feathered champion, its chest puffed out ever so slightly more than it had been the evening prior, and, dare he say, a slight pomposity to its gait. As Hugh smirked down upon the fowl that had seen him fed and bed, in all of its newfound confidence, it turned its head and he could have sworn it exchanged a knowing glance with him. If that was indeed the case, it was not a glance that lasted long.

The man in the blue cloak had appeared quite suddenly, a pointed hood concealing his face, and a shrill charm to his words. 'Good morning to you, traveller,' the greeting announced his presence as he emerged from the thicket bordering the stables, sneaking up behind Hugh. The dagger announced his intent. It was a particularly short and unquestionably sharp blade, which the man had pressed firmly against Hugh's jugular before his greeting was fully spoken.

Hugh was little less than a stride away from his donkey when the man made himself known, another moment and he'd have been atop it, and a moment after that he'd have been away, back on the open road. Then, the man with the cold steel blade held to his throat turned Hugh, so that he was facing a brown-haired steed; the only other mount tethered there.

'Wouldn't happen to be your horse, would it?'

'I… no.'

There was a pause. 'The donkey is yours?'

'Yes.'

'Curious. Wouldn't have thought as much from the look of you. No matter.'

Hugh had at first thought that perhaps the man had been amongst the disgruntled spectators of the day before's deathmatch, though something in the way he spoke – at least in the few words he had spoken so far – told Hugh that this was not your run-of-the-mill ruffian.

'I've not much in the way of coin,' Hugh said, trying his best to remain calm.

'A man of your standing?' the blade-wielder responded, feigning surprise. 'I should think you've more than most who frequent this inn.'

'It's yours if you spare my neck.'

The man chuckled.

'Does that amuse you?' Hugh asked, trying – and failing – to catch a glimpse of the man by looking as far over his shoulder as was possible without moving his neck.

'I'm afraid it's not simply your coin that I'm after,' as the man spoke, Hugh heard something of a rustling sound. 'Now, no sudden movements or loud noises.' Just as suddenly as it had appeared, the cold steel was gone, no longer pressed against Hugh's throat, as the man grabbed hold of his wrists, right first, then left, and began binding them behind his back. They were tightly tied in a matter of seconds – the man had clearly done this before. Then Hugh felt a rubbing against his waist, as the man used his dagger to saw through the strap that attached his sheath to his belt. A moment later the sheath, and the sword inside, fell to the ground, and the hand behind him swiftly snatched it away, out of both Hugh's sight and reach. 'Would you do me the courtesy of stepping backwards, one foot at a time.'

'Why... why do you want me to step back?'

Hugh felt the tip of the blade press against his throat again. The response was clear enough. Hugh obliged, one foot at a time, and he could feel that he was no longer stood on the slightly sodden soil of ground touched by morning dew. He glanced down and saw the coarse brown fabric of the sack, his feet in the centre of it, and at the same time the blade once again left his throat, the man's hands reappearing seconds later and performing the same binding to his ankles as his wrists. The man gave the ankle ropes a final, securing tug, causing Hugh to almost fall flat on his face, though the man grabbed hold of his tunic and held him up right.

'Thank you kindly,' he said. 'And now, the final touch.'

With that he brought a torn piece of rag over Hugh's face and pulled it firmly across his mouth, tying it as tightly (if not tighter), than the two preceding bindings. Then the sack which Hugh stood upon began to rise around him until it had engulfed him completely, blacking out a still not quite fully risen sun.

'Ah,' the man said, some seconds after. 'What are we to do about you?'

Hugh knew not to whom he spoke. It certainly did not sound as if the words were directed at him. Had his snatching been spied upon? If so, now was surely his chance to—

'You'll do to feed a mouth or two,' the man continued.

A moment later Hugh heard the sound of what would have been a caw, the very same caw that his winning rooster had so fervently effused as it fought for its life the evening prior, sparing Hugh from a great deal of discomfort in doing so. But before it was a caw, a sudden snapping cut it short.

Hugh didn't bother to struggle during the journey. He'd taken an educated guess that his kidnapper had, after binding and bagging him, stolen the horse rather than the old donkey Sybil had lent him, the rhythm in which they rode being unfamiliar to Hugh (though this was the first time he had been stowed across a hind as if he were the carcass of a freshly hunted deer). At least the thief had afforded Hugh the courtesy of not blindfolding him, which allowed him to keep a vague track of the time of day. He'd been able to make out the slowly brightening sun through the fabric of the sack, if not much else. The thief, it transpired, was a constant whistler, and a particularly loud one at that. Whether or not this was intended to drown out any would-be grunting protests from Hugh was unclear, though it was inarguably impressive how long the man was able to maintain a tune; ranging from low hum-like renditions of recognisable melodies to jolly, high-pitched whistles of vaguely familiar ballads. On a couple of occasions Hugh even caught himself instinctively attempting to hum along, but was quite unable to on account of the gag.

An hour or so had passed them by when the thought-to-be-horse came to a halt. The light that made it through the sack had lessened during the last stretch of their journey, and the hoof-fall had grown muffled, leading Hugh to believe they'd ventured deep into the woodlands. Hugh's captor's whistling had not subsided, however, at least not until the horse stopped, and then it did indeed cease, with the man dismounting and a moment later dragging Hugh from the horse's hind. He hit the ground with a thud, landing chest first, knocking the breath out of his body.

'Oops – frightfully sorry about that,' said the man, though he sounded somewhat amused. 'You're heavier than you look.' He crouched down beside Hugh. 'As far as passengers go, you're certainly more well behaved than most. That was quite the pleasant journey. At least I found it so.' A pair of hands grabbed Hugh's shoulders and rolled him over. 'I'm going to release you from that sack now, though I must warn you once more against struggling or giving into the urge to scream or cry for help or simply make any loud sounds. This would of course prove fruitless on your part, and I would find it rather annoying and would likely react violently. And seeing as you've been so well behaved up until now, I would hate to have to do that.'

The coarse burlap rubbed across Hugh's face as the man dragged it from beneath him. He instinctively found himself squinting as his surroundings became visible, though there was little need to. They were, as he had suspected, within the forest, and well within it at that; surrounded by nothing but tall trees and thicket, quite shielded from daylight. Once the sack was fully off, the man calmly folded it into a neat square before tucking it into a pouch hanging from his waist. Then he grabbed Hugh by the collar and stood him up. Hugh tried to examine his face, though the hood still very much concealed it

'Now,' he said. 'There remains little left of our journey, but the route is not suited to horseback. I shall tether this creature to a tree, as I'm sure I'll have use of it still, and then I am going to unbind your legs, for our path would also prove quite challenging if you were to attempt it hobbling. I must once again stress, that should you make to flee, I will be forced to draw my dagger. Understood?'

Hugh nodded slowly.

'There's a good lad.' An ever so slightly visible smirk revealed itself from within the cloak, and then the man, true to his word, tied the horse to a tree before untying Hugh's ankles. 'Walk,' he ordered, holding his dagger to Hugh's back, nudging him in the direction of what appeared to be the tricky-to-traverse path.

So, Hugh did just that. His captor directed him through the forest, the pointy end of his blade acting as an ever-present encouraging nudge. The path was narrow and laden with waist-high bramble and snagging scrub, roots both bulbous and snarling snaking along the ground they walked, with Hugh finding it to be just as impractical a route on foot as the man had made it out to be on horse. Still, a short while after embarking, the two of them arrived in what seemed to be a den of thieves, which was to say that about this particular patch of woodland satchels were scattered beside basic bedrolls, barely visible beneath the leaf-litter. Just how many thieves inhabited this den wasn't quite clear at first – they were deep in the woods and the men blended in with their surroundings – but as Hugh stepped into the somewhat less overgrown opening that this band of outlaws occupied, there were at least ten faces with eyes now fixed on him. One of these faces belonged to a man perched on a tree branch, likely on lookout, who drew back the string of his bow the second Hugh stumbled into the den, aiming at him. He appeared to relax ever so slightly seconds later, however, as he noticed the man behind.

'Look what I found at the cockpit,' Hugh's escort spoke loudly, announcing their arrival.

'A nobleman's boy?' one of the faces asked. 'Stumbled into the wrong tavern, did ya lad?' he chuckled.

'I'm not a nobleman's boy,' Hugh said. 'I'm a squire.'

A few of the men shot each other glances of mild concern. It occurred to Hugh that perhaps he should have made this known sooner.

Hugh's captor nudged him forwards, so that he stood in the centre of the den. 'A squire whose master will no doubt pay a pretty price to ensure his safe return, eh lads.'

Hugh sighed.

'Tired of us already, boy?' one of the men asked.

'So it's a ransom you men are after,' Hugh replied.

'As you can tell,' the captor intervened. 'This one catches on quickly.' Now more of the men chuckled.

'I hate to disappoint you,' Hugh said. 'But I no longer serve a master.'

Some more chuckling followed this, though they seemed unsure of themselves. 'A squire with no knight?' the man who had spoken a moment ago enquired. 'How does that work?'

'I suppose I am… *between* knights,' Hugh said.

'So you *did* serve a knight,' the captor replied. 'And might I assume you now seek another?'

Hugh gave an apprehensive nod.

'Even better!' the captor beamed, 'We have two knights to demand a ransom from.'

'I'm afraid the knight I until recently served is unlikely to pay a penny towards my release,' Hugh said. 'And the one who I am on my way to serve – or *was* on my way to serve, before you kidnapped me – will also be, I imagine, quite unable to meet your demands.'

'So what you've brought us here, Shaft,' the same man said, addressing the captor, who Hugh now knew was Shaft. 'Is a squire to two knights, neither of which will give us nothin', which makes this lad worth exactly…' he paused, mockingly making out as if he was tallying numbers, before announcing loudly, 'Piss-all.'

There seemed to be more faces appearing from the thicket now, or perhaps Hugh was only just noticing them. The lookout in the tree had lowered his bow, and wore on his face the same unimpressed look that his fellow ne'er-do-well wore, though now they were directing their attention towards Shaft.

Shaft cleared his throat. 'Now, let's not be hasty, friends,' he said, turning to Hugh. 'I'm sure our young knightless squire here can think of *someone* to whom we can make our demands known. Of all the chivalrous persons he's crossed paths with, surely there is at least one who would see to it that no harm was done to him.' He leaned in closer to Hugh, speaking quietly into his ear now. 'I sincerely hope you do know someone, my boy. We have little use of a worthless squire. And I'm afraid the lads here tend to dispose of things they have little use for. Not all of them are as well-mannered as me, either. They can be rather…' he paused. 'Nasty, about it.'

'Please,' Hugh said. 'I'm telling you the truth. All I can offer you is what's on my person.'

'Naturally we'll be taking that,' Shaft said. 'But a half-full purse was hardly worth the effort I've put into procuring you. We really do need the name of a willing patron.'

'I don't know anyone with—'

'We're not fussed what form this payment takes. Jewellery. Gemstones. Be assured, we are open to accepting all manner of valuables in exchange for your life. Isn't that so, gentlemen.'

The thieves that Hugh could make out nodded in response to Shaft's words, their sneering, scowling faces slowly jouncing, faces that were so at odds with Shaft's well-spokenness that it only served to make them seem more unsettling.

Hugh swallowed deeply. 'There's no one.'

Shaft frowned. 'Think on it,' he said. With a nod of his head, two of the men from the den grabbed hold of Hugh and dragged him over to a tree, shoving him against it. One held him in place, whilst the other bound him to the trunk. Then Shaft walked over to him, holding a small black hood.

'You've until nightfall. Give us a shout when you've someone charitable in mind.'

He pulled the hood over Hugh's head and everything went dark.

Chapter 10
A Favour Returned

Hugh's predicament was only exacerbated by the fact he now had no idea just how long it was until nightfall. Unlike the burlap sack, no light made its way through the black fabric of the new hood that covered his face. The only measurement he had to mark the passing of time was a worsening thirst. More than once he asked whoever might be nearby if they would do him the courtesy of affording him a drink (his waterskin having been stripped from him, not that he would have been able to bring it to his mouth), though his pleas were met with little more than an eerie silence. At first he thought the bandits were simply ignoring him, though soon it seemed more likely they had retreated further into their makeshift woodland hideout.

When he was quite sure that no one was watching, he struggled and squirmed, and tried almost everything to free himself from the bindings, but they were too tight. So Hugh waited a while before attempting to escape again, this effort also proving unsuccessful, and so he waited some more and so on and so forth. All the while he was thinking long and hard – as Shaft had bid him to – of anyone that might meet the as yet to be determined demands of his captors. The only person that came to mind was dear Sybil. But Hugh had little hope that a handmaiden would have much in the way of whatever riches they were after.

His thoughts wandered whilst he waited, bound and alone, to Guilliam. Although escape was seeming increasingly unlikely with each attempt, even if he were to somehow break free, precious time had been wasted. It wasn't just his own life that hung in the balance, that these bandits threatened, it was the life of his friend too. And then he thought on Sir Leland Lockwood's words.

"I'd be surprised if you survive the road."

The knight's prediction was proving ever more accurate with each passing moment. This had been a foolhardy endeavour, Hugh was under no illusion. He did not know if he would be able to save Guilliam's life. But he had, at the very least, thought he might make it to the village, to this Crooklingsham, that he might have had the chance to try. He had not so much as considered that he would be a target, travelling alone in clothing fit for those of a more noble disposition. He had only ever travelled alongside knights and their retinues, well equipped men armed to the teeth, that no bandit would dare bother. But alone, he was just a fresh-faced lad whose conspicuous attire drew too much attention.

He had lost track of how many times he'd tried and failed to break free of the bindings when he heard footfall. It was faint at first, a quiet crunching of leaves beneath boots, but whoever the boots belonged to was approaching him.

'Shaft? Is it nightfall already?' Hugh asked, but no answer came, though the person approached still. 'There truly is no one else who can pay my ransom. Write to Sir Leland Lockwood if you must, for all the good it will do. But he will not give you what you want.'

The footfall stopped. Hugh turned his head, unsure as to the direction precisely whoever it was had stilled.

'You have to believe me,' Hugh went on. 'What good is it to kill me? You will gain nothing from it. I have already offered you what little wealth I possess.'

'It is not,' the voice that spoke was soft and unfamiliar to Hugh.

'I beg your pardon,' Hugh replied, unsure what exactly was *not*.

'It is not nightfall. Not quite.'

'I… who am I speaking with?' Hugh could place where the softly spoken person was standing now, though still could see nothing through the black hood.

'It took me a while to place you,' the person said, quietly. 'I couldn't quite remember earlier, when Shaft brought you in. But I knew I'd seen you before.'

'Who is this?'

'He wasn't lying. They will kill you. They're not all too keen on moving unless they have to. And they tend to move after they collect each ransom. If there's no one'll pay for you, setting you loose would mean wasting a perfectly good spot.'

'How is it you know me?'

'And I must admit, this really is a very good spot. They're not all that easy to come by. I s'pose I can't entirely blame them for choosing to kill you.'

Try as he might, Hugh couldn't place the voice. 'Perhaps you could take my hood off?' he asked.

'I'd stop talking if I were you. If one of them hears, we're both dead.'

'I—' Hugh began, though promptly took the advice.

Silence followed. And then whoever had been speaking took hold of the bindings and loosened them. That's not to say he untied them, Hugh was still very much bound, though he now felt he had a certain amount of wriggle room.

'All I can do for you, I'm afraid. The rest is up to you.'

Immediately Hugh began once again to twist and turn, only this time he actually seemed to be freeing himself. He heard the footsteps retreating.

'Wait,' Hugh was sure to whisper. The footsteps paused. 'Who are you?'

But there was no answer. A few seconds later, the rope that had secured him to the tree fell loose. His back pressed against the bark, Hugh slid against the trunk, and then brought his still tightly bound wrists over his legs, so that they were in front of him once again. He ripped the hood from his head. It was not quite nightfall, but it was fast approaching. He stood, and as he did he caught a glimpse of the figure who had saved him, disappearing back into the brush, deeper into the den. The figure turned to face him for a fleeting second, before vanishing completely. He seemed young.

But Hugh didn't hang around. He was away, quietly fleeing at first, desperately striving to recognise any would be landmarks from the trail into the den. It took some aimless wandering, but he soon had a vague sense of the way back. The further he got from the den, the faster he fled, his hands still bound. And then he seemed to emerge from the tricky-to-traverse path, and was back at the spot where they had dismounted earlier that day.

The horse was not there. His heart sank, but his legs didn't stop moving. He kept on going, the sun now almost fully set. But it wasn't completely gone, there were still slivers of light, fast fading hues creeping into the woodland, piercing the gaps between distant trees. So Hugh ran towards them. He didn't know where he was, but he knew he had to get out of the woods whilst he still could.

He was panting and coughing, tripping and slipping, and he could swear now that he heard distant footfall. He was exhausted, yet he ran faster, towards the last of the light, making for what seemed to be the border of whatever woodland this was. Between the stumbling steps and frequent glances over his shoulder (he was sure the bandits would be upon him any moment, but luckily the distant footfall remained precisely that – distant) he somehow managed to make it to the threshold. As he stepped foot back into the open, leaving the forest behind, the sun disappeared, almost as if he had timed his emergence to the split second. Now it was dark. He stood on a path, which stretched further than he could make out, both to his left and his right. He did not know which way to go, but knew he had to go quickly. And so he chose left, and began to follow the path, running as fast as his tired legs would allow.

The woodland was far behind him when he realised that he could no longer hear his pursuers, and his staggered sprint slowed to a stilted stroll. He knew not what path he was on, but at least, he thought, there was one for him to follow, for surely it would lead him somewhere.

He walked for an hour or so more before finding a small opening off the road; an area that appeared to be a naturally formed shelter, a soft patch of grass beneath a cluster of curving branches acting as a canopy. This seemed a suitable place to try and sleep, and hopefully secluded enough from the eyes of any late-night wanderers. He lay down and sighed with exhaustion, staring into a largely starless sky. Then he closed his eyes, and thought back to the softly-spoken bandit who had set him free. He pictured his face, that fleeting glimpse. There was something about it, something vaguely familiar. As he drifted into a much needed sleep, it suddenly came back to him. It was a face he had seen before. Three years before, in a market square in Smithfield, only then it had belonged to a boy.

A small boy, with long fingers.

Chapter 11
The Passing Cart

The stench of stale breath woke him, as his eyes unsurely unpeeled themselves to the sight of a drooling tongue. Hugh shot up with a fright, his body stiff and sore from the night. It took him a moment to register that the breath, and the drool that accompanied it, belonged to a dog, and another moment altogether to register that it was now daytime. The dog was sniffing him with a calm curiosity. Hugh sat upright and stroked its head before brushing the animal aside. It was a large copper-coloured hound with a flat face and pointed ears. He was vaguely familiar with the breed, it was similar to the sort a nobleman might use to run down wandering wild boars brazen enough to encroach on their estates, though perhaps too much a mongrel to belong to one. Yet despite its size, it seemed gentle enough. A nearby whistling summoned the dog, which in turn trotted off towards the source of the sound, leaving Hugh with a trail

It was an uneventful half-day's travel atop the back of Martin's cart, of which Hugh was thankful for. Still exhausted from the business of being kidnapped, he had found himself nodding off once or twice, though by the time they started passing periodically placed signposts for Crooklingsham, Hugh figured he felt as rested as was possible.

Soon they had reached the edge of the village. Stepping off of the cart, Hugh once again thanked Martin. 'I owe you more than you know. And more than I am able to offer in my current circumstance. I know not what awaits me on the next leg of my journey, but should I be fortuitous enough to come into more coin, I shall see it sent to your farm.'

'It's no bother, lad,' the farmer smiled. 'If Holly hadn't sniffed you out, I'd have rode right on past you, so really it's her you ought to be thanking. And she's got no need for coin.' Hugh gave the dog an affectionate pet and then Martin and the two Hollies were on their way, leaving him standing before the village of Crooklingsham. He found himself in that moment, once again, thinking back to Sir Leland's remark.

"I'd be surprised if you survive the road."

Perhaps the knight's words weren't intended to be as cutting as they'd sounded. Sir Leland was, after all, nothing if not a plain-speaking pragmatist. And Hugh knew very well that it was mere happenstance and good fortune that had seen him escape the bandit's bindings. Regardless, he was still here, albeit far less wealthy and far more weary a man than he had been upon setting off. But at the very least, he had so far – if only just – proven his former mentor wrong.

Of the villagers who were out and about, walking what little Crooklingsham had to offer in the way of streets, or tending to of glistening saliva dripping down his half-awake face. Seconds later he heard the dog bark, and then someone spoke.

'What is it? Found something, girl?' It was a man's voice.

Hugh panicked as the events of the day before came back to him. Had the outlaws set the hounds on him? He cursed himself for not travelling through the night, for not getting as far away from their dreaded den as possible. But no one came bursting through the brush that concealed the makeshift bed chamber. Rather, a man calmly parted the bushes, peeping in with a curious expression on his face. He was a short, stout man – somewhat hunched – with unflattering wisps of grey hair hanging from his temples, beneath a head that was completely bald.

'It would seem you have,' he said upon noticing Hugh.

The first thing Hugh asked for was water, which the man did not have. He did, however, have on his cart a leather costrel three quarters full of ale, which he offered to Hugh, who gratefully accepted, helping himself to a generous gulp, ignoring the sickly thickness of the liquid, simply happy to quench his lingering thirst. The second thing Hugh asked was the man's name. The man was called Martin. He was a farmer and was, when he'd stumbled upon Hugh, returning from a market atop his horse and cart. As well as his dog, which was called Holly, he had brought along his daughter, a pallid and apparently timid young girl, no older than seven or eight by Hugh's estimate. She was also called Holly.

'Wasn't always her name,' Martin said to Hugh (who had left the opening and now stood facing the three pausing passers-by), gesturing to the dog as he introduced his travelling companions.

'Named her Wolf at first, but she never took to it. Then whenever me and the wife called after this one here,' he nodded at the girl, 'the bitch came running. After a while we just took to calling her Holly too, it being all she answered to. And I must say, one less name to remember makes my life easier.' Martin chuckled to himself and Hugh managed a half-hearted smile. For a moment there was silence. 'Anyhow, enough about that. What's your name, lad?'

'Hugh,' Hugh answered. 'Hugh Brombury.'

'You look like you've seen better days, Hugh Brombury.'

'Aye, that I have.'

'Not that it's any of my business, but might I ask why it is you chose the side of this here road to catch some shut-eye? It's just, beneath all that dirt, those clothes of yours seem awfully fine. Finer than the sort you'd think would be worn by a lad who sleeps by roadsides, that is.'

'I—' Hugh cleared his throat. 'I ran into some unsavoury sorts on my travels. They stripped me of my sword and coin, and meant to ransom me.'

'Ransom you?' Martin appeared quite genuinely shocked at the thought. 'Can't say I've ever been in danger of that myself.'

'Nor had I, until yesterday. And I'm afraid it's on account of these very clothes that I drew their attention. I wandered into the wrong inn, looking the wrong way, it seems.'

'Seems you escaped, though.'

'Yes, and ran as far as my legs would take me once I did. Which was here.'

'Well, Hugh Brombury, you've had quite the night,' Martin exclaimed with a well-meaning chuckle. 'If you don't mind my asking, where is it you're travelling to?'

Thankfully the bandits had not stripped Hugh of all his pouches, only the one containing coin. Attached to his person was another small leather pouch, and from it he withdrew the map which Guilliam had left him.

'I'm making for a village called Crooklingsham,' Hugh handed Martin the map. 'I don't suppose you've any idea how far from *here* it is? Only, I've lost my bearings since… well…'

Martin squinted as he brought the map close to his face. 'You're in luck,' he said after a moment of musing. 'S'about half a day by cart, and it just so happens to be along the road me and mine are taking.'

Hugh let out a sigh of relief. 'I don't mean to presume, but am I to take that as an offer of—'

'Aye, lad,' Martin said with a kindly grin. 'Hop on back.'

'Thank you,' Hugh bowed his head. 'As I say, my coin has been robbed. Perhaps I can offer you the cloak on my back. Though it is muddied, it is of fine quality.'

Martin chuckled. 'Keep your cloak, young master, I need no payment. It's blind luck you ought to be thankful for, this village you're headed to being on the way to my farm. Not that it is *my* farm. It's Baron Turbert's land, 'course, and so is this village of yours, mind you. But my family's worked the farm for long as anyone can remember—' aware he was rambling, Martin paused. 'Suppose that's neither here nor there to you,' he smiled, 'I'll not bore you anymore, on you get now.'

Hugh bowed his head again before promptly obliging Martin, taking a seat on the cart in between the farmer's dog and daughter who shared a name.

the duties that inhabitants of such humble villages tend to, their attention was soon drawn to the newly arrived squire, shooting suspicious glances and cynical side-eyes his way as he made for the church. There were none so suspicious, however, as the man who waited inside. As Hugh opened the wooden doors and wandered in, a man dressed in a long white garment, covered by a black cloak, stood before him.

'Good afternoon,' the priest spoke. There was something unwelcoming in his words.

'Good afternoon,' Hugh replied. 'Forgive me, I did not mean to intrude. But I wish to speak with Father Roger Dobbe. It is you, I presume?'

'Yours is a face unfamiliar to me,' the priest replied. He was a very tall, very slender man in build, yet his face somehow simultaneously appeared as plump, with bloated cheeks cradling a pair of peering, beady eyes, and a sag of neck skin which was almost vulture-like. The light that shone through the sacred scenes depicted on the stained glass windows met the top of his head with a gleam, it being completely bald, with hair growing like a grey horseshoe around its sides. 'What brings you to this humble house of God?'

'My name is Hugh Brombury.'

This did not seem to mean anything to the priest.

'I am a squire.'

'A squire?' the priest asked. 'And where, pray tell, is your knight?'

'I believe he is in your gaol, Father.'

A cloud must have blocked the sun from shining through the stained glass windows at that very moment, the priest's hairless head losing its gleam as it did.

'On what business do you seek this heretic?' his tone had turned from unwelcoming to accusatory.

Hugh stepped forward.

'I have come to clear his name.'

PART III

The Village of Two Names

Chapter 12
The Clergyman of Crooklingsham

Having been the most (and only) literate person residing in the village of Crooklingsham up until that point, Father Roger Dobbe had taken an even greater disliking to the retired knight upon reading the message he had allowed him to write, only to discover there were words within that even *he* could not comprehend. Of course, it was to be expected that this man would have been afforded an education – being of noble lineage – and yet the good Father couldn't help but find it irksome that this non-believer possessed a superior understanding of the English written word than he himself had developed in the monastic schools of days gone by. Perhaps, Father Dobbe pondered, if they had spent less time studying scripture in Latin and more time writing in the vernacular of their countrymen, he would have been able to decipher a great deal more of the newly anointed pagan's scribblings. And perhaps he would have known to expect the squire.

Alas, the lad's arrival had come as quite the surprise to Father Dobbe, as it had to the good God-fearing people of his parish, who had duly expected that the knight-turned-non-believer locked away in their modest gaol was to be executed for the murder of poor Ethel come week's end. Baron Turbert himself had arrived in Crooklingsham only the day before, accompanied by two of his personal guardsmen no less, and there was even some speculation amongst the more gossip-prone parishioners that they would get to witness a beheading as opposed to a hanging, with the offender's social standing affording him such a punishment.

Granted, Father Dobbe had given the man called Guilliam a chance to clear his name, and it appeared that his chance had arrived. But, in truth, his leniency was intended as no more than a gesture. Being a holy man, after all, he sought to be seen as just and merciful in the eyes of his congregation and he had hardly expected anyone to respond to Guilliam's summons. Having been unable to make out more than half of the words written on the parchment, he had naively hoped that no man of good standing and the Christian faith would wish to defend a blasphemer, let alone a pagan, especially one found guilty of committing such a wicked crime. Of course, Father Dobbe wasn't entirely sure just what information Guilliam had disclosed in his writing, but he had made a point to be seen reading it to himself in front of the entire village (umming and ahhing and nodding as he did) immediately after it was written, after which he announced to them that Guilliam had requested aid from an acquaintance (an educated guess), but that they need not expect anyone to actually show, for no knight (another educated guess) in service of God and the King would defend a murderous heathen.

Though some villagers took umbrage to allowing this request for aid, Father Dobbe assured them that whilst he was indeed no longer a knight, Guilliam still came from noble stock, and thus it was only right and proper that they, being of the peasantry, were seen to afford him a fair chance at disproving their verdict, lest they risk the wrath of a disgruntled lordly relative. So it was unanimously agreed that the period of one month would be granted to their prisoner, which would be enough time for him to at least send word for help, and let it be known that – to whomever he sent word to – the people of Crooklingsham had allowed him a fair chance. That is to say it was *almost* unanimously agreed.

There were two amongst the village who had believed that Guilliam should have been hanged there and then, to see him swiftly pay for the life he had taken with his own. They were Ethel's father, Elias, the innkeep, and the poor girl's betrothed, Hammond, the blacksmith's boy.

'I'll do it myself, Father,' Elias had protested with a bellowing cry, causing quite the stir amongst the gathered villagers who had filled out the church, the welling tears in his eyes held back only by his unrelenting rage. It was a rage that was perhaps not befitting of a man of his build – being short and slight, and even slighter since the death of his daughter had caused his appetite to disappear and his sleeping to cease. 'I'll see that heathen hanged before nightfall.'

'Patience, Elias, patience,' Father Dobbe spoke calmly once the utterances of those the innkeep had swayed to agree with him had died down. 'As I have explained, whilst there is no doubt in my judgement, we must be seen to give a man of his lineage a chance to clear his name. *Even* in light of his renouncing the Lord and his awful, savage doings. But fear not, and have faith in God. This heathen will answer for what he has done.'

'Have faith in God, you say,' Elias had responded with what was almost a laugh. 'First God lets fever take my eldest. Not a year after, my wife is taken from me in childbirth, and God does not even spare the baby. And now—' his voice cracked. Unable to utter the next part, he looked down and shook his head. When he looked back up into Father Dobbe's eyes, tears were streaming down his face. 'I have no faith left in God, Father.' His words were met with gasps as he turned and marched out of the church, stopping only to afford Hammond a glance.

As the church doors closed behind Elias, a silence fell over the congregation.

'He grieves for his daughter,' Father Dobbe spoke softly. 'He knows not what he says. We will continue to pray for him, and for Ethel, whose spirit has returned to our heavenly Father, may she now rest—'

'I too would see the murderer hanged on this day,' the cry was less rageful this time, more unsure of itself. It was Hammond who spoke up. His father, the blacksmith, placed a meaty, calloused hand firmly on his son's bulging shoulder in an effort to quiet him. But Hammond shrugged it off. 'I found her. The way he left her. Her skin covered in cuts and scratches. He must have dragged her through the woods… he did not give Ethel a chance. So why should we give this monster a chance?'

Once more there was chatter amongst the congregation, as those who agreed with the sentiment made their voices heard.

'Forgive him, Father,' the blacksmith bowed his head.

'It is alright, Hal,' Father Dobbe replied, then looked to Hammond.

'I understand, son. You and Elias have reason more than most to see this man answer for his crime. This man robbed you of a wife-to-be. And believe me when I say, he will face justice.' The priest looked about the church, and spoke up as he addressed the gathered villagers in their entirety. 'He will spend his last month in our gaol and, God-willing, each and every waking moment of his final weeks thinking on his terrible deed. And may he find it in his black heart to ask the Lord for forgiveness before we deliver him to the next life. Though I must admit, I doubt that one such as him, who has renounced our Lord, would find Him again in a lifetime, let alone a month. And so, when the time comes for him to pay for his crime, take comfort in knowing that we will not be sending this heathen to the eternal embrace of our Lord, but to eternal torment in Hell,' Father Dobbe paused and once more looked directly at Hammond. 'So I ask you to have patience, son, for the coming month. For compared to an eternity of suffering in the fiery abyss, one month is but a fleeting moment.'

Hammond lowered his head as those around him nodded in and voiced their agreement. The blacksmith again placed a hand on his son's shoulder, and this time the lad let it guide him to his seat.

'Now,' Father Dobbe had said as the voices died down. 'Let us pray.'

Chapter 13
An Unwelcome Arrival

Word spread around Crooklingsham in no time at all, due to it having no further to travel than the twenty-nine houses inhabited by its not quite one-hundred villagers, just under half of who were in The Unpleasant Pheasant when the wanderer arrived. At first he was thought to have been a mere vagrant, an educated guess on account of his appearance and apparent lack of personal possessions. And where would a vagrant wander besides to a house of God. Christ taught, after all, that compassion was to be shown to those living in vagrancy, and the good people of Crooklingsham certainly fancied themselves as students of Christ, more so now than ever, what with the looming heathen spectre posed by the pagans of Ealdgeat. It came much to the distress of those in The Unpleasant Pheasant, then, to discover that it was no drifter who had wandered into their village that afternoon, but rather the squire of the very heathen they hoped to hang (or behead, God-willing). A hanging (or beheading, God-willing) that this very squire intended to prevent.

The news was delivered by Benjamin the bellringer, a boy of nine whose father, Benedict, had performed the same role until a year prior, when he had met an untimely and unfortunate demise by falling from the very tower which housed the bell he'd spent his life ringing (Benedict's own father, Bertram, had been the bellringer before that, but was subject to a similarly ill-fate when – so the story goes – the bell tower partially collapsed and the bell itself crushed him). Fortunately for the village, however, they were not left without a ringer to mark the hours of the day or to call them to prayer, or to gather them for a very occasional important announcement. See, Benjamin had been assisting his father in the act of bellringing since he was only just out of infancy, so when the position was once again vacated due to morbid circumstance, he was more than capable of handling the duties himself, having developed above average strength for a boy of his age – on account of all the assisted ringing – and stepped into his father's role. Thus, having been at the bottom of the belltower in the church when the apparent vagrant had arrived, Benjamin had been privy to his conversation with Father Dobbe, and it was that very conversation that he frantically relayed to the vast majority of villagers present in The Unpleasant Pheasant, who then went about frantically relaying it to the minority who had not been present.

Following said word having spread about Crooklingsham, it also did not take long for a mob of locals to assemble – ranging in temperament from irritated to incandescent – outside the church, which in turn drew the attention of the village's other recently arrived visitors: Baron Turbert and his guardsmen.

The Baron made a point to ride through the crowd towards the doors of the church, dispersing the mob perhaps only because it pleased him to do so. His guardsmen followed on foot several paces behind, but were given just as wide a berth by the villagers, if only because their appearance warranted it. They were a ragged pair, ill-fitting mail draped over their barrel chests, with not a mouthful of teeth between the two of them, who looked, in truth, more like mercenaries than vassals. Father Dobbe was not too pleased by the manner of this entrance, as it seemed to serve only in riling the gathered men and women of Crooklingsham further, after he had spent a great many minutes assuring them that the squire's arrival was nothing to worry about.

'Quite the commotion out there, Father,' a hint of amusement festooned Baron Turbert's statement as he strode into the church as if it were his own chamber, removing his round-brimmed, feathered cap before peeling off a pair of leather riding gloves, without so much as affording the priest a glance. A plump, middle-aged man, the Baron's pointed brown beard was the sharpest feature of his otherwise round face, which itself was nowhere nearly as rounded as the rest of his overfed frame. 'What's all this I'm hearing about a squ—' Turbert stopped mid-sentence as his eyes found Hugh, who stepped into the nave, emerging from the shadows of the dimly lit rear of the building.

'The folk here can be excitable, at times,' Father Dobbe seemed to be considering his words.

'I'm to take it that it is you that has them riled,' the Baron spoke past the priest, addressing Hugh directly.

'It was not my intention, My Lord,' Hugh replied.

'Though not surprising, surely. You are here at the behest of a blasphemer and murderer, yes?'

'I came to speak on behalf of the knight I once served, My Lord.'

'*Former* knight,' Father Dobbe spoke up. 'The man in our gaol renounced his title.'

'And every last shred of chivalry along with it, from what I've been told,' again the Baron addressed Hugh directly.

'I received word from him that the good Father here had granted him a chance to clear his name. That someone might speak on his behalf. He requested that I do so. I am simply answering his call, My Lord.'

Turbert looked to the priest. 'This is true?'

'It is, My Lord,' Father Dobbe replied after a moment's hesitation.

'I was to believe you had tried him already. You summoned me here to make an example of this man, no? To have my own personal guard end his wicked life, no less.'

'That has not changed, My Lord.'

'Then why, pray tell, is *he* here?' the Baron pointed to Hugh. 'Why would you call on me if you intend to allow this boy to speak for him?'

'An unfortunate oversight, on my behalf. Admittedly, I did not anticipate anyone to speak for the perpetrator of this evil act. But, given his lineage, I thought it only right we afford him the opportunity to send word of the predicament – a predicament of his own doing. – that has befallen him. He may have renounced his title, but he is still of a noble household. Far be it from me to bring the ire of his house down on the good people of Crooklingsham.'

The baron took a moment to ponder these words, stroking the wispy dark goatee he wore on the first of his two chins before slowly nodding to himself. 'A sensible decision. Though quite unsensible to summon me so prematurely, Father. It's a two day ride from my keep, and now I'm expected to wait for the boy to carry out his own inquiries, I suppose?'

'I permitted our prisoner no longer than one month to clear his name, My Lord. Come the morning, that month will be over. Unless the lad here can promptly provide you with irrefutable evidence that his former mentor is innocent, then I see no reason why we cannot proceed tomorrow, as intended.'

'That's not enough time!' Hugh protested. 'Word took some weeks to reach me as it was, and my journey two-and-a-half days thereafter. I beg you, grant me an extension.'

Both men cast their gaze simultaneously over Hugh.

'I must say, you don't look much like a squire,' the Baron remarked.

'The road proved… tricky, My Lord.'

The Baron sniggered. 'Beset upon by brigands, were you?'

'An astute observation.'

'And they took you for all but the clothes on your back, by the look of things,' the Baron once again spoke with a smattering of mockery.

'I have arrived with far less in my possession than I set off with,' Hugh said, his cheeks somewhat reddening.

'Unable to defend yourself then, boy?'

'I was… taken by surprise.'

The Baron guffawed aloud at this. 'Well, at the very least I'm to infer that this knight you served was a rather futile fighter? Or maybe just an inept mentor?'

'On the contrary, My Lord,' Hugh said. 'Sir Guilliam was an excellent mentor, and in his day, a formidable fighter.'

Baron Turbert's brow furrowed at the mention of the name, and for a moment or so seemed to be contemplating what he had just heard. And, then his eyes widened. 'Sir Guilliam, you say?'

'Aye, My Lord,' Hugh replied.

'As in… Sir Guilliam the Great?'

Hugh responded with a nod and the Baron turned suddenly to Father Dobbe.

'You failed to mention,' he said, with some degree of vexation, 'that the man I'm to have beheaded is the once finest tourney knight in all of England.'

Father Dobbe smiled softly in an effort to calm the Baron. 'Forgive me, My Lord. Clearly you are more well-versed in your knowledge of tourney knights than I, which of course is to be expected.'

'You would have me believe that you've never heard of Sir Guilliam the Great?' the Baron barked. 'Are you an ignoramus, father? Or perhaps a charlatan of a clergyman, who takes me for one?'

'I assure you, My Lord, neither is true. Whilst the name is vaguely familiar to me, there was little time to learn of tourney champions during my priestly tutelage. I was perhaps too preoccupied in the study of Latin, theology and philosophy to pay attention to such things.'

The Baron grimaced. 'You mock me, now, Father.'

'Forgive me, My Lord, but you mistake my words for mockery. I am merely explaining as to why the name Guilliam did not strike me as particularly significant.'

A tense silence followed, in which Father Dobbe bowed his head towards the Baron, which seemed to go some way in alleviating his agitation. All three stood unspeaking for some slow-passing seconds thereafter. Then the priest continued.

'Still, the man he *used* to be seems of little consequence to me, given the nature of his crime. I'm sure you would agree, My Lord, that he is not above the King's justice, or the God he has denounced, despite his reputation.'

The baron once again stroked the goatee of his first chin, clearly considering how best to proceed. The stroking persisted for a moment or so, stopping only as he appeared to arrive at a decision. He looked at Hugh.

'No doubt you are aware, *squire*, that on more than one occasion your former mentor jousted before the King. I was witness, myself. Perhaps it was you that had armoured him.'

'It's likely, My Lord.'

'What is your name, boy?'

'I am Hugh Brombury, My Lord.'

'Brombury… Not a name I'm familiar with.'

'Few are.'

'Well, Hugh Brombury, perhaps this is your chance to change that,' he turned to face Father Dobbe. 'Guilliam shall be given a chance to clear his name, as promised to him by the priest,' he turned back to Hugh, 'and you shall be given the full month. From now.'

'My Lord, that's—' Father Dobbe began.

'You asked me here to pass judgement, Father. This is how I judge it best to proceed, given all I have learnt from young Master Brombury,' the Baron began to pull his gloves back on, making for the doors once he had. Upon reaching them, but before leaving, he turned again to the priest. 'You are quite right, of course, in noting that even a man of Sir Guilliam's renown is not above the King's justice. But far be-it from me to take the head of his most favoured tourney knight imprudently.' Then he looked Hugh directly in the eye. 'Let us hope that this poor girl did indeed meet her unfortunate end at the hands of another, for the sake of your mentor. And know that beheading any one of those heretical hermits I've heard tell of, *other* than the erstwhile knight, would certainly save me a lot of grief.'

At that, Baron Turbert left. Hugh and Father Dobbe stood in silence. Though he hadn't outright said as much, both of them knew what the Baron was getting at.

'Well, Hugh Brombury,' Father Dobbe broke the silence, not even glancing at Hugh as he spoke. 'It would seem you've managed to afford yourself some time.' He began to walk towards the altar. Atop it were a number of unlit candles, as well as a small pouch. Upon reaching the altar, the priest removed a flint and steel from the pouch. He held them above one of the candles and began to strike the items together, producing sparks, though the candle did not light. 'Of course, Baron Turbert's judgement is of little consequence. It is only the judgement of God that matters.' Again he struck the items, but still the candle didn't light. 'And I will see to it that His judgement is delivered.' Steel struck flint yet again. This time the spark caused a flame. The candle began to burn. Father Dobbe turned to Hugh. 'You'd best get started.'

Chapter 14
A Dimly Lit Reunion

The gaol that held Guilliam let in little in the way of natural light. Of course, it was more of a solitary chamber than a gaol, the sort you might rightly expect to find in a village the size of Crooklingsham, in which the need to detain more than one malefactor at any given time was, at best, a rarity. Thus, there had never been reason to build a bigger gaol, theirs surely no larger than a cartwheel and perhaps twice its length, offering little space for movement within and certainly lacking the means for its present inhabitant to have laid down during his near month-long confinement. A bolted-shut wooden hatch was the room's only window to the outside world, offering fleeting glimpses on the occasions it was opened, to drop in meagre helpings of stale bread and lumpy porridge, or flasks half-filled with water of questionable cleanliness.

It was Father Dobbe himself who unbolted the hatch now, being the highest authority in the village and thus de facto gaoler when the occasion called. A rectangular beam of light spilled into the enclosure as the hatch swung open, revealing little more than a scrawny, scab-coated ankle, with the man to which it belonged concealed by darkness in the dim corner of the claustrophobic cell. Father Dobbe stepped aside, allowing Hugh to peer into the gaol. He was, as his nose neared the opening, reminded of the stink he himself had picked up in the process of performing the punishment that Sir Lockwood had subjected him to prior to their return from Crécy, and could now sympathise with the decision which saw him sent below deck. Nonetheless, the experience had left him accustomed to tolerating a nasty stench, and so he could manage to put up with it at present.

'Sir Guilliam,' Hugh spoke into the shadows. Initially the figure remained unmoving. Then a face emerged from the darkness. It was gaunt, and the once white hair that Hugh remembered was darkened by dirt so much so that it was a blackish-grey, uncleansed and unkempt, growing down past cheekbones – that were more pronounced than Hugh recalled, on account of the gauntness – and meeting an even more matted beard, with unruly moustache strands concealing the mouth. Above that, sagging eyes which sat atop heavy bags barely opened past a squint as they blinked over and over, the sudden dose of daylight clearly taking some time to adjust to. Some seconds passed and the blinking slowed, and after that came a prolonged peer, in which an almost unrecognisable face studied the person looking into the hatch.

'Hugh?' his voice was raspy, the sound strained.

'Yes, Sir Guilliam, it's me.'

'You came?' he spoke as if he didn't quite believe it, as if he were unsure of what he was seeing.

'I received your message. I'm here to help.'

Guilliam let out a faint sigh of relief. 'You came,' he said again, allowing himself to believe it. He clambered to his feet, letting the light reveal more of himself. His stained clothes hung loosely from his underfed frame. The sight did not sit well with Hugh, who had, until that very moment, remembered Guilliam as the strong and unwavering man that he had been. Despite knowing of his imprisonment since receiving word, it had been that proud and able person that he had pictured in the gaol cell, not the frail, stinking, broken man that now struggled to stand before him.

'I suppose I look different from when last you saw me,' Guilliam said, as if he had heard Hugh's thoughts.

'You've certainly seen better days.'

Guilliam almost managed a chuckle at the gentle jest. 'If it's any help, my spirit's not quite fully broken. Not now you're here.' Suddenly, his eyes dropped. 'Though I fear, dear Hugh, you are too late. I was granted a month to clear my name. By my count that month ends tomorrow.'

'I beg to differ, Sir,' Hugh smirked.

Guilliam did not speak in response, simply a questioning expression befell his face.

'Baron Turbert, who was to preside over your execution,' Hugh went on, 'has granted me a month more.'

Guilliam raised his head slowly. The questioning expression gave way to one that resembled something of relief, or as close to it as was possible, given the circumstance. Then Guilliam's eyes shifted to the right. 'Dobbe,' he said, announcing his awareness of the lingering priest's presence. 'I wish to speak with my squire alone.'

'That shan't be possible, I'm afraid.'

'Why not?' Hugh turned to Father Dobbe. 'Surely I'm to be granted a private audience with Sir Guilliam, given I am here to clear his name?'

'Security is my primary concern.'

Hugh all but gestured to the gaol before them with the expression of bewilderment he made in response to this. 'He appears to me to be quite secure.'

'How can I be sure, were I to allow you to converse privately, that you shouldn't conspire to help him escape?'

Guilliam almost managed a laugh. 'You flatter me, Dobbe. Though rest assured, had I foreseen a way to free myself of these shackles and the dankness of this wretched room, I would have done so already, rather than write to my old squire pleading for his aid in investigating this sorry affair further on my behalf, quite unsure as to whether or not that word would indeed reach him, and if he were to accept, whether or not he would make it in time.'

Father Dobbe stood still for a moment after this, before simply saying, 'When you put it like that, I suppose fortune has favoured you on this occasion, Guilliam. Discuss what you will, in private if you must,' he turned to Hugh. 'If it is not already clear, Master Brombury, the people of this village expect to see this man answer for his crime. I can't imagine the extension afforded to him by the Baron will come as welcome news. I would recommend keeping your distance from the villagers, as not to displease them any further.' He looked unblinkingly into Hugh's eyes. 'Do be sure to bolt that hatch when you're done.' And with that, the priest turned and walked away, leaving Hugh and Guilliam alone.

'Charming fellow,' Guilliam said through a laboured smirk. 'Say, you wouldn't happen to have any food on you? They've had me on nothing but scraps of stale bread and sludge since locking me away.'

'I'm afraid not, Sir,' Hugh frowned. 'All my provisions were robbed on the road.'

'Ran into a spot of bother, did you?'

'More than a spot,' Hugh lowered his head. 'I'd spent not two days on the road before I allowed myself to be taken to a hideout of brigands by a cut-throat. I would likely be dead, if not for the fact that the young street urchin from Smithfield was one of them.'

'Smithfield…' Guilliam pondered on this. 'You mean the little thief you thought had nabbed my pendant?'

'The very same. I couldn't place his face at first, but I believe it was him. I'm near certain of it, in fact. He set me loose. Had he not recognised me, I very much doubt I'd be talking to you now.'

'Oh Hugh,' Guilliam chuckled, albeit faintly.

'My shortcomings, at the very least, offer you some amusement.'

'I'll admit, there's little that's amused me this past month. And it is nice to know I still possess the ability to smile. But don't mistake my mirth as laughing *at* you. Fate is a funny thing.'

'You believe in fate?'

'That would surprise you?'

'Well, it's only… when you say fate, I can't help but think it's no different an idea than that of God's will. Since you renounced your faith, I just thought…'

'There are other forces at work in this world, Hugh.'

'Other forces?'

'You'll see soon enough,' his lips curled into a slight smile. 'As to whether or not I believe in fate,' he shrugged. 'You say had the lad not recognised you, you'd be dead. His very being there saved your life. A crucial coincidence, at the very least. Perhaps that's all fate is. Simple chance. Though I'd hesitate to give fate, or chance, or whatever it is, all the credit for your lucky escape. After all, had *you* not shown kindness to the boy, as you did those years back, then he would have had no cause to help you.'

'There is some truth to that, I suppose.'

'And good thing you did too. For if not for you, who would help me?' Guilliam looked about his cell. 'We really ought to figure out just how you're going to do that.'

'Yes, and I mean to. Though I would ask your advice as to the best place to begin in uncovering the truth behind this girl's death.'

'Ethel,' Guilliam said. The expression on his face had once again turned solemn. 'Her name is Ethel.'

A silence lingered as Guilliam seemed to gaze past Hugh, as far out into what distance the small rectangle afforded him.

'Forgive me, Sir,' Hugh continued after a moment. 'But in your message, you said they found her – Ethel, that is – with your pendant. And when you were asked as to why this was, you did not say. Am I to take it that someone framed you for the killing? That they stole your pendant and placed it in her hand? Is this what I am to investigate?'

'No,' Guilliam said.

'No?'

'You may be right in thinking that the monster responsible for this also wishes to see me dead. But no one took the pendant from me, Hugh.'

'Then how is it that Ethel came into possession of it?'

'Because I gave it to her.'

'You *gave* it to her?' Hugh could hardly believe his ears. He knew just how much the heirloom meant to Guilliam. 'Why?'

Guilliam looked deep in thought for a moment, as if he were carefully choosing his next words. 'I—'

'Pardon the interruption,' the voice of Father Dobbe cut in. Hugh turned to see the priest approaching once again, his slender frame casting a long shadow against the backdrop of a setting sun. 'I should have mentioned. There shall be no conversing with our prisoner after dark,' he turned to glance at the sky. 'And that rule is quite non-negotiable,' he gave a shrewd grin and said, 'As you were,' before turning to leave once again.

'Best not push our luck, ' Guilliam said once the priest was out of earshot.

'What was it you were about to tell me?'

'I...' Guilliam's eyes widened ever so slightly as the light that shone through the hatch dimmed. 'It can wait until morning. It's best that you hear the whole story. Have you a room for the night?'

'Not yet. Nor the coin for one. Not that the locals would take me if I did, knowing why it is I'm here, what with Ethel's father being the innkeep. '

'No, I don't suppose that would go down all too well,' Guilliam pondered for a passing second. 'Ealdgeat,' he said. 'There'll be a bed spare there. Namely mine.'

'With the pagans?'

'They'll put you up, once you explain who you are. The woods are a short walk north-west of here, just beyond the pasture.'

Hugh peered over his shoulder. Dobbe was lingering, his beady eyes flitting between the sinking sun and the cell. 'I shall return first thing tomorrow,' he said. 'And you can tell me the whole story.'

'I'll tell you everything.' Guilliam brought his hand to the opening and reached out. Hugh took a hold of it. 'It's good to see you, Hugh,' he said.

'You too, Sir.'

And then he clasped Guilliam's hand and the two shared a knowing smile.

A few moments later, Father Dobbe began a slow walk towards them, the sun sinking lower. Guilliam nodded to Hugh, silently bidding him on his way lest they give the priest the satisfaction of separating them. Leaving the hatch open and unblocked, Hugh walked past the priest, who shot him a shrewd side-eye. As Dobbe marched towards the gaol, to see to it that no soon-to-be moonlight might make its way in, Guilliam called out.

'Hugh,' he beckoned, and the squire turned. 'They prefer *druids* to pagans.'

Chapter 15
Druidic Dwellings

It did not take Hugh long to reach the pasture, what with the village of Crooklingsham being the size it was. His short stroll through its streets, however, did not go unwatched. For as short a walk as it indeed was to the pasture, it was nonetheless fraught with a palpable tension, with the odd passer-by pausing in their passing-by upon seeing Hugh, offering him a scowl or a malicious mumbled remark. It seemed, too, that in every other house that Hugh passed, there was, standing by the window, a villager (or indeed *villagers*) ready and waiting to afford him at best an inhospitable stare, if not an outright hostile glare. More than a couple of the older occupants made their thoughts on his presence abundantly clear, hocking spatters of phlegm in his general direction as he passed their abodes. He decided it best to give the inn a wide berth, hearing that it was lively and not caring to find out what insults – or indeed more material projectiles – his passing by its windows might inspire those inside to send his way. No doubt his arrival was talk of the inn, it having deprived all the patrons within of bearing witness to the supposed justice they had been eagerly anticipating be delivered to Guilliam.

Thankfully, Hugh had reached the pasture before any of his hecklers had managed to organise another angry mob – one which would be full of ale and far quicker to anger than the earlier assortment who had protested outside the church. By the time his hurried stride had taken him across the stretch of grass, he could hear distant threats addressed to him coming from a possibly re-forming rabble in the village.

Despite now finding himself facing the woods, Hugh could see little in the way of another village amongst its outskirts, namely the one that supposedly sat between them, as Guilliam had alluded to. All that appeared before him were the vast woodlands. They seemed to stretch out as far as the eye could see, never-ending, or at least appearing to be, now that it was dark. There was something inherently unwelcoming about this woodland – quite aside from the vastness and darkness, though Hugh couldn't quite put his finger on what it was. Against his better judgement, he took a step towards the trees, and heard a crack beneath his boot. He looked down to see a wooden plank, snapped clean in two by his pressing foot. And then his eyes were drawn to another, nearby, and then another, and then he could see that all about him there were wooden planks of all sizes, broken up into pieces. But not just broken. There were piles of ash, and where the wood was not snapped at the ends it had been burned.

He was standing amongst a wreckage.

A crudely marked out track appeared to offer the only path that seemed to lead anywhere other than back the way he came. That *anywhere* was a narrow opening in the woods that lay ahead, which itself appeared to lead into complete blackness. So, with nowhere else to go, Hugh took one step towards the woods.

An instantaneous urge came over him to turn back – a shiver making its way through his entire being. But nearby the taunting cries of far-from-pleased piss artists seemed to be growing increasingly frequent, the name "heathen friend" apparently having been bestowed upon him (alongside a slew of less easy to decipher slurs, on account of them being largely, well, slurred). With no desire to face the not-too-distantly gathering patrons with a particular distaste for him, Hugh brushed aside the sudden unease that the thought of stepping into the woods had stirred in him, and did just that.

His first thought was that he really ought to have brought a torch with him, as he began to slip and stumble over roots and into branches, though no sooner had the thought entered his mind when, a few feet before him, a small burning ball appeared. Hugh stopped in his tracks, and the ball became larger as it grew nearer, as did the face behind it that he could just about make out. A pair of large, dark eyes were all he could see. Suddenly there was a swoosh. An arrow flew past the ball of light and narrowly passed Hugh's own face, the slicing hiss abruptly becoming a snap as it pierced a tree directly behind him, bark splintering off in all directions.

'Another step and you'll no longer be in Crooklingsham,' it was a woman's voice. 'I would suggest you don't take that step.'

'I… I mean you no harm.'

'You have driven us back once already. You will not do so again.'

'I am looking for Ealdgeat. I was sent here. I was under the impression I would find it on the outskirts of these woods. I see that it is no longer the case.'

'You are *not* welcome.'

'You mistake me. I was sent here. By Guilliam.'

The pair of large dark eyes squinted. The ball of light moved towards Hugh, the face with it, and brown eyes bore into him. He could make out more of her now. She seemed young, around his age, perhaps. Her face was fierce yet somehow delicate; her hair was yellow and wild, its tangled ends curling as if they were waves beneath a bright sun, and her skin seemed to glow in the torchlight. Beneath sporadic patches besmirched by dirt, it looked soft, and it had the hue of sweet honey, and her lips were the colour of ripe berries, the sort that might grow in the very woods she had appeared from. She was beautiful. But there was a fearlessness to her face too, and despite her beauty it was almost unsettling enough to make Hugh want to run in the opposite direction.

'You're not from the village,' she said.

'I am not.'

'Who are you?'

'My name is Hugh Brombury. I was once squire to Sir Guilliam.'

'Guilliam. He is to be executed.'

'I have come to clear his name. I've been granted an extension of one month to do so. By Baron Turbert.'

'How can I know you speak the truth?'

Hugh slowly raised his arms. 'I am not armed,' he said, speaking loud enough in the hopes that the unseen archer would also hear. 'Guilliam wrote to me. He wrote of your village, of Ealdgeat, and of its people. You are the druids he spoke of, yes?'

The girl gave a single nod.

'He informed me of his imprisonment, and the crime he has been accused of. He was given one month to call on someone who would speak for him. He requested my aid. But I only arrived in the village today. He was to be executed soon, yes. Only the Baron wasn't aware that he was to preside over the execution of *Sir Guilliam the Great*, giving him cause enough to grant me more time.'

'And Guilliam told you to come to us? Why?'

'A bed for the night, if it pleases you. I daren't try the local inn. The villagers are… less than happy at my coming here.'

She snickered, albeit bitterly.

'Has my request insulted you?' Hugh asked.

'You are right about Ealdgeat,' she replied. 'It was to be found on the outskirts of these woods.'

'What… what happened here?'

'There is no village. Not anymore. The people of Crooklingsham saw to that.'

'You mean to say they—'

'Tore it down,' another, deeper voice cut in. It belonged to a man. 'A fortnight back.' A face followed the words, as the man who Hugh assumed had fired the arrow stepped into the flame's light. 'They came with clubs and pitchforks and torches and chased us into the wode.'

Hugh could make out the face of the man now. His beard – the top half of which had been knotted into separate smaller sections, nestled atop a big plaited bulk that almost reached his belly – appeared to be grey and his hair was at least as long as it, similarly twisted into several strands. Creases lined his forehead, his face forlorn and battered, the face of a man who had clearly seen many seasons. Hugh thought back to Guilliam's message, of the names mentioned in it.

'Are you… Eotenfrēond?'

'Guilliam spoke of me?'

'He did. And of your daughter,' Hugh turned to the girl holding the torch. 'Ber…?' he began, struggling to recall the name precisely.

'*Beorh-twyn,*' the girl huffed, sounding it out for him.

'That is us,' Eotenfrēond confirmed. He took another step towards Hugh, looking him in the eyes. He stood for a moment, unblinking and expressionless. Then he turned and began into the woods. His daughter lingered for a mere moment, then she followed, as Hugh stood still, taken aback by their sudden withdrawal.

'Where are you going?' he called out as they disappeared into the woodland, the small circle of torchlight shrinking. A reply came a moment later.

'Come.'

And so Hugh began after the ever-moving light, each step carrying him further into a forest that felt increasingly foreboding.

They moved quickly. To keep the light in his line of sight, Hugh picked up the pace, every few steps almost stumbling over a shrub or rolling his ankle on a root.

'Wait,' he found himself beckoning, his breathing quickening, each inhale ever so slightly more noticeable than the last. But the torch kept moving. In fact, it appeared to move more swiftly. It was as his brisk walk became a slow jog that Hugh remembered Guilliam's words: *Before long I could not tell if I had been following for mere minutes, or if I had been in those woods for days.* It occurred to him that he too had lost track of time. All he knew was that he had been following the druid and his daughter, but for how long now he couldn't quite determine. Had it been only a matter of minutes? Or even hours? He began to wonder how far they'd delved into the woods, glancing over his shoulder to see if perhaps he could still spy the opening, if a sliver of moonlight might make out the woodland's border. But behind him was blackness, nothing more. When he turned his head back, the flame was further away again, and so Hugh began to run after it now. He thricely swerved shy of charging headfirst into a tree trunk, his eyes still adjusting to the darkness of his surroundings, and soon he was having to avoid trees every few seconds as he dashed determinedly, worried that he might lose sight of the fire and very possibly his way out of the woodland. Fortunately, the ball of fire began to grow larger once more, and as it did so too did a light ahead. It was moonlight, and it was creeping through the trees. The torch ceased moving and Hugh could make out the silhouettes of Eotenfrēond and Beorhtwyn, who had now stopped in their tracks, a backdrop of moonlight piercing the trees behind them, casting long shadows. A series of strides saw Hugh standing before them, and now he could tell that just beyond the row of trees up ahead – the ones letting through the light – there was a small opening in the forest, a patch of treeless ground, soaked in the soft illumination of the moon.

'Where are you leading me?' Hugh asked, hiding the fact that their brisk departure had irked him, not wanting to affront his guides, worried that he perhaps had already, simply by stepping foot in the forest.

'To where you seek,' Eotenfrēond answered. 'Or what has become of it, at least.' And with that he entered into the opening, followed by his daughter.

Hugh followed, stepping into a glade of tall, green grass, the tips of its blades nearing his knees. It was as if he had quite suddenly walked into an altogether different place, the disorientation he had felt not a moment before washing away in an instant, as if purged by the lunar luminescence that filled the space. Wildflowers of every colour he could name grew here, and the sound of a nearby stream flowing freely carried through the space. Around them were a number of crudely erected tents, though apparently not enough to shelter the number of people congregating in the opening, many of whom were sitting or laying on bedrolls. And now, it seemed, every face in the opening had turned to Hugh. They had fallen silent. There were mothers and children still awake, young men around Hugh's age and some slightly older, all of them dressed in simple garments and furs, most of the men sporting shabby beards and the women wearing tangled, knotted manes, much like Beorhtwyn. He estimated perhaps thirty or forty people in all (of whom he could see), each studying him with a curious apprehensiveness, reassured only that he posed no threat thanks to Eotenfrēond's presence.

In the centre of the opening lay a crackling fire, and it was around this fire two more faces could be found. Eotenfrēond approached those sitting beside the flames and gestured for Hugh to follow with a nod. He did just that, each and every person he passed affording him a stare, their heads turning, following him as he followed the elder druid. When Eotenfrēond reached the fire, he faced Hugh and held his arms out.

'Welcome to what remains of Ealdgeat, Hugh Brombury.'

'You… you all live here?' Hugh asked, seeing now that it was a man and a woman sat by the fire. Each one of them looked to be old, older than everyone else he could make out in the opening, though younger than Eotenfrēond. The man's beard, which was greying but still lined with streaks of dark brown, was tied into one large plait, and the top of his head was completely bald, though hair grew freely from the sides, its crudely cut tips touching his shoulders. The woman, who sat opposite him, wore her hair wildly, it being shabby and matted and decorated with what appeared to be twigs and twine.

'There were more of us,' Eotenfrēond said. 'Until recently.'

'Who is this you've brought to our woods?' the woman by the fire spoke up. It was then that Hugh noticed, sitting perfectly still atop her shoulder was a bird. He squinted, wondering if he had seen it right. Indeed he had. It was a kestrel – by the look of its size and black-spotted, brown plumage – perched, unmoving, almost as if it were a part of her.

'He is a friend to Guilliam. And I might remind you, Fugolcwēn, these are not *our* woods.'

The woman with the kestrel bowed her head slightly. 'Of course, Eotenfrēond. I did not mean to infer so. My guard is up, is all.'

'As it is for us all,' Eotenfrēond replied.

The woman – Fugolcwēn – turned her attention to Hugh. 'He knows what has become of his friend?'

'What *will* become, unless I can help him,' Hugh spoke up.

Fugolcwēn and the other man by the fire glanced at Eotenfrēond.

'The Baron has granted our guest one month to clear Guilliam's name,' the elder said.

'And Guilliam thinks *we* can help you?' the man asked Hugh, with something of an accusatory nature to his tone.

'I would be grateful if you could,' Hugh replied. 'As would Guilliam, no doubt.'

The man sniggered, mockingly.

'This amuses you, Eoforgār?' Eotenfrēond asked.

'I am far from amused.'

'You take issue with my bringing the boy to our camp?'

'Guilliam brought naught but ruin upon us,' Eoforgār scowled as he spoke. 'We should never have allowed him to join us. Nor should we allow this boy anywhere near us. How do you know he is to be trusted?'

'I did not know you'd been chased into the woods, that your village was torn down,' Hugh said. His words were met with no response, so he cleared his throat and carried on. 'Nor does Guilliam. I spoke with him today. As far as he is aware, Ealdgeat still stands. It is not my intent to offend you with my presence. I merely wish to save Guilliam. I was his squire, some years ago. I left the service of another knight to travel here... but... but I do not know how I can help him. I only know that I do not believe he committed the crime he is accused of, and I should like for him to keep his head. And so I must try. Tomorrow, I will begin my inquiries. Naturally, those who believe he is guilty are far from pleased with my intervening in his execution, and so I cannot stay in Crooklingsham. Not tonight, at least. Guilliam told me to seek you out, and so I have. I know you owe me nothing,' he looked about the camp, and spoke up upon noticing that all around were listening closely. 'None of you do. All I can do is ask that you afford me a bedroll and allow me to share in your fire, and trust that you are the good-natured folk that Guilliam has me believe. But if the answer is no, I understand. These woods are vast. I will make my own camp, if I must.'

'I wouldn't go wandering too deep, lad,' Fugolcwēn said. She looked unyieldingly into Hugh's eyes, and as she did the kestrel on her shoulder finally moved, its head turning to face Hugh, the creature mimicking the woman on whom it was perched, its black pupils piercing him.

An uneasy silence followed her words, broken a moment later by Eotenfrēond. 'You may stay here, Hugh Brombury.'

'We did not agree—' Eoforgār began, but Eotenfrēond raised his hand, cutting the dispute short.

'For one night, you may stay. After you have begun your inquiries tomorrow, however, it is best you do not return. You were not followed by the villagers this evening, though once you start looking into their affairs, I imagine they will have even more reason to rid themselves of you. And they will surely keep keener eyes on your movements. I am afraid I cannot risk you leading them to us.'

'Thank you,' Hugh bowed his head. 'All of you. I will leave at sunrise.'

'You will require passage to find your way back,' Eotenfrēond said.

'It's no bother.'

Eotenfrēond smirked. 'Tell me, how long did it take you to follow us here?'

'I... well. I can't quite say. Though I'm sure I can find my way in daylight.'

'Travelling to and from this grove is not as simple as you think. A guide is required.' Eotenfrēond glanced over to one of the tents, of which his daughter sat outside. She was looking back, directly at Hugh, through narrowed and wary eyes. 'Beorhtwyn will lead you.'

As evening turned to night, many of the forest-dwelling folk retired to their tents. Hugh spent those transitory hours sat in solitude, on what could be considered the outskirts of the glade, though he was still very much subject to the stares and glares of the druids. The children amongst them seemed to study him with an innocent curiosity – there were even those who wandered towards him only to be stopped by their parents and sent back into their tents. The two whom he had conversed with by the fire – Fugolcwēn and Eoforgār – remained by the flames and continued to discuss matters with Eotenfrēond, every now and then turning to Hugh, Eoforgār even pointing at him from time to time. But eventually they seemed to settle, and of the three, Fugolcwēn was first to retire, followed by Eoforgār and finally Eotenfrēond, who spoke to his daughter before entering his tent.

Beorhtwyn, who had kept her eyes on Hugh, having lingered outside of her tent since their arrival, seemed somewhat disgruntled with the words her father had left her with, but accepted them with a single nod nonetheless. Once Eotenfrēond had departed to his tent, Beorhtwyn again settled her squinted gaze fixedly on Hugh.

He decided it was time to speak with her.

'I take it your father informed you that you're to guide me back to the village come morning,' Hugh said upon approach. Now that he was near, she finally turned her attention away from him, opting not to look at him as she spoke.

'He did.'

'And I take it that this displeases you.'

'You shouldn't have come here, Hugh Brombury. Why my father allowed it, I know not.'

'I wasn't followed. That's what you're worried about, isn't it – what everyone is worried about? I understand, too, with what happened to your previous settlement.'

'I am not worried about you having been followed. Had you been, then you certainly would not be here.'

'Then what is it?'

'What is what?'

'The two by the campfire, their main concern with my being here was that I might bring folk from the village. But you… have I offended you?'

She turned to Hugh. 'These woods are no place for outsiders.'

'And why is that, exactly?'

Once again she turned away.

'In Guilliam's message, he told of travelling to this place, mentioning things he could not write of. Then the woman with the kestrel, Fugolcwēn, she warned me of wandering too deep. And now your father tells me that finding my way back is no simple matter, that you must guide me. So tell me, what waits in these woods?'

For the first time since Hugh had set eyes on her, Beorhtwyn seemed to smile. That's not to say it was a warming, or kind smile, more so the sort of smile a parent might give upon hearing their child ask a question to which they have no business asking.

'Get some sleep, Hugh Brombury,' she said. 'We leave at sunrise.'

'Perhaps I shall find out for myself.'

At this Beorhtwyn broke out into a laugh. 'By all means,' she mocked. 'Get yourself lost and save me the journey come morning. Now I think I shall sleep, even if you shall not.'

'One final question, if I may,' Hugh called after her as she made for her tent. 'You let Guilliam in. Showed him these woods, when he was an outsider. Why was that?'

She stopped, and seemed to think on his question a moment, before turning to him.

'Most who wander into these woods are bound to lose their way. But there are those, too, who are lost long before they come across them. And it is only once here that they are truly found,' she looked about the opening, her eyes examining the many trees that surrounded them. 'Or so my father says. I suppose he thought Guilliam needed to be found.'

And with that, Beorhtwyn retired to her tent.

Chapter 16
An Early Inconvenience

The druids were gathered round the fire when Hugh woke, helping themselves to servings of what seemed a stew of sorts, simmering in a large pot.

'Will you breakfast with us, Hugh Brombury?' Eotenfrēond asked.

'I wouldn't wish to intrude anymore than I have already.'

'There's plenty to go around,' he reassured. 'You'll be better suited to help Guilliam on a full stomach.'

Not having had a hot meal since his evening at The Fighting Cock, Hugh gracefully accepted the offer, taking a bowl of stew; a hearty concoction of root vegetables and surprisingly tender meat (by his reckoning venison, with a little pigeon). As it had last night, his presence drew the attention of the entirety of those camped out in the opening, and he sensed a great many of the druids were irked at his enjoying a serving of their breakfast. But also as it had been last night, Eotenfrēond's word seemed final, and despite some dour dispositions, none vocalised their discontent.

Beorhtwyn was ready and waiting for Hugh once he had finished eating, just as enthusiastic at the thought of accompanying him back to the border of the woods as she had been leading him to their camp the evening prior. Before leaving he thanked Eotenfrēond for his hospitality, and the elder druid wished him good luck.

'It will grieve Guillliam to know what has become of Ealdgeat,' Hugh said as he prepared to part.

'As it grieves us all, Hugh Brombury.'

'If I might ask, before I go…'

'Yes?'

'Is there anything, anything at all, you can tell me that might go some way in helping me clear Guilliam's name?'

Eotenfrēond smiled softly. 'If I could help save him, I would. But the people of Crooklingsham made up their minds the moment they found that medallion of his in the poor girl's hand. They were looking for any excuse to drive us out, and he gave it to them. I did tell him, once he started staying with us, that he ought to put a stop to their… meetings. Especially with her being betrothed to another.'

'Meetings?' Hugh asked, unsure if he had heard right.

'He was quite infatuated, I suppose—'

'You mean to say they were courting one another? Guilliam and Ethel?'

'He… he didn't tell you?'

'There was no mention of it in his message. And yesterday our chat was cut short.'

'Forgive me, I assumed you were aware.'

'Their relationship… it was a secret, I presume?'

'I… I have said too much. Best you hear it from Guilliam himself. It is his tale to tell.'

'Yes… of course,' Hugh nodded. 'Thank you again for your hospitality, Eotenfrēond.'

With a nod and gentle smile, the elder druid bid him farewell, and then Hugh approached Beorhtwyn.

'I am ready,' he said.

'Keep up,' she answered, barely giving him a chance to register the words before beginning into the woods.

As she had the evening before, Beorhtwyn kept Hugh on his toes during their journey back to the village, and just as it had then, a feeling of disorientation began to creep over him, a certain uncertainty hindering his sense of direction and perplexing his perception of time. Remaining just within his sight, but always several steps ahead, Beorhtwyn turned her head every now and again, likely to make sure he hadn't got himself lost, but also affording him the chance to catch up to her. It appeared that she was entirely unaffected by this sense of directionlessness; lithe and graceful as she guided him through the thicket. It was to be expected of one familiar with the forest, of course. Still, to Hugh there didn't seem to be so much as even a vague path to follow. It was as if she were privy to some invisible compass, pointing her in the right direction in what he found to be an increasingly wildering woodland.

Eventually, the opening at the edge of the woods, which Hugh had entered the evening prior, appeared before them, though he had no notion of just how long it had taken them to reach. Beorhtwyn stepped aside, gesturing for him to follow the path out of the forest.

'You have my thanks,' he said, before heading towards the treeline. Before reaching it, however, he turned. 'What will become of your community? Do you mean to stay in the woods?'

'For now,' she said, gazing out of the opening, at the place where the village of Ealdgeat had once stood. Her wide, dark eyes seemed to droop ever so slightly. 'We'll move on eventually.'

'I am sorry for what happened to your village, for what it's worth.'

'It doesn't matter. Those who did it will see no punishment.'

'I could… if you wished for me to, that is… I could speak with the Baron, on your behalf?'

Once again that cutting laugh left her lips.

'He granted me a month to help Guilliam. Perhaps he will hear your plight, too. Perhaps you could have your justice.'

'Guilliam was a knight of noble birth, Hugh Brombury. And *you* are a squire. We, here, are heathens. Those who uphold the justice you speak of do not care for us. Not in these lands.' She looked back into the depths of the woodland. 'I must go,' she said, before offering him a parting glance. 'I hope you find the truth you seek.'

With that, Beorhtwyn turned and walked away, disappearing into the thicket.

Hugh headed for the gaol. The morning was fresh; grass gleaming with a coat of dew, glistening amidst a wispy mist that seemed to be dissolving beneath a recently risen sun. He passed the pasture and soon vague shapes of dwellings in the distance grew clearer, and he could almost hear the crispness of the moisture of the mist which hung to them like shrouds made from see-through silks, which meant that the village was yet to wake. Indeed, the patrons of The Unpleasant

Pheasant who had distantly taunted him last night were nowhere to be seen, no doubt sleeping off their ale-induced animosity. They would, he presumed, be just as unhappy to see him when they did eventually stir, but daylight brought with it a certain sense of security, and once the villagers learnt that Baron Turbert had permitted him to go about his business, he felt assured they would largely leave him be. He still had little hope of them welcoming him in the inn, mind you, and with the druids warning him against returning to the woods, he would have to find somewhere nearby to stay. Guilliam would be able to direct him to the nearest neighbouring hamlet, at least he hoped. Though as far as questions for his former mentor were concerned, directions weren't the first he sought to ask. As Hugh now approached the gaol, he knew precisely what he meant to ask the man inside.

He needed to know the truth about Ethel.

'Guilliam,' Hugh said aloud as he reached the cell, unbolting the wooden rectangle covering the hatch on the door. There was no answer. He opened the hatch and poked his face into the gap. At first he thought it was simply darkness that concealed Guilliam. But then his eyes adjusted.

There was no one inside.

'Guilliam,' Hugh called, knowing full well that simply saying the name louder wouldn't make his mentor reappear, though finding it to be the only thing he could think to do as it dawned on him that the gaol was empty. It was only then, as his hand found the handle, that he discovered the door to be unlocked. Someone had come for Guilliam.

Minutes later, Hugh was banging on the doors of the church.

'Father Dobbe,' he called. 'I must speak with you at once!' Morbid thoughts were filling his mind as he knocked repeatedly. What a fool he was to leave Guilliam unguarded last night! How naive to believe that the Baron's word would simply be accepted. For all he knew the villagers had seen to the execution themselves. To think he took the people of Crooklingsham for honourable folk, despite knowing nothing of them!

It took a minute's more banging before the priest opened the doors, seemingly in no rush to do so, appearing quite unconcerned as he stood before Hugh.

'Master Brombury,' he said calmly. 'Whatever commotion it is you now wish to cause, I would politely posit that it is far too early for it.'

'Where is he?' Hugh snapped.

'Come again?'

'You know of what I speak. Guilliam has gone.'

'Hmm,' Father Dobbe began pondering, quite unalarmed by the revelation. And then, a moment later: 'Gone, you say?'

'Yes.'

'Show me.'

And so they returned to the gaol, where Guilliam was indeed no longer imprisoned. Dobbe walked around the building at a leisurely pace, inspecting little more than bricks, before doing the same within.

'Ah,' the priest uttered matter-of-factly following his dawdling inspection. 'How curious.'

'Enough of this,' Hugh retorted. 'Is he alive?'

'Last I saw, he seemed to be.'

'Don't play the fool, Father. This is your doing, I'm sure of it.'

'Are you now, young man?'

'He is no longer in your gaol. Who else should have the authority to move him but yourself?'

'Yesterday evening, the two of *you* were talking. Privately. You might recall my objecting to it, for fear of your plotting an escape. And now your friend is… gone.'

'I… he has not escaped.'

'Is that not precisely what one who aided in his escape would say?'

'I… no, I did nothing of the sort. I was to speak with him this morning. He was to tell me—' Hugh paused. 'I was to begin my inquiries.'

'I see. He called after you yesterday, as you left, no?'

'What of it?'

'I believe he said *druids*. Is that where he sent you? To find his heathen playfellows?'

Hugh remained silent. It dawned on him what the priest was doing – whatever he said would be turned against him.

'It is, isn't it?' Father Dobbe smirked. 'Now why would he send you to them? Perhaps… perhaps he sought to get word to them. A message that might have aided in his escape.'

'He hasn't escaped,' Hugh retorted, locking eyes with the priest.

Dobbe turned to the empty cell. 'I do wonder what Baron Turbert will make of all this. To know that you have used the extra time he so generously afforded you, to help Guilliam escape the King's justice.'

'You…' Hugh uttered, though couldn't find the words to finish. He began to slowly back away, but with each step he took, the priest took another towards him.

And then Father Dobbe lurched.

Hugh stumbled backwards, but Dobbe's spindly fingers, outstretched as if suddenly a spider, grabbed a hold of Hugh's gambeson. He was surprisingly strong for such a slender man, the sudden grasp pulling Hugh off balance.

'Get off!' Hugh cried.

'Easy boy, you'll wake the village.'

Hugh tore away from the priest, that crooked smirk remaining on Dobbe's face as he snatched after him. But this time Hugh managed to swerve the elongated appendages, which only just brushed him as he set off with a sprint, dashing past the gaol. The priest didn't bother chasing, but Hugh could hear him chuckle as he ran away. Once he was well out of reach, Hugh turned to see Father Dobbe simply standing there, watching. He looked about the village. The mist was sinking now, falling off of the houses it had shrouded. And as it faded, villagers were beginning to wake. He could see faces appearing at windows, faces beset by unsettled expressions as they caught sight of his unexpected stand off with the priest. And then some of the faces disappeared from their windows and moments later doors were opening. Then came the chatter, murmurs shared amongst neighbours, and looks of alarm began to spread about the spectators. He had no choice but to start running again. Where to, he knew not, but he needed to get away from the village. And so he let his legs carry him where they might, and before long Hugh was once again approaching the pasture. He hadn't even thought to look behind him, though it appeared the chatter had died down. This didn't see him stop though, he was headed straight for the woods. He gave little thought to running back in that direction, other than it was the nearest place he knew of which might provide him somewhere out of sight to stop and surmise his next steps. And of course, the druids were there. Despite Eotenfrēond making it clear that they could offer him no aid, his only option seemed to be to return. If Guilliam was indeed still alive, he would need help in finding him, and he would need it quickly. There was no one else he could turn to.

Chapter 17
The Good Fellow

A dizzying wave washed over Hugh. It had taken no time at all for forest to swallow him, for it to close in around him, and now it seemed as though the branches above had knitted themselves together, the morning sun struggling to squeeze through the twisted matrimony of trees. Still, he stumbled deeper into the darkness, with gnarled roots and notched rocks faltering his footsteps. He called out for Beorhtwyn and Eotenfrēond. No one called back.

Peculiarity perforated the passage of time, just as it had previously. But now there was no one to escort him, no torchlight for him to follow. He understood now just why Eotenfrēond had insisted on him having a guide. Guilliam had alluded to the wonders of the woods, but Hugh found little in the way of wonder as he wandered aimlessly. He was still calling out the names of the druids known to him, but his voice had grown hoarse and his words uncertain.

'Is anyone there?' He found himself pleading with an indifferent environment, entirely unsure as to who he was even talking to. Perhaps he was simply trying to trick himself into thinking someone would hear, that help might still appear. And so he continued to ask the question, merely out of routine if nothing else. At some point he found himself to be both sweating and shivering simultaneously, caught between a stark breeze weaving itself between the trees, but also an inescapable, smothering humidity. Such a concoction of confounding sensations were wearying at best, and fast-proving to be quite debilitating. He had to rest his body, to gather his thoughts. And so he stumbled towards and then slumped against the nearest tree. His back pressed against its trunk, he let himself slide down until his haunches were beset firmly upon the dampish earth.

'Anyone… there…' he murmured still.

Naught but that intrusive, biting breeze answered. At least, at first.

'Lost, my good fellow?'

Hugh's neck jerked, his head snapping up, eyes suddenly widening. The voice, a man's, had been – as with most every incompatible occurrence within the woods – both distant and nearby at once, its cadence one of charm and tease.

'Hello?' Hugh replied to the speaker, looking about his surroundings as he clambered to his feet.

'Over here,' he said, which of course made finding him no easier, Hugh not able to distinguish *here* from *there*, or, for that matter, anywhere. This must have been apparent from his attempting to place the source of the speech, as the man, again with a touch of good-natured jest to his tone, continued: 'I see you've a case of acute incertitude.'

'Who's there? Are you with the druids?'

'Quite common in these parts,' he continued as if Hugh hadn't asked his questions. 'Especially amongst your kind.'

'Is… is this a trick?'

'Hmm… A trick. One way of looking at it… *Your* way, that is to say.'

'I… I don't understand.'

'Yes. Yes, I suppose what separates this place from the places you know could be thought of as *trickery*.'

'Did Dobbe send you?' Hugh glanced about frantically now, eyes wide but unable to focus, searching desperately for the source of the voice. Had Father Dobbe's mob caught up with him? Were they simply toying with him? 'You… you're from the village?'

'Village?' If this was feigned confusion, it was feigned convincingly. 'I do not dwell in such places.'

'You are with the druids, then?'

'I've known those who deem themselves druidic in demeanour, here and there. This is true of you?'

'I… no. I'm no druid.'

'No, don't seem the sort. If you don't mind my prying, what – besides from lost – are you?'

'I will not answer your questions until first I can see you.'

'Was it not you who asked for *my* help, but a moment ago, good fellow? You could at least afford me an answer. For I should like to know who it is I am helping.'

'You are playing tricks on me! Not helping.'

'I assure you, I can help you. I *will*, in fact. Surely my assistance is worth you sharing your name?'

'Show yourself first,' despite his mounting anxiousness, Hugh sought to speak with some authority.

'Why, my good fellow, I have not been hiding.'

'But I… I cannot see you.'

'I am where I have been this whole time.'

'Where's that?'

'Behind you.'

All of a sudden the voice was painfully obvious to place. It was a whisper in his ear. Perhaps it had been the whole time. Hugh startled forwards, spinning on his heels, stumbling back, tripping on a bulbous root. He landed with a thud, the wind whacked right out of him. The fall was dizzying, discombobulating his senses even more so than they already were. He winced, now sprawled on the bed of brown leaves that coated the ground, struggling to draw in a full breath. He was staring up, through the branches, at specs of dust floating in the strands of sunlight that pierced through the seemingly tethered treetops. But it wasn't just dust – the specs floated lazily through the air, so lazily that they had almost stopped completely, in fact, as if the forest was holding its breath as he struggled to regain his own. And they were shimmering too, subtly, that is to say, but undoubtedly coruscating countless colours. As the impact of the fall eased, Hugh propped himself up with his elbows, so that he was able to face the tree that he had had his back against. He had expected to see the man standing, looming over him, but naught but the tree itself was there. It made no sense. The whisper had unmistakably come from behind him.

And then he saw the face.

It was the face of a man, but it wasn't a man he was looking at. Sure enough, the tree was the only thing that loomed over Hugh, only the tree was looking at him with a pair of near-black eyes. Accompanying the eyes were features which, though now seemed so sharp and pronounced, were apparently part of the tree bark itself. Tufts of tangled foliage sprouting above had the look of an unruly head of hair now, and then there were crusts of moss that clung to the tree – Hugh had felt their powdery dampness pressed against his back only moments before – which looked remarkably like a beard. And beneath the bearded face he could now make out the outline of a lithe torso, which appeared to have been pressed into the tree almost, embossed as if it were a human sized seal, taut and rigid, stuck in a state of strenuous suspension, palms open, pushing, long fingers splayed wide, blemished by knots and whorls, as if caught and frozen still mid-quiver, itching to burst out of the bark at any moment.

'Wh… what are you?' Hugh uttered.

'Good fellow,' the mouth, moist with wood rot, moved. 'My state of rootedness has startled you, I fear.'

'Is this real?' Hugh was quite sure that the forest had driven him mad.

'Regrettably so. It is an unfortunate embrace indeed. But, I hope, an impermanent one.'

'My wits have surely left me,' Hugh found his feet, brushing himself down, though not peeling his eyes away from what was before him.

'Fear not, they seem intact to me. I should be more concerned if you did not think yourself mad, conversing with me in my current condition.'

Hugh turned around quite suddenly, holding his breath, his fists clenching and body tensing. Perhaps, he thought, if he simply looked away, the apparition might cease to be.

'Are you ailed, my good fellow?' the voice persisted.

'You are a fantasm,' Hugh's back remained to the tree.

'I assure you, beneath this bark I am very much formed of flesh and bone.'

Hugh turned slowly. The outline of the man in the tree was still there. 'You… you're a… man?'

'In parts. Now, seeing as I have shown myself, you shall share with me your name, yes?' he asked this through a faint smile, in a tone which was disarming in many ways, familiar almost. It would have put Hugh at ease had he not suspected that was the very intent behind it, that it was more than just a benign request.

And yet, for some reason he spurted it out. 'Hugh. Hugh Brombury,' he spoke as if compelled to. A moment later he cleared his throat, composing himself. 'And yours?'

'Ah, now that was not part of our bargain.'

'Bargain?'

'You requested I show myself in return for your name. And now our terms are upheld.'

'You are shrewd for a tree,' Hugh eyed him up and down, 'I did not realise we were bargaining.'

'Oh, but everything is a bargain, my good fellow.'

'Is that how… how you ended up like this? The bad end of a bargain?'

The moveless man chuckled. 'You're hardly lacking in shrewdness yourself, Hugh Brombury. Alas, it was no bargain that bound me here. Though maybe striking one with you might see me freed.'

'I do not wish to bargain with talking trees anymore than I already, unintentionally have.'

'You have not yet heard the terms.'

'I am not interested. And still unsure if my eyes deceive me. Now, I should take my leave.'

'And go where, Hugh Brombury? You are lost.'

'I shall find my way.'

'Your way out?'

'I… that is none of your concern.'

'How long has it taken you to find your way so far?'

Hugh did not answer.

'Minutes, maybe? Or is it hours? Dare I say, days? You know not how long you've wandered these woods, nor which way to go. How do you suppose you'll leave whilst lacking such senses?' Again the tone was over-familiar, charming. 'I know the way out. I could show you, if only you cut me free.'

'This is your bargain? Passage out of this place in exchange for me setting you loose?'

'It is a fair one, wouldn't you agree?'

'And how do you suppose I would cut you out?' Hugh humoured him. 'It seems to me it requires more than the swing of a simple wood axe to uproot you. Not that I possess one at present.'

'You are quite right on that count. No ordinary woodman's axe will do. Fortunately, a condition of my constraint was the forging of an axe that would indeed bring an end to it. A single, special axe that can cut me free. What's more, it is to be found in these very woods.'

'You mean to say whoever trapped you in this tree also forged an axe that can release you?'

'Aye.'

'And that it is left unguarded in the very same forest?'

'A malicious addition to the pitiless state assigned to me. To leave the only means to my freedom so near, yet me unable to move to acquire it. I can tell you where it is, Hugh Brombury. If you would but fetch the axe and free me, I will lead you from this place.'

'Such an agreement would require me to trust you.'

'You don't?'

'I am still yet to determine whether or not you are real, or merely a figment of my mind.'

'It is not a question of trust. I am bound by bargain, and this is a bargain plain as they come. Ensure my freedom, and secure your own. It is as unambiguous as an arrangement could be. There is nothing, surely, to distrust.'

'The druids with whom I camped last night cautioned against my wandering these woods alone. Perhaps it is you they were warning me of.'

'A superstitious bunch!' the tree declared merrily, amused by Hugh's suggestion. 'Though t'was a warning you'd have done well to heed, for their words were not without merit. I for one can attest to the perils lingering in these woods, though I assure you, I am not one of them.'

'But you are from these woods, are you not?'

'I am from all woods.'

'You wish for my trust yet you seem only to allude rather than answer,' Hugh spoke with a furrowed brow and began to gently rub his temple. 'You say you are *part* man, as if it were perfectly natural to be so, and attempt to convince me that freeing you is my only means of leaving this place, all the while you evade revealing both your name and the reason behind your entrapment.'

'Answer me this, Hugh Brombury. Have I sought to know *your* reason for being here?'

'I… I suppose you have not.'

'And nor will I, for it is not my business. The preconditions of your predicament are not mine to know, no more than mine are yours. I simply see an opportunity for each of us to aid the other in our respective plights, and seek to take advantage thereof.'

Again the man in the tree appeared to have it all thought out, to be one step ahead of Hugh in his reasoning. And it was reasoning that Hugh could find no fault with. For all the apprehension he felt towards the proposition, he feared further aimless wandering was all that awaited him without the bark-bound man's guidance.

'Tell me of this axe,' Hugh said. 'Where can it be found?'

'Am I to take this as acceptance of the terms?'

'If you hold true to your word and help me find my way,' Hugh paused, 'Then yes, I shall cut you loose.'

'And so it is,' the tree replied, the charm and cunning of his cadence clear in equal measure. 'The axe is set firmly in the stump of a felled tree, and has left in its path a trail of further felled trees, signposted by stumps, each shorter than the last. 'Tis only a short jaunt from here.'

'I've come to think that there exists no such short jaunts through this forest.'

'Verily so. Which is why you must follow the felled trees, Hugh Brombury. They shall go some way in assuring you stay steadfast.

The first can be found yonder, I can see it from here. Straight ahead it waits.'

Hugh turned and studied the spread of sprawling woodland which lay in wait. It took him a moment to spot it. The man in the tree spoke the truth, it would seem. Amidst a cluster of green-leafed timber towers reaching skyward sat a solitary stump, cleanly relieved of its top three quarters.

Hugh took a deep breath, glanced once more at the wooden man, and then walked towards the stump. Upon reaching it, he could see just how evenly the wood had been sliced; the exposed insides of the tree were as smooth a surface of wood as he had ever seen, and a perfectly level one at that. Compelled simply by the sight, he ran his fingers along the top of the stump, letting them glide along the immaculately exposed ligneous fibre. It felt as though he were brushing a polished steel blade. Pondering the need whichever woodsman responsible would have for such refinement, Hugh eyed the forest for the next stump. After a moment, it too was apparent in the distance, and sure enough shorter than the first. As he neared the next it was clear that this tree had also been flawlessly felled – it sat just as smooth as the last. This was true of the following stump, and the stump after that, and so on. Each stump led him to the next, each cut shorter than the one before. Once they were roughly knee height in their diminishing, Hugh saw it. The last stump; more apparent than any of those felled before thanks to the shimmering steel of the axe head half-stuck in it. All he need do now was remove it and return to the man in the tree.

He neared, and as he did, he heard a sudden rustling. From behind. He whipped around. Save for forest, he saw nothing. Cautious, he paused, noticing leaves that looked to have been crunched beneath feet. Surrounded by bushes of all sizes, there was ample undergrowth offering obscurity for what he suspected to be some sprightly animal that had darted past him. A rabbit or deer, perhaps. As the thought occurred to him however, he realised that he was yet to see such a creature in the woods. Other than the man in the tree, in fact, he had yet to see another living thing since returning to the woodland that morning.

Footfall again.

'Hello?' Hugh called, thinking now it may be more than a simple critter. But there was no reply. He waited in silence for a moment before continuing towards the axe. In a matter of strides he stood before it. It was sunk deep into the exposed wood of the stump before him, penetrating an otherwise perfectly cut tree. The surface was smooth and supple, and the way in which the axe sat in it reminded Hugh of a knife in softened butter. As for the axe itself, the steel appeared to be pristinely polished, its edge freshly sharpened. It had to it an odd bluish hue. The handle, however, retained a certain rawness; fashioned from what looked like naturally winding wood, not shaved or smoothed, with streaks of split grain and sap running along its length.

Hugh reached out slowly for the axe, weary of any would-be splinters. But before his hand touched the rustic wood of the handle, he felt a pinch at his left ankle, a sharp nip accompanied by the same scurrying sound from moments before. Releasing a brief shriek of pain and shock, he turned quickly, but his biter had already made off, scampering away from him. Whatever moved blended into its surroundings – it was almost indistinguishable from them, in fact. It was only the manner in which it scurried that gave it away, though it looked almost as if it were a moving bush, shaped, however, like something limbed, squat in stature, yet agile.

Hugh was able to gather little more than a glimpse of the creature, but having at the very least determined its size, felt less threatened now than he otherwise might have. A moment of silent stillness followed, broken by a fissle in the foliage ahead.

'Shoo,' Hugh started towards the bushes. 'You little nipper!'

But then it appeared again, bursting from the bushes it had vanished into, darting towards Hugh with its head bowed. Only now he could make it out more clearly; atop its head grew a pair of antlers – the sort you might find on a young stag – which threatened to stick his midriff. Hugh leapt aside, his body clumping on the ground as the creature propelled forwards, missing him by mere inches. It was coated entirely in what looked to be coarse hair – no, not hair, but branches, as might be found on a bush barren of leaves. Having missed its target, the twig-covered creature turned, its eyes – wide eyes of rich green – meeting Hugh's, to which he gasped, for its face resembled a persons. Scrambling to his feet, Hugh turned and made for the axe, if only for means of defence.

He lunged for the handle, but the antlered creature charged him again, mouth open wide. A set of pointed teeth caught Hugh's wrist, only pinching the skin, but it was enough to make him flinch.

'Away, goblin!' Hugh shouted as he drew his wrist back and kicked at the creature. Of course, *goblin* was no more than a guess as to the nature of this thing, with Hugh having never seen a goblin before, nor believing in their existence until that very moment. But this time the bramble-furred beast did not dart away. It had placed itself between Hugh and the axe, and was poised, ready to pounce, to charge him with its antlers. Hugh managed to clamber backwards a little, and he saw more of the creature now, namely its tail, which, by his reckoning, was no different than that of a beaver's.

Hugh jolted forwards, only to pull back a second later, hoping to startle the creature. It flinched, but stood – yes, it seemed quite capable of standing on two legs – its ground. He thought back to Ethel, how Guilliam had described the state in which she'd been found, scratched and cut as if dragged through thorns. Could this beast's branched-fur have been the cause? But this thought lasted only for a second, because, looking at it as he now did, this was no beast. It had nipped him, yes, but barely seemed capable of killing, it being no taller than a child. And curiously, for all of its resolve, it appeared to be quite terrified. There was, about its oddly human face, an unmistakable expression of fear. Hugh was suddenly aware they had become ensnared in a shared stare, with the forest around him dimming, fading into a blur as he held the creature's gaze. In that moment he couldn't help but pity it, as it trembled ever so slightly before him. Perhaps if he could simply show he meant it no harm, the creature would leave him be.

With a delicate nod, he gestured to the axe. Remarkably, the creature responded, shaking its head softly in return.

A steady patter of feet disturbed the staring. Both Hugh's and the creature's heads snapped towards the source of the sound. A figure neared. Might this be another one of these, whatever *these* were? But then the figure came into focus, approaching with haste, pushing through the thick tangle of brush and untamed bramble, and it was clear they were taller. It was a person, and it was a person Hugh knew.

'Hugh Brombury,' Beorhtwyn stopped in her tracks, somewhat surprised to find him. A hunting bow was slung across her body, and a quiver of arrows hung from her belt. She appeared to be about to wield the weapon, but then she caught sight of the creature. Hugh expected it to either charge her, as it had him, or perhaps rush away and disappear into the brush. But neither of those things happened.

'It's ok,' Beorhtwyn spoke softly to the bramble-bearded being, crouching to its level and raising her left arm slowly, reaching out. 'He means no harm.'

The creature looked to the axe again, and then back to Beorhtwyn.

'He will leave it be,' she said, assuringly. Beorhtwyn glanced at Hugh, gesturing for him to come to her. He carefully made his way over, keeping his eyes on the creature. It appeared calmer, as if comforted by Beorhtwyn's words, even if not understanding them. Once Hugh reached her, Beorhtwyn nodded to the creature. It returned the gesture.

'Come,' she said to Hugh, her eyes still on it.

'What… what is that thing?'

'It is afraid,' she turned to Hugh, a slight furrow in her brow and a pout that more than expressed her displeasure with him. She began to back away. Hugh followed. As they backed into the brushwood Beorhtwyn had appeared from, the little twig-haired creature grew smaller, more distant.

And then it was out of sight.

'I told you not to wander these woods alone,' Beorhtwyn rebuked the second they'd ceased in their retreat.

'I… it's Guilliam,' he said. Of course, he had so many questions, but time enough had been wasted already.

'What of him?'

'He was gone from the gaol this morn. The villagers… I think they mean to execute him. If they haven't already. Dobbe… he went for me, accused me of helping Guilliam escape. I… I didn't know where else to go.'

Beorhtwyn's expression changed from one of contempt to concern. She stood in thought for a moment. 'You know where they have taken him?'

Hugh shook his head.

'Come' she said. 'Time is fleeting.'

Chapter 18
A Fracas in the Forest

'You knew that... that... *animal* back there?' Hugh asked Beorhtwyn as they made haste through the forest, briar and bramble scratching at his ankles and protruding roots threatening to trip him as the pair pressed through thicket as quick they could.

'They are no animals,' she replied. 'This is their home.'

'*They*? You mean to say there are more?'

'Many more.'

'What are they?'

She did not respond immediately, appearing to consider whether she ought to tell Hugh more of what he had seen. After a moment she said, 'We've taken to calling them dam-dwellers.'

'And you have had dealings with these dam-dwellers?'

'Few to speak of. They know that those from our camp pose no threat to them, and we know they pose none to us.'

'This forest is fraught with beings beyond belief then! And to think I have witnessed two in such short succession.'

Beorhtwyn slowed, turning to Hugh. 'You saw another?'

'Aye, but it was not like this one. And it did not dwell in a dam.'

'What was it you saw?' she stopped running, suddenly sounding more serious than she had thus far.

'Why have we stopped? We must find Guilliam—'

'What was it you saw?' she repeated.

'A man, inside of a tree. He spoke with me.'

'*He* sent you to fetch the axe?'

'In return for passage out of here,' Hugh nodded. 'This troubles you?'

'That was no man, Hugh Brombury. He is a trickster, as cunning as he is ancient. That tree is his prison. You are fortunate the dam-dweller stopped you taking the axe. For if you were to free him…' she did not finish, rather she paused. 'But you are right. We must now focus on finding Guilliam.' With that, she set off again.

The sun was beginning to breach the trees now, leading Hugh to believe it was likely nearing noon. 'How is it you know where we can find him?' he asked Beorhtwyn, running beside her.

'This morning, one of our watchers saw three villagers enter the woods. One of them was being dragged by the other two. For fear of them venturing too deep and discovering us, I set about tracking them. Or so I thought. It was your footprints I actually happened upon.'

'Dragged? That means they've brought Guilliam here to… what if we're too late?'

'Guilliam is more well-versed in this place than they are. Perhaps it will buy him some time.'

'You can lead us to them?'

'If I can find their trail…'

Hugh noticed now that Beorhtwyn was scanning their surroundings as they moved, and had been doing so since they'd started. Best to keep quiet, so that she might focus, he thought. So he followed in silence, as she once again navigated the woodland with the same nuance as she had when guiding him that very morning. Eventually, she stopped, crouching down. She had spotted something. She reached for it and held it up. It was a strip of fabric, torn from a smock or tunic.

'They are near,' she said. Then she looked Hugh up and down.

'What is it?' he asked.

'You're not armed.'

'I… my sword was lost. On the road.'

'When we find them, I will not be able to help you. The villagers cannot know we dwell here still.'

'Well, then I shall face them alone.'

'Alone *and* weaponless.'

'So it would seem.'

Beorhtwyn sighed. With her right hand she reached to her left hip, and pulled out an item which had until then been concealed by her cloak – a crude hunting knife, its blade about the length of her wrist and its handle wrapped in worn leather. Hugh thanked her as she handed it to him, hesitating and stating, 'I want this back,' before letting go of the blade.

Then she was scouring their surroundings again, her eyes narrow. 'Here,' she said after a moment, crouching. 'Footprints. Two pairs. And this,' she pointed to what resembled a raked streak, which had cleared a line of leaves, revealing a travel trail of dirt. 'Someone was dragged.'

They swiftly followed the trail, which soon became obscured again, though Beorhtwyn was, it seemed, an immaculate tracker, able to identify even the faintest of footmark. Hugh followed her as she traversed through the trees, noting that they were nearing the outskirts of the woods, sunbeams brightening by the minute, protruding the edge of the woodlands as the trail that Beorhtwyn tracked led them away from the disconcerting depths. As he found himself further from those depths, his perception of his bearings and the passing of time seemed to correct itself again, the sensation of disorientation that had become near normal for him now remedying with every step. His wits had almost returned in their utmost when Beorhtwyn once more raised her hand, signalling for Hugh to stop. He obliged the instruction in an instant, standing silently, following Beorhtwyn's lead as she crouched.

A moment passed. Then he heard it. Voices, not far away. Beorhtwyn began forwards, slowly, carefully, each step deliberate. She was crouched, so Hugh crouched too, keeping close as she tactfully peeled back the shrubbery that obscured their view of the nearby speakers. As they encroached on the source of the sound, it became apparent the speakers were ill at ease. Both voices belonged to men, and one seemed to be hurrying the other, sternly stating that they should get on with whatever it was they were up to. Hugh had an idea what this might be. A few steps later, his suspicions were confirmed.

Approaching a row of bushes that were the final barrier between them and the voices, Beorhtwyn gently peeled leaves apart, revealing the scene ahead. There were indeed two men; the two they had heard. And, as reported by the watcher, a third.

It was Guilliam.

He was kneeling. A rope had been tied around his neck and strung around a near-broken tree branch, swaying gently above him, not quite fully snapped, meaning the rope was still slack. The two men appeared to be in the midst of a disagreement as to how to best proceed. Clearly, their first attempt at a reckoning had not gone how they'd hoped.

Beorhtwyn turned to Hugh. 'Can you handle them both?' she spoke quietly.

Hugh watched a moment more before answering. Guilliam's hands were chained behind his back, though neither man appeared armed.

'You mean can I talk them down?' he replied, also in a whisper.

Beorhtwyn simply glanced at the knife she had given him.

'I should like to try and parley, first,' Hugh continued. 'I have no desire for violence.'

'They have already gone to the trouble of dragging your friend from his cage to hang him from a tree branch. You think they can be reasoned with?'

Hugh had no answer for her. He did not know. He slipped the knife between his belt behind him, and took some subdued steps forwards, towards the ruckus, creating enough distance between himself and Beorhtwyn before standing to his feet, emerging from the thicket and approaching the two men with a meaningful stride.

'Good sirs,' he called out.

Needless to say, both men were surprised by the unforeseen introduction. They pivoted suddenly, alarmed by the intrusion and, as they turned to him in their state of startle, Hugh could see them more clearly now. One was a man with greying hair who wore a beard in need of a good grooming and was perhaps in middle-age, though his eyes looked heavy and tired, which made him seem altogether older. The other was younger, no more than a few years older than Hugh, tall and broad-shouldered with thick forearms, and looked as though he might well have been able to hoist Guilliam up all by himself, without the aid of his senior accomplice.

'Stay back!' barked the younger of the two. The older one placed a hand on his shoulder and stepped forwards.

'This doesn't concern you, friend,' he said, squinting. He appeared to be trying to determine whether or not he recognised Hugh, though his squint softened once it was apparent he did not. 'T'is a matter of local justice.'

Guilliam – who was still on his knees and facing away from Hugh – half-glanced over his shoulder. He caught sight of Hugh, meeting his eye, but did not give away that they were known to one another.

'A hanging in the woods. This is how your village sees fit to deliver justice?' As they did not seem to have him for the squire, Hugh presumed they had taken him for a passing traveller, and thought best to assume the role momentarily.

The younger of the two marched forwards. 'Our laws are our own to uphold. Unless you wish to see this murderer hang, you'd best be on your way.'

Hugh was certain now that neither of them were armed. Again, Guilliam afforded him a glance, but this time Hugh could see that he had been gagged. The younger of the men turned, making for the rope. Hugh sighed, stepping closer. 'There shall be no hanging today,' he said.

The younger man, whose brow had deeply furrowed, was about to respond, but the older stepped in. 'I appreciate your cause for concern. But I assure you, friend, this man is a murderer and a heathen.'

'He is neither,' Hugh said. Both of them were perturbed by this. 'He is Sir Guilliam the Great. As for your local laws, your own Baron Turbert yesterday granted me one month to clear his name of the murder you hold him responsible for, though I assure you, he did not commit.'

The younger man clenched his fists, but Hugh continued.

'Now, I would ask you to kindly step away from the rope, and allow me to escort Sir Guilliam back to the Baron, with whom I will arrange to have him gaoled somewhere other than your village for the duration of my inquiries, for I no longer believe him safe there.'

'It's you!' the younger one snarled, flecks of spit accompanying the words, the skin of his face scrunching. '*You're* the squire.'

'I am.'

'Damn this!' the younger one charged for Hugh and dived. With not so much as a second to avoid the burly body that flew towards him, Hugh was driven into the ground, crushed beneath a meaty shoulder.

'Hammond, no!' cried the other man, clearly distressed.

But Hammond was having none of it, wasting no time in grabbing Hugh by the throat. Hugh writhed beneath the weight of him, struggling to slip out from beneath, to no avail. A moment more and he was reaching for the knife, but the instant he drew it, Hammond grabbed his arm, restraining him, and the knife slipped from Hugh's grasp.

The other man made to go to them, but managed no more than two steps before toppling, tripping over the rope which he had moments before been pulling. It was only once he'd hit the leaf litter that it became clear what had happened; Guilliam was up and had darted forwards, using the very rope around his neck to sweep the man's legs from beneath him.

'Hugh!' Guilliam called, having half-spat out his gag, turning around and rushing to his friend. Hammond barely had time to turn and see the shackles, and then a chain was looped over his neck and yanking him away from Hugh. Guilliam must have managed to step over the irons during the distraction, and now his restraints had become his weapon. He pulled them towards his torso with all his might, causing the blacksmith's boy to remove his hand from Hugh's neck and reach for his own.

With Hammond now trying to free himself, Hugh managed to wriggle out from beneath him, propping himself up onto his elbows. Despite his current state of gauntness, in that moment Guilliam reminded Hugh much of his older self, wrestling with – and presently bettering – a man twice his size. Yet Guilliam seemed to have found his strength, as he pulled his captor further and further away from Hugh.

His hand free, Hugh scrambled for the knife. Glancing around the ground, he could see that it had been flung two strides or so away. He crawled towards it. He grabbed it. Then he heard a large crack followed by an *oof*. Blade in hand, he spun around again. The older man had found his feet. And apparently a log. He stood over

Guilliam, whose head drooped, dazed by the blow. His hands fell limp and his shackles hung loosely around Hammond's neck now, and so the blacksmith's boy simply slipped out between them and pushed Guilliam to the ground. He groaned as he hit the dirt, and when Hammond found his feet a few seconds later and gave Guilliam a kick in the ribs, he let out another. Hugh raised the hunting knife, pointing it at the men, their attention now on him.

'Get out of here, boy,' the older man said, sounding far less patient this time. 'Your butter knife's not big enough to stop both of us.'

'I'm not leaving without him,' Hugh said.

'He must pay for what he's done!' the older man retorted, raw emotion in his words and expression now, eyes watering, lip trembling, saliva leaving his mouth as he vehemently voiced his objection.

'I.. I di…' Guilliam uttered, a cough accompanying every vowel. 'I didn't… kill her.'

'You lie!' Hammond barked, kicking him again.

'Leave him be,' Hugh rushed towards them, blade first. He didn't mean to stick either of the men with the knife, merely scare them back some way. It worked. On Hammond, at least, who stumbled backwards, clearing himself from the path of its point.

But the older of the two was either blind to it or simply did not care. Instead of stepping away, he stepped towards Hugh, log still in hand, and swung. Hugh managed to swerve it for the most part, though its notched end nicked his face, cutting him across the nose and sending him stumbling off to the side.

'He robbed me of my daughter,' the older man cried out. 'You'll not rob me of revenge!' He held the log high above Guilliam's head, meaning to bring it down.

A sudden whoosh.

And then the would-be-weapon was no longer in the man's grasp, but on the ground. An arrow lodged in it. Before them appeared Beorhtwyn, a bow in one hand. With her other, she removed another arrow from her quiver and readied it, aiming it at the older of the attackers.

'You boys quite finished?' she said.

Chapter 19
A Discreet Deliberation

Hugh bound their hands with rope as Beorhtwyn kept her bow nocked and pointed at the two villagers, leaving enough distance between herself and her targets that they were within sight, though not earshot.

'I would advise against attempting to flee,' Hugh said, turning the two men around, so that their backs were turned to the lingering archer. 'I don't think she's one for *missing*.'

'They'll hang you too, for this,' Hammond grunted in response.

'I wouldn't be so sure,' Hugh replied. He walked back towards Beorhtwyn. 'Thank you. Again,' he said to her.

Guilliam – who had taken some time in gathering himself – smiled warmly. 'Beorhtwyn. It's good to see you.'

She returned the smile, though hers seemed bittersweet. 'You look awful,' she said. Though she spoke plainly, there was some warmth to the way she said it.

'Worse than it looks,' Guilliam smirked through the pain he was still clearly in.

'What'll you do now?' Beorhtwyn asked the both of them. 'Run?'

'No,' Guilliam shook his head.

'Sir, we have the chance—'

'No, Hugh,' Guilliam cut in. 'I'll not run. Not from a crime I did not commit.'

'They tried to kill you,' Hugh protested. 'And back in the village, Father Dobbe accused me of helping you escape, though I'm sure he knew full well that these men had taken you. They don't care for the Baron's extension granted to me. They've made up their minds.'

'If I flee, there'll be no question. My escape would be as good as a confession.'

'If they don't catch you, what does it matter?'

'Because then,' his voice cracked, 'then they'll never catch who did it. Who killed Ethel.'

Beorhtwyn lowered her head. Hugh frowned, recalling Eotenfrēond's revelation regarding the two of them.

'Hugh, there's something I must tell—'

'I know,' Hugh said.

Guilliam arched his brow.

'About you and Ethel. I found out this morning. Eotenfrēond mentioned it. He assumed me aware.' There was a brief silence. 'I am sorry, Sir. I did not know you were…' he let his words trail off. 'If you will not flee, then what is our course of action?'

'Why, you have already decided,' Guilliam answered. Now it was

Hugh who arched a brow. 'As you said, you will return me to the Baron, with whom you will arrange to have me gaoled somewhere other than the village for the duration of your inquiries.'

'And what of these two?' Beorhtwyn asked, nodding to the villagers. 'We cannot simply set them loose.'

'We can leave them to the Baron,' Guilliam said.

'No,' Beorhtwyn snarled. 'They know we're still here now. More will come to the woods.'

'What do you speak of?' Guilliam asked.

But she didn't answer, or perhaps couldn't. She simply stared at the two men, her fist and the bow it held trembling.

'Beorhtwyn, what is it?'

'Sir Guilliam,' Hugh said. 'The village. Ealdgeat, they… it is no more.'

Guilliam didn't appear to register the words at first, his troubled eyes darting between both Beorhtwyn and Hugh. 'You mean to say—'

'They tore Ealdgeat down. Torched it,' Beorhtwyn said matter-of-factly, her glare and aim unfaltering. She spoke loudly enough so that the men her arrow was aimed at could hear.

'It's no less than you deserve,' Hammond retorted, turning to face them. 'You people and your ungodly practices have no place here.'

Guilliam's gaze met the blacksmith boy's. Behind him, Ethel's father hung his head. Then Guilliam asked Beorhtwyn, quietly, so only the three of them could hear: 'What of the druids?'

'We have taken refuge. Deep in these woods.'

'The way is open?' Guilliam asked. He sounded shocked, and Hugh could not make sense of why this was, nor the meaning behind his words.

'It is.'

'Is it not perilous, to leave it remaining in such a state?'

'Yes. Yet I had no choice. It was the only place we knew to go. But as long as we remain in these woods, the way remains open, and the line can be crossed.'

'You cannot close it?'

'I have never tried from within. And I fear, if I do, we may not be able to return.'

'Forgive me,' Hugh said. 'What is this line you speak of? What *way* is open?'

Guilliam and Beorhtwyn shared a knowing glance.

'He should know,' Guilliam said. 'I had planned to tell him anyway.'

'Know what?' Hugh pressed.

'I suppose you have already *seen* it,' Beorhtwyn replied a moment later, with a hint of resignation. She looked directly at Hugh. Just as they had upon first meeting, her big brown eyes bore into him. 'There are parts of these woods, parts that *you* have wandered, that do not belong to this world. At least not all of the time. You have crossed a line into hidden depths. Those depths – where we made our camp, and where I found you earlier – are closed off to most. But there are some who can sense the lines that separate such places from our world. Those who are able to open the way. And you will know should you stumble across such a place; it is why you forget your bearings, and lose all notion of time when you walk here, and it is why you have seen such creatures as you have.'

Hugh didn't know what to say, nor make, of what had just been told to him, and found himself looking to his erstwhile mentor. Guilliam nodded.

'You mean to say we have… crossed into another realm?'

'You might call it that,' Beorhtwyn said. 'Though more that it has bled into our own. As long as the way remains open, at least.'

'You certainly would not find the *depths* Beorhtwyn speaks of on any map,' Guilliam added.

'And you… you are able to "open the way" as you say?'

'I am,' Beorhtwyn answered.

'This is what you wrote of,' Hugh turned to Guilliam. 'In your message. This is what they showed you. This place.'

'It is,' Guilliam said.

'How is it you…' Hugh turned back to Beorhtwyn. '*Sense* this line? Open the way from our world to here?'

She shrugged. 'I cannot remember how long I have been able to cross into these places. Perhaps always. It was woods much like these ones in which my father found me, as a babe.'

'Found you? You mean to say—'

'Eotenfrēond is not my blood. Though, he raised me as if I were his. Soon after he found me and brought me to his people, the way to the woods in which I was found closed. When I was a child, we wandered this country, seeking out new paths to walk, new ways to open and lines to cross. Here and there, we found some. Not often. Then one day we came upon Crooklingsham, and the woods beyond its pasture. And in those woods, I sensed a line. A line which led to the most vast and verdant of all the hidden places we had ever crossed into.' She looked again at Hammond and Ethel's father. 'We built our village on its border so that we might learn more of what lay in this place. We did, for a while. We never sought conflict with the people of Crooklingsham, but they see us as heathens. Now they have torn down our village, I fear what will become of these woods should word reach the rest of them that we are still here.'

For a moment, no one spoke.

'They must return to the village with us,' Hugh said, decisively.

'You would let them go free? After they sought to string up Guilliam?'

'No, not free. They will be my prisoners.'

'Hugh,' Guilliam said. 'You don't hold the authority.'

'Of all of us here, Sir, I believe I do. I am yet a squire, after all. A squire without a knight to serve, perhaps, but a squire who has been granted legal authority by the Baron, who is lord of this land. These two men sought to undermine that authority, and therefore they shall be my prisoners, and I shall present them to the Baron as such. I will ask that they be gaoled outside of Crooklinghsham for the remainder of my investigation, so that they cannot confer with anyone as to your being here.'

'You put too much faith in this Baron,' Beorhtwyn noted. 'You would do well to remember his interests do not align with yours.'

'No, but nor do I believe they align with Father Dobbe's. You are right, Beorhtwyn, in so far as that Baron Turbert is, I deem, a man of profound self-interest. But upon learning of who exactly *you* were, Sir Guilliam, he became uneasy at the thought of executing you. He even went so far as to suggest I lay blame on any other of the druids. Offer the locals the head of a lowborn and be done with it. Not that I intend to heed this counsel. But it does show that he would rather not have to sentence you to die, if only to avoid the disfavour of the many feudal lords who know your name and admire your many deeds. I believe that in taking these two as my prisoners, the Baron will agree that I am acting within the limits of the authority he has granted me.'

Guilliam took a deep, contemplative breath. 'So be it,' he said a moment later. The three of them now looked at once to the two men bound before them. 'You best go let your prisoners know that they are *your* prisoners,' he said to Hugh.

And so Hugh began towards them.

'You think this wise?' Beorhtwyn asked.

'No,' Guilliam answered. 'But what choice do we have?'

Chapter 20
The Baron's Room

Beorhtwyn accompanied them only to the border of the woodlands. 'Here,' she said, offering her bow and quiver of arrows when Hugh handed her back her hunting knife.

'Beorhtwyn, I couldn't.'

'You'll need it to escort them. You can keep this one. I've another.'

Hesitantly, he took the bow. The face from the battlefield in Crécy flashed through his mind. 'I... I'm not the best shot.'

Beorhtwyn's lips curled into a slight smirk. 'You shall only have to shoot if one of them decides to run,' she said, loudly enough so that Hugh's now prisoners would hear. They were still some strides ahead of them, having been walked to the edge of the woods with Beorhtwyn's arrow nocked and aimed at them the entire while. She looked to Guilliam. 'And you're sure you don't want me to see about removing your chains?'

'As much as it would please me to be rid of these,' he held up his shackled wrists, 'my being manacled betters our chances that the villagers shan't set upon us. It's perilous enough for Hugh to be marching these two back to the Baron with their hands bound. At the least, if I remain a prisoner beside them, it may give the villagers pause for thought .'

'Let us hope so,' Beorhtwyn replied.

'Yet again, my lady, I am indebted to you,' Hugh said, gesturing to the bow.

'*My lady*,' Beorhtwyn near chuckled. 'I cannot say I have ever been called that.'

Hugh felt his cheeks redden.

'Before we part,' Guilliam said. 'I… Tell your father that I am sorry for what happened to Ealdgeat. Tell everyone that I am sorry. I did not know they would…'

She placed a hand on Guilliam's shoulder. 'May fortune favour you both,' she said with a nod. She smiled softly at Hugh. 'And may my bow serve you well, Hugh Brombury.' Then she turned, and walked once more into the woods.

Drawn out shadows sprawled across the pasture, the stains of a fading afternoon. Guilliam led the procession of prisoners who now trudged single-file across the overgrown grass of the pleasantly green field, so that if either Hammond or Ethel's father did decide to run for it, they would have to attempt to pass him first. Though he held no intention of shooting either man, Hugh kept the arrow aimed from behind, which seemed to be enough to encourage their continued compliance.

Before long, Crooklingsham drew near. Hammond and Ethel's father shared a knowing glance.

'Don't try anything now,' Hugh called out. 'We're to find the Baron straight away.'

A woman hanging clothes out to dry from a line stretched between two posts was the first to notice the three men being marched. She immediately called out for her husband, who came tottering out of their abode some seconds later, squinting up until the point the prisoners passed him.

'Hammond? Elias?' he spoke the names of his fellow townsmen, each of them acknowledging him with a glance.

'Fetch the priest,' Hammond said to the man.

'Quiet,' Hugh snapped. Then, turning to the onlookers. 'These men are my prisoners. They tried to take the law into their own hands, and I am bringing them to Baron Turbert, along with Guilliam. Tell me, where is he?'

'Ummm,' the man began, appearing quite unsure what to do at that moment. His wife gave him a sudden nudge and scowled at him. 'What?'

'Get Father Dobbe,' she spoke in a whisper, though Hugh was close enough to hear.

'No,' Hugh retorted. 'Fetch the Baron,

The man seemed at a loss, but another, sterner scowl from his wife saw him make up his mind, and he careened towards the church yonder.

Hugh groaned. Guilliam turned to him. 'Quick,' he said, then rushed over to Hammond, stood behind him and looped his chains around his neck.

'Get off—' Hammond protested, only to be silenced by a sharp elbow to his ribs.

'We'll make for The Pheasant,' Guilliam declared, then addressing Elias: 'Will the Baron be in his room?'

Elias sighed, clearly in no rush to reveal as much.

'Answer him!' Hugh snapped, pulling the arrow aimed at the innkeeper's back in an over-obvious manner.

'Aye,' Elias spoke calmly. 'I would think so.'

'The Pheasant, then,' Guilliam nodded to Hugh.

'And what if he's not there?' Hugh asked.

Guilliam looked past Hugh, and could make out the beginnings of curious villagers making their way towards them. 'Let's hope he is,' he answered.

They began in the direction of the inn. Hammond tried to drag his feet, but a jab or two more from Guilliam saw him move with them, and Elias, with the arrow pointed at his back, put up no fuss. The Unpleasant Pheasant was no more than a couple of minutes away, but now villagers were leaving their homes, lining the streets, watching with bewildered faces and crumpled brows as the four men made for the inn. Those couple of minutes passed before Hugh could make out the signpost bearing the bird for which the inn was named; it creaked as it swayed in the breeze. As they neared the front door of the alehouse, there was the odd jeer, here or there, though the jeers quickly soured into a scornful chorus, catching on as if it were a fast burning match, and along with the hectoring the odd pebble or piece of rotten fruit was hurled.

'Stay back!' Hugh spoke as loud as he could. 'These men are to be brought before the Baron, for taking the law unto themselves. I shall see to it that any man or woman who interferes accompanies them.'

A tomato narrowly missed Hugh's face, the cry of *heathen friend* following it. Forced to barge their way past a group gathered before the inn-front, Guilliam kicked the door open, and he, Hugh and their detainees stumbled into a half-packed alehouse.

'Barricade the door,' Guilliam exclaimed, and Hugh promptly dragged the nearest (fortunately unoccupied) table to it, flipping it over and pressing it firmly against the door.

Lips left flagons mid-swig as the heads of drinkers turned in bewilderment at the sudden commotion. Amongst those present, Hugh noticed the two oafs who had accompanied the Baron to the village. They did not notice him, however, on account of them being blind drunk. One was passed out on a bench, his face resting against wood wetted by a recently spilled flagon, and the other was slightly more upright, one eye closed, head held up by one hand as he gulped slowly from his own mug with the other, apparently oblivious to their entrance.

'Elias?' a man behind the bar announced, upon seeing the proprietor dragged into his own establishment in such an unbecoming manner. A few of the men stood, making towards them.

'It's all right, lads,' Elias assured them, causing them to pause.

'The Baron's room,' Hugh addressed Elias. 'Take us.'

'Elias,' Hammond squawked, Guilliam's chains still around his neck. He shook his head. 'Let's have at them.' This suggestion roused a few cheers.

'Quiet!' Guilliam barked.

But with a reluctant sigh, Elias shook his head.

'Elias!' Hammond protested, his voice strained now as Guilliam pulled him back, the chains digging into his windpipe.

'No,' Elias said. 'I would see the man who murdered my Ethel hang, but this one's just a boy. Not much younger than her.' He looked about the inn, 'No one is to hurt him,' and then to Hugh, 'Ask him to remove his chains from Hammond's neck, and I'll show you.'

They held one another's gaze for a moment, Hugh holding the bow firm.

'He won't try anything,' as Elias spoke he kept his eyes fixed on Hugh's. 'Not while he's in my inn. Isn't that right, Hammond.'

'Right,' croaked Hammond.

Hugh turned to Guilliam. 'Release him,' he said with a nod.

Guilliam reluctantly lifted his chained hands above and away from Hammond. Then he stood next to Hugh, who lowered the bow aimed at the innkeep, though kept the arrow at the ready.

'Come,' Elias said. He led Guilliam and Hugh across the room, between grudgingly parting patrons, to the staircase ahead. They followed him up. The stairs led to a corridor with doors on either side, in which Elias nodded to the furthest on their right.

Hugh approached and knocked.

'Baron Turbert,' he spoke loudly. 'It's Hugh Brombury. The squire.'

There was no answer. He knocked once more.

'I must speak with you as a matter of urgency, My Lord.'

This too was met with silence. Hugh turned to Elias.

'He was in there before I left. Came down to breakfast, then returned to his room.'

'Baron Turbert,' Hugh tried again, his fist pounding the timber. Met with a foreseen silence, he gave the door a nudge. He hadn't expected it to open, presuming it locked on account of the keyhole, but open it did. With the door slightly ajar, Hugh peered inside. The Baron was sat upon a stool, his back to the door, looking out of the window, from which you could see, in the distance, the pasture and the woods beyond them.

'Forgive the intrusion, My Lord,' Hugh said with a startle. But the Baron neither reacted to his uninvited entrance nor turned to face him. 'My Lord?'

Hugh stepped into the room, cautiously approaching the Baron. Once behind him, he gently placed a hand on his shoulder. And then Baron Turbert's head fell back, and hung far lower than any head should rightly be able to hang – with a pair of wide, unblinking eyes staring into Hugh's – for his throat had been slit.

Hugh gasped, falling back, slipping on something beneath his feet – blood. It was blood. And as he fell he pulled the Baron with him, and the corpse fell from the chair and onto Hugh. He cried out, writhing beneath the body to get it off of him.

'Hugh!' he heard Guilliam call.

He managed to get out from beneath the dead man, for the most part, propping himself up on his elbows and wriggling away, his breeches blood-smeared. And as he dragged himself further from the body, his fingers found an object on the floor. He knew just what the cold steel was before he looked at it. But as he did, he now saw Guilliam and Elias, stood on the other side of the open door, staring at the dagger by his right hand.

All three of them were speechless. And amidst their speechlessness he heard footsteps. Footsteps climbing the stairs with haste, then making their way along the corridor. Guilliam and Elias turned to see who they belonged to. And from the look on his friend's face, Hugh had a feeling that precisely the last person he would have chosen to have seen him in that moment had arrived.

'God have mercy,' the voice of Father Dobbe was measured as he looked upon the scene.

Chapter 21
The Priest's Proclamation

It was, of course, the priest's word against theirs. A rabble of men of various degrees of drunkenness had pushed their way up the stairs moments after Father Dobbe, prevented from releasing their frustrations on both Hugh and Guilliam only by Dobbe's command. Elias had remained silent, his head hung low, as the priest painted the picture as to what he *suspected* had happened, for all of the inn to hear. Guilliam's squire, Father Dobbe proposed, had broken him out of gaol that very morning, only to be apprehended by both Elias and Hammond. However, having been afforded a knightly tutelage in the art of combat, he had managed to best them. Then the squire had decided to return to The Unpleasant Pheasant, the men his prisoners, under the pretence that they had, in fact, tried to hang Guilliam themselves. Here he would attempt to frame the unfortunate Hammond and Elias, and in doing so convince Baron Turbert to clear his former mentor of any wrongdoing.

'Perhaps he hadn't initially intended to cut the poor man's throat,' the priest had preached to the inn-goers, who had tripled in number since Hugh had entered. 'I can only assume the Baron didn't accept his version of events, perchance leading to a passionate disagreement that provoked such a violent outburst?'

'Liar!' Hugh cried out, presently restrained by a pair of ale-scented, well-built villagers.

'You saw what I saw, friends,' Father Dobbe spoke as if he were delivering a sermon, as if the words had been rehearsed. 'He stands stained in the Baron's blood. His hand next to the dagger that dealt the cut.'

'His throat was cut when I found him,' Hugh protested. 'Known to you, no doubt.'

'As if framing poor Hammond and Elias is not enough, now the boy tries to place blame on me!' The priest's words caused an uproar amongst the onlookers.

'Tell them,' Hugh turned to Elias. 'You have to tell them the truth.'

Father Dobbe took a step towards the innkeeper. 'We already know the truth. Is it not what I have just spoken?' He placed a hand on Elias' shoulder and looked at Hammond, the two of them now cut free of their bindings.

'Aye, you are right, Father,' said Hammond. 'It happened just as you said.'

Elias' head remained hung, unable to meet Hugh's desperate face. And so Hugh looked to Guilliam, and he once again looked defeated, just as he had when Hugh had seen him in his cell. The crowd began to jeer and taunt.

'Hang 'em both, I say!'

'Take their heads!'

And a dozen more declarations of the sort followed. Father Dobbe waited for them to die down, his expression unremitting, all the while his hand on Elias' shoulder.

'Patience, my friends,' he began as the onlookers fell quiet. 'We must have patience. I would see these men pay for their crimes as much as you. But we must not let wrath cloud our judgement. The victim of this latest killing is of noble birth. The very reason we sought his counsel was because such standing saw him fit to adjudicate the fate of one of similar status,' he glanced at Guilliam as he said this. 'So, we must now send for another lord of like standing. For it is not our place to assume the roles of arbiter or executioner, nor our place to deliver the King's justice. No, we shall let their deeds be spoken of to their peers, that they may be known for the knaves they are to all the lords of the land!' The priest spoke with gusto and the crowd erupted into a great cheer.

'What'll we do with them till then?' slurred one of the men restraining Hugh.

The priest's lips formed a thin smile. 'As of this morning,' he said. 'We've an empty gaol.'

The wooden hatch closed shut and the daylight disappeared.

'Forgive me,' Hugh said to Guilliam. ''Tis a fine mess I've led us into here.'

They were both of them shackled now, wrists and ankles, and sat with their backs pressed against opposing walls, facing one another – though unable to actually make out each other's faces in the darkness – the two of them in a room barely big enough for one. With their knees pressed up against their chests, their feet touched the other man's.

'You are not to blame, Hugh,' Guilliam said, a touch of resigned amusement to his tone. 'We weren't to know Dobbe would kill the Baron.'

'So you do think he did it?'

'Who else? I suspect the truth is not far from what he spoke, a disagreement likely did take place. Only between himself and the Baron, of course. And Dobbe, from what I have seen of him, is a cunning man. A fine coincidence, the Baron's guards being blind drunk at that hour, don't you think? Dobbe's doing too, I'd wager. No, this is not your fault Hugh, none of it is. Besides, you told me to run while I had the chance. It was I who insisted on returning.'

'Your reasons were just, Sir.'

'But my actions were not.'

'Sir?'

'Not at first, I mean. Ethel was betrothed to another. To Hammond. I knew as much, and still I courted her.'

'You and she. What...' Hugh paused.

'You wish to know what happened between us?'

'If you wish to tell me, I would listen.'

'Well, I suppose we've time to kill.'

Hugh chuckled faintly. 'Aye.'

'I know what you must think, Hugh,' Guilliam continued. 'You spent enough time with me. You know my nature. But Ethel was different. She was not just another serving girl.'

'You... loved her.'

Guilliam did not respond immediately. The two of them sat in silence for a moment. And then: 'I did.'

'If it's too painful, Sir, we don't have—'

'No. I want to,' Guilliam said. 'I want to speak of her. I would tell you of the fairest woman I have ever known. I would tell you about Ethel.'

Chapter 22
The Girl from the Inn

Three months ago

The Pheasant didn't seem all that Unpleasant, thought Guilliam, glancing up at the sign swinging above his head in the early evening breeze. Moreover, a plate of pheasant certainly wouldn't *be* unpleasant – though he would find himself more than a touch surprised if an establishment such as the one before him served such delicacy. It was one thing that he perhaps missed, from his old life; the feasts and banquets and cuisine that came along with it. Since setting off from his estate way back when, he'd lived off jerky and hard cheese, taking bread and beer where he could, and on one occasion a small helping of honey, treating himself to a spoonful a day for as long as it lasted. He'd had his share of porridge and stews and boiled meats too, along the way, having lodged at a number of inns in the hamlets and villages he had passed through thus far. And now he found himself in the village of Crooklingsham, a place he had never heard of until reading its letters etched on the wooden post that had led him to where he presently stood.

Within, the inn appeared to be even livelier than it had sounded from outside. Half the drinkers slurred along to a song played by a pair of colourfully clothed minstrels performing in the corner, one with a fiddle, the other tapping a tabor and wearing a set of bells on his feet, kicking them up above his head at points in the ballad that appeared to empassion the inebriated onlookers the most.

A few faces turned to take note of the newcomer as he stepped foot into the alehouse, though most paid no heed to Guilliam. His appearance at present favoured such establishments as The Unpleasant Pheasant; tunic tattered, kerchief creased, cloak's wool lining worn out, leather boots battered and muddied – months on the road had left him seeming suited to a peasant-run pub in a peasant-populated village. It was a far cry from the larger, more illustrious taverns he'd formerly frequented, in the towns and cities, which tended to be full of travelling merchants and artisans and men of the profession he had left behind. Here, instead, he was amongst those who worked the local land; farmers and fishermen, shepherds and herders, blacksmiths and bakers, brewers and barrel makers, weavers and woodcutters. Yes, all around him were earnest men (and some of their women, with them) who had worked the long, hard day, and so it was no wonder none thought to give him more than a moment's glance, for they were enjoying their well-earned ale, and seemed to care not who came in to enjoy it alongside them. Save for one, that was, who did afford Guilliam far more than a glance. From where she stood, behind the bar, her bright blue eyes – emboldened by rosy cheeks and golden hair – met his own and kept with them.

And then she smiled.

***

'A scribe!' Ethel declared as she placed a bowl of piping hot porridge in front of Guilliam.

'A scribe?' he laughed. 'Me? *I* look like a scribe to you?'

'You can read and write, yes?'

'That would be telling.'

'You talk like a man who can.'

'And how is that?'

'Yesterday, I heard you use words which I reckon not a single man in this village has ever heard used.'

'Yet they all nodded along and spoke as if they had.'

'Well, *I* have never heard some of those words, and if I haven't, then I'm certain *they* haven't.'

Guilliam smiled. 'Fine. Yes, I can read and write.'

'So you are a scribe?' Ethel beamed.

Guilliam shook his head with a smirk, to which she sighed. The serving girl had only spoken with him briefly the evening before – between pouring ale – and had taken to guessing just who he was. This began after he had introduced himself as "just passing through" and, intrigued, Ethel asked if she may know his profession.

'I no longer have a profession,' he had told her.

'But you did once?'

'Naturally.'

'And it was?'

At that he had then taken a hefty sip from his tankard, and with a smirk said, 'I will let you guess. And if you do, I shall buy you an ale.'

'But *Guilliam*,' she had emphasised his name, having only just learnt it, 'you already have,' and she had raised the ale she'd just finished pouring with a merry giggle.

'Then I suppose I shall buy you another,' and he had chinked her mug with his, and then said: 'If you guess right, that is.'

Their game was soon cut short, however, thanks to the ever-thirsty inn-goers, to whose thirst Ethel had to tend, and so they picked it up now, the morning after, as Guilliam tucked into his porridge.

'You can read and write, yet are not a scribe,' she wondered aloud. The inn was, at that hour, empty save for the two of them. She pondered a moment more, then said, 'Surely not a holy man?'

Guilliam let out a guffaw.

''Tis a foolish guess?'

'No,' he shook his head with a faint smile. 'No, it's only… I'm far from it, these days. So no, I am not a man of the church.'

'Neither a scribe nor a priest… hmm,' her eyes narrowed as she peered at his chest. 'Perhaps that will give me a clue?'

Guilliam glanced down, noticing the top half of his pendant peeking above his collar.

'Looks precious,' she said.

'The only thing that still is to me.'

'A gift?'

He nodded. 'Tell me,' he covered the pendant, steering the conversation away from it, 'Why do you care to know my profession?'

'Perhaps,' she said, looking into his eyes as her lips curled into a coquettish grin, 'it might impress me.'

Guilliam sensed his cheeks redden ever so slightly. 'Well, whatever I was,' he cleared his throat and glanced around the room. 'I assure you, it is not as impressive as you. A young maiden governing an inn full of rowdy drunkards single-handedly. 'Tis quite a feat.'

Her gaze fell to the ground. 'I am but a serving girl. This is my father's inn.'

'I see. And he is away presently?'

'Oh, no,' she shook her head. 'Why, he was here last night.'

Guilliam looked about the unoccupied room. On every table were empty or near-empty mugs and cups and the odd stew-stained bowl, remnants of the prior night's revelries. 'Your father is here yet leaves you to both tend to the customers and tidy thereafter, does he?'

'His being *here* is why I now labour alone,' she said. 'He is sleeping off last night's…' she paused, looking for the right word.

'Carousing,' Guilliam finished her sentence.

'Carousing?'

'It is what most every man in here last night was doing.'

'Ahh,' she smiled. 'In that case, yes, my father is sleeping off last night's *carousing*.' Again, her eyes met his. 'And you say you're not a scribe.'

He laughed, and so did she. And when their laughter faded, he said, 'If you really want to know…'

'Was that not apparent?' she teased.

'I was a knight.'

A faint blush spread across her cheeks, and she seemed to need a second to find her reply, as her long eyelashes fluttered, the blue of her eyes suddenly seeming, in that moment, brighter. 'Oh my,' she said, softly, walking slowly to the other side of the bench on which she had placed his porridge, pulling back a stall and sitting opposite him. 'I've never met a knight before.' She leaned in close. 'Tell me more.'

* * *

'Closed for the night!' Ethel shouted to whoever knocked, not so much as glancing at the locked door, collecting as many mugs as she could in her hands as to lighten the load of tomorrow morning's tidy. Whilst there was no set closing time to speak of, every man and woman in Crooklingsham knew the rules; The Unpleasant Pheasant stayed open as long as there were drinkers still drinking, and when the last man left and the door closed behind him, no more drinks would be served that night. It had been near on twenty minutes since the last man left – that being Manfred, the brewer, who enjoyed his product more than anyone else most evenings (he was in the habit of insisting on a discount when buying his beer, on account of his having brewed it, an ambitious request which was everytime met with a No, on account of Elias having paid full price when purchasing the product from him).

The knocking continued.

'Whatever it is,' Ethel said, her attention still elsewhere. 'It can wait till the morrow. Now piss off!'

The knocking stopped.

'Always one,' Ethel uttered to herself. She carried the cradled tankards over to the bar and placed them down. Then, there came a voice from behind the door.

'Forgive me.'

She knew the voice.

'I thought I would wait until after the carousing, is all.'

Ethel rushed over to the door and unbolted it. She pulled the handle, and there he stood.

'Guilliam,' she said, unable to hide her smile.

With a smile of his own he raised a finger to his lips. 'May I come in?'

'I… yes,' she said, brushing herself down, mildly flustered all of a sudden.

He stepped inside, checking over his shoulder before closing the door behind him. 'I hope you can forgive my coming at this hour. But… I had to see you.'

'What are you—' Ethel began, but then her expression changed. 'We heard you had taken up with those heathens near the woods.'

'Ah,' Guilliam smiled softly.

''Tis true, then?'

'I… I have beheld certain wonders, since I have been away, Ethel. The druids showed me things beyond reckoning.'

'Druids?' her tone was one of concern. 'They are pagans, Guilliam. And now it seems you are too.'

'Ethel, please—'

''Tis best you leave,' she drew back.

'You don't understand.'

'Father Dobbe told us you were one of them now. I did not want to believe it… But it's true.'

'You must let me explain. Let me show—'

'No,' she snapped, her expression now a far cry from the smile that had first drawn Guilliam to her. 'If such wonders await you in that ungodly settlement, you ought to have stayed there.'

'I intend to,' he replied solemnly. A silence ensued. And then, 'At least for the coming months.'

'Then why come back at all? Why come here?'

'I had to see you.' Guilliam took a step towards Ethel. 'For all the wonders I have seen of late, you have ever been in my thoughts.'

'Guilliam… I…' Ethel's reluctance now faltered as her eyes met his. He leaned nearer. 'I am betrothed,' she announced abruptly. He halted.

'I see,' he answered, after a moment.

'I… I am sorry. I had meant to tell you, before Father Dobbe sent you off.'

'Who is he, might I ask?'

'Hammond.'

'The blacksmith's boy?'

She nodded. In his evenings spent at The Unpleasant Pheasant, Guilliam had enjoyed an ale or three with both the lad and his father.

'He seems a fine young man,' Guilliam cleared his throat, now looking away from her. 'Forgive me. I should not have come. I will return to Ealdgeat.'

He turned to leave.

'Wait,' Ethel said as he neared the door. He stopped and faced her. 'He is handsome, yes.'

'Pardon?'

'Hammond. He is handsome. And strong.'

'No need to twist the knife, m'lady,' Guilliam replied, though with a touch of good humour. She sensed this and chuckled.

'He is also arrogant. And talks of little else other than himself. And…' she approached him. 'He oft carries a foul stench.'

'Ah,' Guilliam smiled. 'Well, you should know that I too have been told, once or twice, that I am fair of face and strong of arm.'

'Is that so?'

'What's more,' he stepped closer. 'I smell foul only on occasion. But one thing I do know,' he stepped closer still, with a smirk. 'I am most certainly not arrogant.'

Their eyes locked. They leaned towards one another. Their lips met and held together for what Guilliam felt to be both a welcome linger and all too brief a moment.

'I am sorry,' Ethel said as she pulled away, albeit unable to conceal a smile.

'Do not be.'

'I… what of your heathen friends?' she tried to hide her giddiness with a change of subject.

'Druids,' Guilliam said gently.

'Druids, then. You mean to return to them?'

'I do. But I can come back here, too. Every fourth night. If you wish me to.'

They stood, looking at one another, silently, in yet another lingering moment.

'I do.'

* * *

The first fourth night came and went, as did the fourth night following that, and the fourth night following that. It was now the fourth fourth night, and this time Guilliam did not need to knock on the door of The Unpleasant Pheasant – as he had knocked, under cover of darkness, on each of his previous visits – for as he made to leave Ealdgeat, he saw a figure approaching from the pasture.

'Ethel,' he spoke aloud as her face grew clear. He looked about. Most of the druids had turned in for the night, and of those who hadn't, their attention was elsewhere. Guilliam, with some sudden haste, left the confines of the small settlement and caught up to her as she strode towards him through the tall grass. She smiled as he neared.

'What are you doing here?' he asked with some apprehension.

'I thought it finally my turn to come see you,' she replied. Noticing his concern, her smile faded. 'Should I not have come?'

'I… no. I am glad to see you, as ever,' as he spoke he glanced over her shoulder.

'I was not followed, if that is your worry.'

He smiled nervously.

'Or,' Ethel raised an eyebrow. 'Is it that you do not wish me to be seen by your druid friends?'

'Ethel… it's not that simple—'

'It would be an embarrassment to be seen with a God-fearing woman?'

'I… we must be careful, is all. Hammond cannot know of… this.'

'I can assure you, Guilliam, the last people anyone back in the village would hear of *this* from are your friends here.'

'Forgive me, seeing you has simply taken me unawares.'

She smiled softly and suddenly he felt at ease. 'I also wondered if I might…' she trailed off.

'If you might…?'

'These wonders in the woods you have spoken of. I thought, maybe, you might show me them?'

Guilliam glanced over his shoulder. The few druids who had not yet turned in for the night had not appeared to notice the two of them. They would be easy enough to slip past, if a wide berth was taken into the woods yonder, Guilliam thought. He looked back to Ethel.

'I… Ethel, I'm not sure it is wise.'

'I roamed those woods countless times as a child, and found them far from remarkable. Yet you speak of them with awe.'

'I speak of parts un—'

'Parts unknown to and unseen by me. Yes, you've said as much. Yet you claim you are unable to put these parts into words. And if *you* do not have the words, then how else am I to picture what you speak of, if I cannot see for myself?'

Guilliam remained quiet for a moment, considering her point. 'No one can know about this,' he said.

'Do you not trust me by now?'

'Of course I do,' he gently brushed her cheek with his finger.

'Then… will you show me?'

* * *

Soon after, every fourth night had become every third. And then every second. And now they no longer met under the cover of night at The Unpleasant Pheasant, nor under the cover of night at all, for that matter. Guilliam had shown Ethel the woods, the parts unknown to and unseen by her, and so it was now there that the two of them would meet and be together. For there, not only were they free from the eyes of the village. They were free from the passage of time as they knew it. In the woods, they were together for what felt like hours upon hours and hours upon that still, only to step out of the deepest shade of the furthest trees to discover that not even half of one hour had passed in Crooklingsham.

'Oh Guilliam,' she had said one late morning, as they lay beside one another, rested against a slight incline that overlooked a stream of the clearest blue that either of them had ever seen. 'I would very much like to stay here. Just me and you. Away from my father's inn.'

'The villagers might have something to say about that, with no one to pour their ale.'

Ethel sighed.

'I have offended you?'

'No…' she shook her head, suddenly unable to look at him.

'It was but a jest, my sweet Ethel,' Guilliam placed a finger beneath her chin, gently guiding her head up so he might meet her eyes. There were tears forming in them. 'What's wrong?'

'It's Hammond,' she said. 'We are to be married next month.'

No words were spoken for a short moment.

'I see,' was Guilliam's eventual reply.

'Guilliam, I… oh, what am I to do?'

He stood.

'Guilliam?'

He reached beneath his tunic, revealing the medallion around his neck. 'You said that this looked precious, the morning after we met,' he lifted it up over his head. 'My mother left it to me.'

'It's very lovely.'

'I've worn it since I was a boy. Around my neck, during every tourney, every duel. I like to think it has kept me on course… steered me true. Perhaps it led me here.' He held it out to her.

She took it and looked it over.

'Do you like it?' he asked.

'It is a pretty piece. Truly,' she said, before offering it back. He did not take it.

'Guilliam?'

'Take it,' he smiled.

'I couldn't possibly—'

'It is yours, Ethel,' he said.

'But you need it. You just said, it has steered you true.'

'A superstition. Besides, if it truly did bring me good fortune in combat, it has served its purpose. Those days are behind me now.'

'Guilliam… your mother would not want me to have it, I am sure.'

'She is long dead. It is but a keepsake by which I have remembered her. And now it can be one for you to remember me… to remember our time together. I shall not ask you to forsake Hammond, only that you not forget me.'

'I don't want to marry him! My heart belongs to you.'

Guilliam smiled tenderly and stroked her cheek gently with the back of his finger. With his hand he closed her fingers around the medallion. 'You are a young woman. Do not squander your youth on an old man such as me.'

'You are a knight!'

'I am a hermit, Ethel. Who will likely live out his days wandering woods much like these.'

'Then I shall wander with you.'

'No,' he said gently.

'Do you not love me?'

Silence hung in the air. Guilliam's eyes scanned their surroundings.

'Eotenfrēond tells me there are more places like this. He wishes to chart them. I am to set forth with him and a small company of druids to seek them in the coming weeks.'

'You… you are leaving?'

'Yes. And you cannot accompany me. Nor will I ask you to wait for me.'

'I do not believe this. The druids have insisted on staying here for so long.'

'It is true, Ethel. I was going to wait until the day before we left to tell you. But it seems the timing has aligned with your own news.' Both of them fell quiet, unable to look at the other. 'I… we should return, now.'

'No…' she shook her head, taking a step back. 'You do not speak the truth.'

'Come, I shall walk you to the outskirts of—'

She slapped his hand away. Though she spoke no words, the look she gave him in that moment said more than they might have.

And then she turned and walked away.

Chapter 23
Two's Company

'It was the next day that they found her,' Guilliam spoke plainly. 'And she was right, of course.'

'Right?' Hugh asked.

'About me lying. Eotenfrēond had mentioned charting other woods, but it was nothing more than an idea. There was never a company of druids.'

'Why tell her that there was?'

'In the hope that it would anger her enough to go back to her betrothed. I suppose it angered her, but I don't think she ever believed it,' Guilliam gazed at a tiny sliver of light as he spoke.

'But you… loved her?'

'I did.'

'Why tell her to leave then? Why bid her return to Hammond? She wanted to be with you.'

'I told her to do those things *because* I loved her, Hugh. I am old and she was young. Of childbearing age. I would have taken from her the chance of a simple life, of raising children. She'd have lived as an outcast. And it would have drawn the ire of the village to Ealdgeat even more.'

'Eotenfrēond told me he had warned you away from her.'

'Aye. And at first I protested. But he spoke sense.'

A moment of unspeaking passed.

'Do you think Hammond...' Hugh began, insinuating his speculation without finishing his sentence.

'You mean to ask if I think he killed her?'

'Maybe he saw the two of you?'

'I have wondered, Hugh. When Dobbe and his mob came and dragged me to the village, Hammond was amongst them. He was weeping the whole while. If he had seen us together, he did not say then, and still has not. But if he did, I do not think he... I do not think he would have hurt...' his voice cracked. 'No, I do not believe he did it.'

'How can you be sure? He tried to kill *you*.'

'He did so because he loved her. Even if she did not love him back. I do not believe Ethel died by his hand, though. Call it a... a *feeling*.'

'You defend him, and yet still he holds you to blame. All because she was found with your medallion. If you were to but tell them what you told me—'

'I cannot. I will not ruin Ethel's name, I will not have them think her unchaste.'

'You and her...'

'Nay. We shared our lips with one another, no more. Still, they would brand her a harlot.'

'Sir, with all respect, she is gone now. What does it matter, if it might save you?'

Guilliam let out a defeated chuckle. 'Even if I were believed about Ethel, Dobbe now strives to see our heads taken for what befell the Baron.'

Hugh sighed and a silence hung over them for some time. Eventually, he said, 'Who do you think it was, Sir? If it was not Hammond?'

'I do not know. 'Tis why I did not wish to flee earlier, Hugh. I must know who, or what, has done this to her.'

'What about…'

'What about what, Hugh?'

'I saw a creature. In the woods. Beorhtwyn called it a dam-dweller.'

'I know of what you speak. They dwell deep in the woods. I never did see the dam they are named for, though I have spotted them from afar, on occasion. But never have I known them aggressive. They keep their distance from folk, to my knowing.'

'I do not mean to suggest that it was the dam-dweller's doing, but if the woods truly are another realm, as Beorhtwyn says, it stands to reason that they are not the only other creatures that inhabit it. Might a fiercer beast have been responsible?'

'It has crossed my mind. Though there are beasts fierce enough from our own world that one can be unlucky enough to cross paths with. I had wondered if a wolf had found her, but it surely would have sunk its fangs into her. Then I thought of a boar, but she was not gored. She had been *dragged*, not stuck or bitten. Unless you know of any creature capable of dragging without leaving mark of its teeth?'

'None that I can think of. The only other encounter I had in those woods was with a man – if you could even call him a man – quite incapable of moving, let alone dragging.'

'You met a man who couldn't move?'

'He seemed to be stuck in a tree. I have not yet had a chance to tell—'

'You saw *him*?' Although it was too dark to see his face clearly, Hugh sensed Guilliam's sudden alertness.

'I… yes. This morning, when I came seeking you. I was lost and he bade me fetch him an axe—'

'Hugh, please tell me you did not chop—'

'Worry not. That was when I saw the dam-dweller. It stopped me. And then Beorhtwyn found me. She told me he was a trickster, cunning and old. But that is all. Do you know more of him?'

'Little other than that. The druids warned me of him, too. How he came to be trapped in that tree, none know for sure. I was simply told that should I ever come across *He Who is Held in the Tree*, to be wary of his words.'

'Do you suppose that Ethel… met him too?'

'I hope not. Though if she did, what could he have done?'

'Other than try to bargain with her, as he did me, I do not know,' Hugh answered. 'His body was stuck, his mouth and eyes were all he seemed able to move.'

'This bargain he offered you, what was it?'

'He would guide me out of the woods, in exchange for cutting him loose. I did not trust him… but I was so lost. I was fortunate that the dam-dweller stopped me, knowing what I now know. Nipped my ankle, it did. I can feel it still. Though… I wonder if it really did

happen. If I really did see them. Such peculiar creatures that did not, to my knowledge, exist, until I witnessed them with my own eyes this morning. Yet even my memory feels… distant.'

'As if it were a dream.'

'Yes. Like a dream.'

'The woods have a way of doing that,' Guilliam sounded somewhat saddened.

'They were real? Weren't they? The things I saw.'

'Yes. Even though they may seem distant now. Much like my time spent with Ethel. It *felt* as if it were many months, but by our measure of time… barely days.'

'I see now why you could not mention such things in your message,' Hugh said. 'I would have thought you had caught a case of madness. Woods of worlds beyond, branch-furred beasts and men trapped in trees.'

'Aye,' Guilliam sighed. A moment later he said, with a hint of light-heartedness to his tone, 'I wonder if this tree-man's trappings are more comfortable than ours.'

'Less cramped, at the very least.'

'We'd best get used to it. We won't be moving much until Dobbe's new judge arrives.'

'You've no plan to get us out of this one, then, Sir?'

'*You* were my plan, Hugh,' he replied with a tired titter.

'I am sorry I was not able to help.'

'I am the one who is sorry. For dragging you into all of this. I should have known my fate was sealed from the moment my medallion was found in Ethel's hand. It gave Dobbe the excuse he was long looking for. I should never have called on you.'

'I am glad you did, Sir, in truth. Despite our present predicament. My most recent master was not all too fond of me.'

'No?'

'I think he despised me, in fact.'

'Then he surely does not know the meaning of the word loyalty.'

'He favoured faculty over loyalty. Of which, as you are no doubt aware, I lack. I do not think he thought me fit to serve.'

'Nonsense. You are the finest squire I ever did know, Hugh Brombury. Clumsy, at times, yes. And fair to say, not the fiercest fighter. But never have I known one with a better heart than you. If your last master could not see that, then he was not fit to mentor.'

'It is kind of you to say, Sir.'

'It is true! What was that swaggerer's name again? Sir…'

'Leland Lockwood.'

'Ha!' Guilliam guffawed. 'No more a knight than a status-seeking swordsman. An upstart who married a mare-loving maiden. He would be no more than a mercenary if her father had not been so desperate to marry her off!'

'He was a hard master, nonetheless. Glad to see the back of me too, when I set off to aid you. And now I fear his parting words to me were right.'

'What were they?'

'He told me I would fail. An accurate assumption, it would appear.'

'I suspect he merely meant those words to dishearten you. Do not let them.'

'That may be so. But he said something else too. He said that once I have failed, the name Brombury would be forgotten.'

No words were spoken for a while.

'Have courage, Hugh,' Guilliam said. 'Even in the face of death. Do not let them take that from you.'

Two servings of slop per day was all that they had to measure the passage of time. They presumed perhaps a week, or just over, to have passed when the rider arrived, with their reminiscing receding with each estimate of a day drawing to a close, along with their strength. Despite this, Hugh had held on to Guilliam's words, holding onto his courage – if only a sliver – the only thing that seemed to give him some small hope that they would yet find a way out of this.

That was until, for the first time in however many days they had been locked in the cramped and dank room, the door swung open. Before them stood two figures, impossible to identify at first as their eyes adjusted to the sudden spill of daylight.

'I thought you might like to know that your justiciar has arrived,' the words were unmistakably spoken by Father Dobbe, his appearance becoming clearer as their sight tailored to the brightness.

Behind him, the other figure stepped into the fore. It was at that very moment Hugh felt the courage he had clung to for all those days in the darkness suddenly leave him.

'Still trying to get yourself killed, I see, Brombury,' said Sir Leland Lockwood.

Chapter 24
The Trial

In the centre of the village there was a well, and around that well the men and women of Crooklingsham had gathered. They had been summoned there by Father Dobbe, who had announced to them the arrival of Sir Leland Lockwood and the imminent trial he would oversee. Amongst the not quite one-hundred villagers were Hammond, who stood tall, his face a permanent penetrating scowl, and Elias, whose own head was bowed for the most part, though those who did catch glimpses of his face would surely note the vacant look that had overcome it. The crowd had parted as the knight rode into their village, his horse slowing to a canter as it made its way from the gaol to the well. He wore a wine coloured cloak which partially covered a breastplate displaying his heraldry – two rearing horses, one black and one white, either side of a tower – and a helmet with a plumage of a similar shade, the visor lifted up so that his face was visible. Following him, atop a horse of smaller stature, was his squire, a blonde haired, lanky lad.

Not far behind them, two of the burlier villagers dragged Hugh and Guilliam towards the well by their shackles. The crowd cursed and hissed and spat at the pair, eager to see the justice they had long waited for be served. Sir Leland Lockwood dismounted as they were stood next to the well.

'Gilbert?' Hugh said as he was pulled past the lad, surprised to see his former fellow squire. Of course, it made sense that Sir Lockwood would have one of his aides accompany him.

Gilbert Giffard said nothing to Hugh. He simply glared, as if that were all he were permitted to do. Then Father Dobbe began to speak, announcing to all in attendance the accusations as if he were delivering a sermon, spending some time detailing the state in which he'd "found" Baron Turbert. After his piece was said, Sir Leland called upon Hammond to step forwards.

'You found the girl?' he asked.

'I did,' Hammond nodded.

'In what state was she?'

Hammond looked to Father Dobbe. 'Did you not tell him?'

'I am sorry, my son,' the priest said. 'It is merely a necessity, for the sake of proceedings.'

Hammond nodded, taking a breath. 'She was cut all over. Her dress torn. Muddied. Skin split. And the blood, from the cuts... there were so many cuts and scratches. She'd been dragged through the woods, I could see that much...' his lip began trembling. He looked at Guilliam, tears in his eyes. 'And you. *Your* medallion was in her hand!' he made to lurch towards Guilliam in that moment, but was held back by many a hand. Once he had calmed, Sir Leland approached the prisoners.

'You stand accused of murder,' he addressed the both of them. 'Guilliam, of the girl, Ethel, and Hugh Brombury of Baron Turbert. What say you in your defence?'

'It is not true, Sir,' Hugh answered. 'Guilliam did not kill Ethel. And the Baron did not die by my hand. The priest lies. He was dead upon our entering his room.'

'And what evidence do you have in your favour?'

'My word, Sir, which is no less than the priest's.'

Sir Leland considered this silently for a moment. 'You are a fool, Brombury, there is no doubt in that,' he said. 'Though I cannot in good conscience say I have ever known you to be a liar.' He turned to Father Dobbe. 'I must make further inquiries into the circumstances surrounding Baron Turbert's demise before I can pass judgement.'

'But of course,' the priest bowed his head cordially as the crowd muttered.

'In regards to the girl,' Sir Lockwood spoke loudly, the crowd falling quiet as he looked to Guilliam. 'She was found with your pendant, yet you still deny she died at your hand.'

'I do.'

'And you have offered no reason as to why she had your pendant in her possession.'

'Other than the reason I have already given, I have not. I gave it to her, and that is all there is to it.'

'Liar!' Hammond called out.

Sir Leland turned his head sharply. It took little more than a look from the knight for Hammond to fall quiet – a look that Hugh was all too familiar with.

'I am asking the questions now,' he said. Then, facing Guilliam, 'Though your lack of elaboration is undeniably suspicious.'

Father Dobbe stepped forwards and added, 'Given Guilliam's affiliations, who is to say he did not subject the poor girl to some sort of ritualistic desecration.'

'Therein lies the issue, Father,' Lockwood said. 'Who is to say, indeed?'

'Forgive me, Sir,' the priest seemed surprised by the question. 'I do not follow.'

'Your theory, as I see it, is mere speculation. Why go to the effort of killing the girl, dragging her through the woods, only to leave his medallion clutched, so apparently, in her hand?'

'Sir Lockwood—' Father Dobbe began, speaking through a laboured smile, behind which his teeth were gritted.

'Based on the accounts I have heard, both today and in the message you had the late baron's men deliver me,' the knight continued, cutting him up. 'I can only conclude her cause of death as indeterminable.'

The priest scowled. Onlookers gasped. Hugh and Guilliam glanced at one another, sharing looks of disbelief. Was Sir Leland Lockwood speaking in favour of them?

'However,' Sir Lockwood continued. 'The priest is right to raise the issue of your affiliations. A band of pagans, I am told. This is true?'

'A peaceful community of druids, Sir,' Guilliam replied.

'They are no longer of concern,' Father Dobbe said. 'We saw to it that their dwellings were torn down. I believe they have retreated deep into the woods.'

'You mean to say you let a band of known heretics flee? You of all people should know the seriousness of such a charge.'

'I… we do not possess the capacity here to detain a whole community, Sir Lockwood. You have seen our gaol.'

'And you,' Sir Lockwood turned to Guilliam, dismissing the priest. 'You openly renounce God, too?'

'I do.'

'Then you admit that you are guilty of heresy, at the very least,' Sir Lockwood looked around, taking in the faces of the crowd. 'Yet, it would be remiss of me to overlook your standing in the realm. I myself have witnessed Sir Guilliam the Great's skill in tourney, and heard tell of your bravery in battle. I know of none even now who might surpass the knight you *once* were. And so I would make you an offer. Lead us to your merry band of druids, as you call them. For let us not forget that heresy is a serious crime. Take me to these heretics and you shall be granted exile, and be permitted to live out your days in peace.'

Guilliam remained silent.

'What say you?' Lockwood pressed.

His lips curled into a gentle smile. 'You are generous in your praise of me, Sir Lockwood,' Guilliam said. 'But I think you already know my answer.'

'I am to take that as a refusal of my terms?'

'I would never lead you to them.'

'So be it. I do hereby declare you, Guilliam, guilty of heresy. Sentences for such a crime do vary, of course.'

'And what, pray tell, sentence do you deem fit for me?'

'Some are simply fined. Though it strikes me as fruitless to fine a man who has renounced all of his possessions. Others are imprisoned, until such erroneous beliefs are renounced. I would deem a continuation of your current circumstance a suitable sentence, until you come to such a renouncement. Of course, I shall see to it you are moved to a more appropriate chamber.'

'If I may, Sir Lockwood,' Father Dobbe spoke up. 'Heresy is an offence against the Church.'

Guilliam noticed, in that moment, that something in the priest's manner had changed. It was as if a great revelation had all of a sudden occurred to him, and he seemed barely able to contain himself.

'It is. You would dispute my verdict?'

'Guilliam has admitted his guilt. The conviction is undeniable. But...'

'What are you getting at?' Sir Leland asked impatiently.

'I am simply stating, Sir Lockwood, that the crime of murder – of which you are yet to find Guilliam guilty – is very much *yours* to convict, and the punishment *yours* to decree. Your status affords you that power, and 'tis why I called upon you. But in cases of crimes against the Church, the punishment is for the Church to decree. Would you agree?'

'That stands to reason,' he replied, his words considered.

'And I presume you would also agree that it is the duty of knights, such as yourself, to uphold the Church's decree, in these instances?'

'My duty is to the King.'

'Of course, of course. But you took an oath, did you not, Sir Lockwood?'

The knight nodded.

'Whilst I am not familiar with its exact wording, you surely swore to defend the faith in your oath, no? I was to believe all knights do so, lest we forget the Inquisitions of the past.'

Lockwood exhaled, his eyes fixed on Father Dobbe. 'Something like that.'

'Then we are in agreement that, as a man of the Church, it is *my* duty to sentence this heretic before us, and *your* duty, Sir Lockwood, to see that sentence carried out.'

Sir Leland blinked slowly. 'What sentence did you have in mind?' he asked.

'You are right that it is suitable to simply fine or imprison a heretic. Though, in those instances, the heretic must renounce his heresy and return to the true faith. In cases where it is clear the offender will not return to the true faith, however...'

'Go on,' Sir Lockwood said.

'I trust you will uphold your oath, Sir Lockwood, in seeing my sentence enforced?'

'Out with it, priest.'

'In my judgement, Guilliam has made it clear he will not recant. By decree of the Church, there is only one thing for it,' Father Dobbe turned from Lockwood to Guilliam, his eyes narrowing and the corner of his lips curling into a wry smile. 'Purification of the soul.'

'And just how is one's soul purified?' Sir Lockwood asked.

'It's simple,' Father Dobbe replied. 'By burning at the stake.'

The eyes of the prisoners and the crowd alike fell onto Sir Leland Lockwood. He was hesitant to respond. He considered the priest's words for a moment.

'I have heard of such sentences, outdated as they might be,' he spoke less assertively now. He looked to Guilliam. 'Repent your sin for all to hear. Proclaim your faith in God, and imprisonment shall be all you suffer.'

'It is too late for—' Dobbe began.

'Do this now,' Sir Leland interrupted, his gaze fixed on Guilliam. 'For the sake of your life.'

Guilliam sighed deeply. He looked around, taking in all of the faces staring at him. A resigned smirk befell his face.

'Sir,' Hugh uttered to his friend. 'Please.'

'Sorry, Hugh,' Guilliam replied. Then, to Sir Leland, 'I've many sins to repent for. It is true. But I'll not repent this.'

Sir Leland Lockwood exhaled. 'So be it,' he said.

Chapter 25
Gathering Wood

Anumber of men from the village, Hammond amongst them, had begun collecting wood to build a pyre. As the villagers set about constructing it, Guilliam and Hugh were returned to the gaol.

'You can't do this!' Hugh had cried out, his protest directed at Sir Leland.

'You heard the priest. Heresy is a crime against the Church,' the knight had replied matter-of-factly. 'The punishment is the priest's prerogative. I am but its enforcer.'

Behind Sir Leland, Father Dobbe appeared almost giddy as the door shut on Guilliam and Hugh. This time, the rectangular hatch remained open, offering a clear line of sight to the growing wood piled in the distance.

'Please, Sir,' Hugh called. 'I beg you—'

'Hugh,' Guilliam said softly. 'It is fruitless. The decision is made.

And the charge is true. I am a heretic, there is no denying it.'

'So that's it then?' Hugh asked with some despair. 'You will let them burn you alive, will you?'

With a faint smile, Guilliam shook his head.

'I do not understand.'

'You will soon see, Hugh,' he said, gesturing with a nod to the open hatch.

Still unsure as to what he was getting at, Hugh looked between Guilliam and the outside. Every so often a villager would pass, headed towards the slowly rising pyre, a pile of sticks held between their arms.

'See what?' Hugh asked.

'Watch a while longer.'

And so, in silence, Hugh did just that. He peered through the rectangular opening in the iron door, and watched as villagers walked back and forth with armfuls of firewood – small logs, twigs, broken branches and the like – each batch extending the height of the pyre that Guilliam was to be burned on. For some time he remained unsure as to what exactly he was looking for, but eventually he noticed.

Whenever a lone villager ventured off to gather wood, there would be something different about them upon returning. They wore the same clothes, but their faces were largely concealed by the brush piles they carried. Looking closely, it became clear what Guilliam had alluded to. They were coming back ever so slightly taller, or shorter, or perhaps rounder. And almost always with a longer beard.

'The druids,' Hugh said with some disbelief. 'What are they—'

'Infiltrating, it seems to me.'

'How… how could you know they'd come?'

'I noticed Beorhtwyn slip into the crowd whilst Dobbe was rambling. Always been one for staying unseen. No wonder she's so skilled a hunter.'

'But how are the others…'

'All this wood has to come from somewhere, Hugh,' Guilliam replied.

'So they are waylaying the villagers in the woods, donning their clothes and returning here disguised,' Hugh was grinning now. 'They mean to rescue us.'

'Here's hoping.'

And so it went on, with Hugh noticing at least a dozen villagers making for the outskirts of the woods, only for a different person to return wearing their clothes. After a while, a familiar face, peering from behind a pile of sticks stacked high, walked by the gaol and glanced in.

'Ready yourselves,' Eotenfrēond said quietly, in passing.

The time that passed between his words and what happened next felt, to the two of them in their cell, much longer than it likely was.

They heard a shout first. Then, a ruckus.

Then they saw a group of villagers, who had not yet been replaced, charging to where the ruckus sounded likely to be, and then some running back, and then forth, and then a mixture of both. Soon after, the grappling began, and it became more tricky to distinguish villagers from imposters. Then the villagers were arming themselves with what looked to be farming forks or flails and even the odd scythe and sickle, and those without immediate access to farming tools simply dropped whatever logs they had thus far accrued save for their largest. Amidst the altercations that were now well under way, a figure approached the gaol with haste.

It was Beorhtwyn, dressed also in disguise (having stolen the clothes from a man much bigger than herself, by the look of her) and she was holding a set of keys. She placed an iron key into the lock, turned it and pulled the door open.

'I've not got one for the shackles,' she said, ushering them out. 'Hurry, we make for the woods,' with that she turned and nodded to her father, who, nearby, had just managed to separate a scythe from the hands of a villager. In turn he nodded to another of their number, and so on and so forth, and within minutes the druids began to fall back.

Following Beorhtwyn's lead, Hugh and Guilliam were running, the chains around their wrists rattling as they fled the village.

'We're leading them straight to the woods,' Hugh posited. 'You'll give up your camp.'

'Not if we all make it back first,' Beorhtwyn replied, pausing momentarily to glance over her shoulder, taking note of the druids who were following, counting their number to herself. 'We are all counted for,' she said, running again now.

'But they'll surely follow us,' Hugh stated.

'Not if they can't.'

It took a moment to occur to Hugh precisely what she meant. 'The line,' he exclaimed. 'You mean to—'

'Close it behind us.'

An arrow flew through the air, landing just shy of them, followed by a plethora of less piercing projectiles – rocks, rotten vegetables (some ripe ones, too) and the like – that nonetheless saw the retreating druids dodging and ducking. As they approached the pasture, Hugh glanced over his shoulder, noticing that a fair few villagers had fallen back, though there remained two dozen or so still in pursuit, with Hammond leading the charge. Thankfully, thus far, it was only his roars and taunts that had reached them.

And then came a great neigh.

Hugh had barely a chance to hear the galloping hooves pounding the ground before the black steed sent him flying, its charge launching him through the air as if he were no more than one of the rocks lobbed by their pursuers. Fortunately he landed in a particularly tall tuft of grass, which went someway in cushioning his fall. He scrambled to his feet to see the horse cantering towards him now, mounted by the man who, until recently, he had been in the charge of.

'Give it up, Brombury,' Sir Leland said, his visor now very much down, making the pair of eyes Hugh could only just see appear even more penetrating. The horse slowed to a trot as it neared. Sir Leland unsheathed his steel.

'You mean to use that on me, Sir?' Hugh asked, attempting to mask, in his voice, the genuine fear that he might.

'I mean to escort you back to gaol. If I must bloody my sword in the process, so be it.'

But the both of them knew that Hugh would not go willingly. Even as Sir Leland spoke, Hugh was making to turn and run, as unlikely as escape now was. As he set to flee, Sir Leland raised his blade, angling it in a manner that signalled he meant to bring its hilt down upon his once squire. Though it was clear he didn't mean to kill, the knight held no reservations when it came to hurting. But before it struck, Hugh – who had now half-turned – heard a ringing clang. Metal on metal.

Between them stood Guilliam, brandishing an iron sickle.

'Run, Hugh!' Guilliam spoke without taking his eyes off the mounted knight with whom he was now in a bind, Sir Leland's shining steel blade pressing down against the rusted curved iron he gripped tightly on to.

'But—'

'Now!'

Though Sir Guilliam was no longer a knight, and Hugh no longer served as his squire, the tone alone told him that this was no mere request. It was an order. So, Hugh obeyed.

Even armed with only a sickle, held in shackled hands, Guilliam was able to parry Sir Leland's swordstrokes. Hugh heard the horse neigh again as he fled, and turned to see it rearing, standing tall on its two hind legs. It was at that point Guilliam struck Sir Leland's midriff with his improvised iron weapon, and though the knight's armour spared him from a flesh wound, it was a blow powerful enough to send him from his horse. But the sight had served to attract attention. The mob of villagers who had been chasing down druids were now headed for Guilliam, and in the time it took Sir Leland to find his footing they had surrounded him, pitchforks pointed at him from all sides. One of the villagers ran at Guilliam from behind, the rusted ends of a fork set to stick his unarmoured back. But the would-be impaler was stopped in his charge by Sir Leland, no less. He stepped between the peasant and his target, shoving him so hard that he lost both his balance and his fork. He then picked up his own sword, and shot a scowl to the rest of the encircling mob, making it clear that this was a melee between himself and Guilliam, and it was not to be interrupted.

But Hugh was not deterred by this unspoken warning, by Sir Leland Lockwood's want to test his mettle. In a last ditch, likely hopeless, attempt, he readied to rush to Guilliam's aid. It was Beorhtwyn's hand, grabbing his shoulder, that stopped him.

'Hugh,' she urged. 'We must go.'

'I cannot leave him!'

'There's too many of them!'

She was right. More of the mob had reached them now, and those not surrounding Guilliam were piling onto the slower of the druids.

'I…' Hugh began.

Then a *whoosh*.

Another arrow flew past Hugh. A sharp breath left Beorhtwyn. She groaned, and stumbled forwards, Hugh catching her.

'No!' came the nearby cry of Eotenfrēond. His head turned between his daughter and the villager armed with the bow, now in the process of drawing back another arrow. Hugh did not recognise the man who had fired the shot, but he did recognise the bow. It had been the one Beorhtwyn had left him with.

'Get her to the woods!' Eotenfrēond called to Hugh. Then he charged back into the fray, weaving his way through the amassing mob and swung the long wooden stick he held, striking the bowman before he had a chance to fire another shot. And then, just like Guilliam, he was surrounded.

'Come on,' Hugh had no choice now.

Beorhtwyn grimaced, stumbling as Hugh helped her onwards, one of her arms flung over his shoulders for support as her other hand pressed against the fresh wound in the centre of her chest, the back end of the arrow poking out between blood stained fingers.

The stragglers amongst the druids had seen this too, and some had taken to following her father's lead, giving up their escape to stop the villagers from reaching the elder's injured daughter. It gave them the chance they needed. As the villagers surrounded the remaining druids, Hugh and Beorhtwyn made their way over the pasture and slipped away into the woods beyond.

* * *

It took no more than a few minutes to quell the stragglers, the mob of villagers overwhelming and surrounding them. In that time Guilliam had been disarmed, with two or three of the villagers tackling him to the ground, much to the ire of Sir Leland, with whom he had been mid-melee. Along with Eotenfrēond, he had been herded with the remaining dozen druids, and the mob now encircled them, the pointy ends of their improvised arsenal aimed at their persons, prodding and poking them.

With a furious stride Father Dobbe fought his way through the mob, emerging in front of Guilliam. He looked about the villagers, his eyes stopping on Sir Leland, who stood back ever so slightly from the crowd, and wore on his face an expression of annoyance, for having been robbed of his fight.

'It looks like you've brought your fellow pagans to us after all, Guilliam,' the priest did little to hide the malevolence in his manner. 'We shall require *more* wood, it seems, to purify so many corrupted souls.'

The mob cheered.

'No!' Guilliam defiantly declared.

'You are in no position to barter. Your sentence has already been passed.'

'I will not see these people condemned without contest.'

'They condemned themselves when they forswore God.'

'Then let it be your God who decides their guilt,' Guilliam barked, and then he looked past the mob. 'Sir Lockwood, let us finish our duel.'

Sir Leland raised an eyebrow, his curiosity piqued.

'What is the meaning of this?' Father Dobbe appeared perplexed.

'Grant me a trial by combat. Should Sir Lockwood strike me down, then you will know for certain it is the will of your Lord that these people are to be punished. But should I win, then it is surely His will that they go free,' he was looking only at Sir Leland now, unblinkingly, challenging the knight as much with his eyes as he was with his words. 'What say you?'

'Sir Lockwood,' Father Dobbe said at once. 'You can not indulge such folly—'

'I accept,' Sir Lockwood's words cut through the priests. Many in the mob gasped, looking to the Father.

'Sir Lockwood—'

The knight shot him a stern glance.

'I… very well,' Dobbe uttered. 'Someone fetch this man a sword, and let us see this matter settled once and for all.'

'Not now,' Sir Leland said, without taking his eyes off Guilliam.

Dobbe sighed, gritting his teeth. 'Why, not now, pray tell?' he asked.

'There is no honour in that. He is underfed and exhausted, and has taken a beating from more than one of you on this day.'

'When, then, might we assume this duel to happen?' the priest pressed.

'Would a fortnight suffice for you to find your strength?'

Guilliam gave a single nod.

'So it is,' Sir Leland said. Then he simply turned, and made towards his horse.

'Sir Lockwood,' the priest rushed over to the knight, speaking in lowered tones upon reaching him. 'I would ask you to reconsider. Why risk your life when we can—'

'You do not think me capable of besting him, priest?'

'I... no, it is not that.'

'It is his right to demand such a trial. And my duty now to honour it. If God is good, then he shall indeed grant me strength.'

'But... the heathens. We have not the space to imprison all of them. And certainly not for a fortnight!'

Sir Lockwood stood still, and pondered for a moment before responding, 'Your church seemed rather spacious, Father,' speaking for all around them to hear, making to mount his horse as he did so.

'You cannot mean to—'

'Yes, Father Dobbe. Let them be chained up in the church,' he pulled himself up onto the horse. 'Who knows, maybe they will come to know God once more.' His horse began to trot, carrying him away from the crowd. 'Now, if you would excuse me,' he called back, turning to afford Guilliam a final glance. 'I would return to my keep before the fortnight is up.' Then he called aloud, 'Giffard!'

Moments later, his squire appeared, hastily making his way through the crowd. 'Sir?'

'Gather my possessions. And your horse. We ride for Ragstone.'

As the squire scurried away and Sir Leland Lockwood rode off, Guilliam let out a sigh, and with a slight smirk, he fell to his knees.

Chapter 26
The Bargain

Hugh stumbled as he helped Beorhtwyn along, deeper and deeper into the woods. The druids who had made it out of the village had – by Beorhtwyn's insistence – gone ahead of the two of them.

'Here,' Beorhtwyn uttered eventually. 'This is the crossing. Set me down here.'

She winced as Hugh gently helped her sit, her back rested against the trunk of an oak tree. Her face had turned completely white now, and her hand, though still pressed against the arrow and the wound it inflicted, had lost its strength, and was doing little in the way of applying pressure. Noticing, Hugh pressed his own hand on hers. Again, she winced.

'I must find you help,' he said.

'I must close the crossing first,' she spoke through laboured breaths. 'We cannot let them through.'

'Beorhtwyn… you told Guilliam that you had never tried to close it from *this* side. That you feared…'

'It might remain closed.'

Hugh held her gaze.

'Yet now,' she wheezed. 'I have no choice.'

Hugh could hear nearing calls. Their pursuers approaching. Looking into her pained eyes, he knew she was right. He nodded.

'You should stand back for this,' she said.

As he backed away, Beorhtwyn placed both her hands upon the ground, digging into the dirt with her fingers, calling on what little strength she could muster. She closed her eyes and began to breathe deeply, melodically almost, though it was clear it pained her to do so.

At first it appeared that nothing was happening.

But then Hugh noticed it.

The plants were suddenly growing. And not just the existing plants. New stems were sprouting, rising swiftly through the soil, and within seconds of doing so they were flowering, petals peeling open, wildflowers of all shades and sizes surrounding them. All around them, the thicket became thicker and tree branches broke off into further branches, and on those branches leaves appeared. Hugh's eyes widened with wonder as this ever-growing forest engulfed them, not noticing when exactly the sound of their pursuers ceased, but knowing only that they were someplace separate now.

But then he was brought back to the present as Beorhtwyn began to cough. He rushed over to her.

'You've done it,' he said softly, smiling.

Her eyes hardly open, she returned his smile best she could, though seemed so sapped of energy now that she could barely curl her lips.

'I… I…' she tried to speak.

'Shhh,' he replied, finding his own lips starting to tremble. 'Save your breath. Now we must find you help.'

'I… can't feel…' her eyes rolled shut and her head slumped before she could finish her words.

'Beorhtwyn,' Hugh leaned in. 'Beorhtwyn, please. Please, I need you to tell me where to go, where to find aid. Beorhtwyn, you must stay awake.'

She murmured a string of not-quite-words in response. She was still breathing, but fading fast. Hugh looked frantically about this newly grown forest.

'Help!' he cried out, hoping one of the other druids might hear him. Though call as he might, no one came. Knowing that she had little time left, Hugh had but one idea. He took a deep breath and scooped Beorhtwyn up, cradling her and rising. Taking note of their surroundings, he began heading in the only direction that appeared vaguely familiar to him, dismissing the disorientation that had befallen him, the same feelings of directionlessness he had experienced when last he trod this path. But he was determined now, desperate, and as a result his senses were sharpened. In his arms Beorhtwyn groaned sporadically, and each one spurred him on. He knew where he was now, yes, he had walked this way before. More importantly, though, he knew where he was going.

No sunlight found its way through the treetops this time. Darkness lingered now, clung to the forest, as Hugh approached the man in the tree.

'Lo, behold,' he heard the voice before he could make out the form. 'The boy who breaks his bargains. And who is this he carries? A girl, barely drawing breath?'

'I wish to strike a new bargain,' Hugh replied, following the sound of the voice, made tricky by the fact it now sounded to be coming from varying directions. 'Your help in return for freedom.'

The man in the tree laughed, a laugh as equally callous as it was giddy. 'We struck that bargain once already. And yet still I am stuck. Now you seek to trick me again?'

'No tricks,' Hugh said, turning as he spoke, trying to spot the man in the tree. 'None from me, nor you.'

'Ha! You are a brazen boy indeed. And what, pray tell, makes you think I would entertain bargaining with you again?'

'Because our last bargain was not an honest one. I knew not what you were then. But now I do. I was warned to be wary of you by this girl I hold in my arms. Now that I do know of your nature, I propose we strike an honest bargain.'

Suddenly, the tree that Hugh happened to be looking at at that moment changed before him. There was, once more, the man, his palms pressed against their wooden prison. 'I am listening,' he said.

'Save this girl's life, if it is in your power, and I will free you. I will fetch the axe and cut down the tree that binds you. But there can be no curses nor trickery.'

A smirk befell the wooden face. 'A tempting offer.'

'You can save her, then?'

'I am most certainly her best chance. Though I can only accept this bargain on one condition.'

'Out with it,' Hugh was losing patience.

'You must first free me.'

'How can I trust you will uphold your end?'

'A question I should rightly be asking *you*! It is you, after all, who failed to honour our last bargain.'

Hugh grimaced. Beorhtwyn's breathing was slowing by the second.

'Regardless, I would be of little use to her bound as I am now. To apply what powers I possess in their fullest, I must be freed from these wretched roots.'

'So be it,' Hugh said. Hesitation was no longer an option, and though he did not trust the man in the tree – unsure that it even was a *man* – it was now his only chance of saving Beorhtwyn's life. He gently set her down, resting her against another tree trunk. 'Hold on,' he spoke softly into her ear. 'I will be back soon.'

And then he was off, headed once again along the trail that led to the axe, only now running as fast as he could. As he had before, he followed the gradually shortening trees, and just as they had before, they led him to what he sought.

The old axe was before him, its shimmering steel sunk into the wood, the metal boasting as pristine a finish as it had when last he laid eyes upon it. He went straight for it, surveying his surroundings as he reached out, half-expecting the dam-dweller to appear again and nip at his heels to attempt to prevent him from taking the axe. But there was no creature, not this time. He gripped the raw wood of the handle with both hands.

He pulled.

Upon his return, Beorhtwyn's head was slumped, her eyes barely open and her breathing slowing, life slipping away with each excruciating exhale.

'Hold on,' Hugh willed her, albeit under no illusion that she was aware of his words. He held the axe before the man in the tree, his arms raised, ready to swing. 'You wish for me to slice you?' he asked.

'Yes, yes,' the creature spoke excitedly through a wide grin, and although he could not move, his palms appeared to be pushing more against the wood than they were before, desperate for the axe's touch. 'Swing, my good fellow! Do not hold back.'

Hugh swung the axe.

It sliced through the bark as if it were warm butter. So clean a cut Hugh had never made with a blade, nor butterknife, in fact. And as it came through the other side of the trunk, he witnessed something truly weird. The top half of the tree, now felled, toppled backwards, and as it did so the man remained precisely where he was stood, in the very same stance. It was almost as if the tree moved through him, as if he were made of water at that moment, but an unmoving water, undisturbed by objects passing through it. And then, as the trunk landed with a mighty thud, the man moved his arms, for what seemed to be the first time in a very long time. His actual appearance was revealed, now he was not so bark-covered; his face was distinctive, pointed, with defined cheekbones trailing down into a long, narrow chin. In fact, most everything about his face was pointed. His bushy brown eyebrows were arched, the unblinking eyes beneath resembling large almonds in shape, though they were near-black in colour. His nose was elongated also, ever so slightly upturned at the tip. Most strikingly, the tops of his ears pointed, their tips poking out through the curly mess of dark brown hair that sat atop his head. His long torso was exposed now, too. Both his face and body were pale, but he had about him a greenish hue, though not in the slightest a sickly one.

His fingers wriggled, stiffly to start with, his hands scrunching and un-scrunching over and over as they felt the free air. Despite his top half now being on show, Hugh had struck the tree at the point of the man's waist, and as such his legs were still bound in bark. But then, once the man had limbered, he pressed his palms down against the wood that wound around his waist and began to push. He was pushing it away from him, lifting himself out from what remained of the tree, his slender arms straining as he did so. Slowly he began to rise, releasing himself from his wooden wrappings, revealing his lower half as he did. To Hugh's surprise, his legs were not pale and bare, but covered in long, matted hair, and in stark contrast to his lithe torso, his thighs seemed wide and robust, and as they emerged from the stump, he could see that they were goat-like, and that in place of feet were cloven hooves.

'It is true, then,' Hugh said as the half-man, half-beast finally stepped out of the stump, standing tall. 'You are no man… you are a demon.'

'I have been named many things, my good fellow. Demon, to some, yes. To others, faerie. It is all but a matter of perspective, you see.'

'I care not what you are, then. Just that you will keep your part in our bargain,' Hugh turned to Beorhtwyn.

The creature looked at her too, and then gave Hugh a smirk in turn. 'But of course,' he said. A single stride brought him to where Beorhtwyn lay. He held a hand over her. His finger nails were as pointed and sharp as all the features of his face. Crouching, he placed his hand around the arrow that was still stuck in her, and gently began to remove it.

Hugh stepped towards him, but the creature paid him no attention, it simply continued to pull. And then, as the arrow came out, Beorhtwyn let out a spluttering cough, before falling silent.

'What have you done?' Hugh demanded.

Still the creature ignored him. It rose and took a step back from Beorhtwyn, and Hugh crouched beside her. For a moment, all was still. And then her eyes opened and she took a deep breath. Instinctively her hands shot to the middle of her chest, where the arrow had been but a moment before, her stolen tunic still wet with blood. She tore at where it had made a hole in the fabric. The wound was gone. Both startled and confused, she looked at Hugh.

'I… what happened?' she uttered.

'Worry not,' Hugh smiled. 'You are mended.'

Then she turned, taking note of the creature that stood before her, that loomed over the both of them, and the look on her face changed from confused to afraid. 'You…'

'M'lady,' the creature bowed. He shot Hugh an unsettling smirk. And then he simply backed away, into the thick cluster of woodland, disappearing into the trees.

Hugh knelt beside Beorhtwyn, helping her to sit upright. 'Softly, softly,' he said.

'Hugh,' she uttered, a stark look on her face now. 'What have you done?'

'You were dying.'

'You made a bargain. You felled the tree.'

'It was the only way. And he has kept his word. Your wound is no more. You are saved.'

She sighed. 'I fear it is not so simple,' her expression changed, as if she had suddenly remembered something. 'My father. Did he—'

'He brought us time,' Hugh said gently. 'But he…'

'Where is he?'

'He did not make it past the crossing. I am sorry.'

Her eyes saddened.

'Nor did Guilliam,' Hugh went on. 'I have failed him.'

They sat in silence for some moments.

'Not necessarily,' suddenly the sadness in her eyes had gone, and now they seemed to gleam with contemplation.

'I am sorry, Beorhtwyn. But they were outnumbered…'

'Perhaps they still are.'

'I do not understand.'

'How long have we been here?'

'I… I couldn't say, exactly. You know things are strange in this place.'

'What does it *feel* like? Hours? Days?'

'I… not quite an hour. What does it matter? We fled. It is done.'

'You said it yourself. Things are strange in this place. You cannot say how much time has passed, because time works differently here. Slower. You have felt it. An hour here, in these woods, may pass as but a few seconds elsewhere. All the more so when the way is closed.'

Hugh nodded. 'Guilliam spoke of this to me. It was during his time spent on *this* side that he and Ethel fell in love. They spent months with one another, yet in the village all that time amounted to days. '

'Then you see my meaning,' she stood as she spoke, Hugh offering his arm so that she might steady herself. And then, once she had risen: 'There remains a chance, Hugh. That we might still save those who were left behind.'

'You think you can open the way again, from within? From this side?'

She nodded to herself, albeit unsurely. 'We shall soon find out,' she said.

Chapter 27
A Parting of Ways

They had returned to the point of the crossing. Just as she had done when sealing the passage between realms, Beorhtwyn once again dug her fingers into the soil. Hugh stood behind her, still holding the axe – a weapon would be useful, after all. They had gathered what druids they were able to as they made their way back to the crossing, and now another six stood with them. They had been rallied by Beorhtwyn, but half of those she had asked for aid refused, having so recently failed in their first rescue mission. She did not begrudge them. Those willing to go back with her, to help save her father, now followed behind her and Hugh, readying to return to the village once more. Amongst them were both Eoforgār and Fugolcwēn – her kestrel still perched on her shoulder.

'You are hurt?' Eoforgār had asked Beorhtwyn once they had regrouped.

'A flesh wound, nothing more,' she had insisted.

He had taken her word for it, but during their journey had kept a close eye on Hugh, clearly suspicious of the axe in his hand.

Soon enough they were back at the crossing. Beorhtwyn and Hugh shared a glance as she readied herself.

'You can do this,' Hugh assured her.

She closed her eyes and crouched, her hands finding the soil. Taking a deep breath, she dug her fingertips into the dirt. Nothing changed. Not at first. But then came a faint rustling. Branches began to contort. Soil started to subtly shift beneath their feet.

'It's working!' Hugh exclaimed.

Before, when sealing the way, trees had grown all around them. But as Beorhtwyn now opened it, they began to shrink, with trunks sinking into the soil as suddenly as they had sprouted. As much of the surrounding shrubbery subsided, Hugh felt again that the air around him was changing, that the path that had been closed was opening up. Soon the sunlight of the world Hugh knew was once again piercing through the trees, and alongside the six druids who had joined them, he stepped back into his own realm.

They had barely made it a stone's throw when Beorhtwyn began to slow. She groaned.

'What is it?' Hugh asked. 'What's wrong?'

Suddenly her knees buckled. She fell to the ground and her hand shot up from the soil to the centre of her chest, where her wound had been. She looked down to her hand, and then to Hugh, her face white. She was bleeding again.

As she stumbled, Fugolcwēn stepped to steady her. Behind her

Eoforgār watched. 'That is no flesh wound,' he said.

'I… I was fine,' Beorhtwyn began.

Hugh's face fell, and a heavy sigh escaped him. 'And there it is,' he said. 'The catch.'

'What is happening here?' Eoforgār demanded.

'We must return,' Hugh continued, ignoring him, approaching Beorhtwyn. 'And you must close the way again. You cannot be in this world.'

'My father…'

'Beorhtwyn,' he looked to her hand, pressed against the wound and the blood that was bleeding from it. 'You will not make it to him.'

'So, this is the gain from treating with a trickster,' she said through a sorrowful smile, spluttering after speaking the words.

'What is this you speak of?' Eoforgār pressed.

'Please' Hugh replied. 'We must return and the way must be sealed.'

No sooner than it had been reopened, the way was closed again. The six druids watched in awe as the wound disappeared. Removing her hands from the soil, Beorhtwyn. turned to face them.

'That axe,' Eoforgār gestured to Hugh. 'You used it to free He Who is Held in the Tree.'

'I did,' Hugh answered solemnly.

'And he healed you in return?' Eoforgār looked to Beorhtwyn.

She nodded.

'I never took you for a fool, Beorhtwyn.'

'Eoforgār, calm yourself,' Fugolcwēn said.

'You have set loose a demon in these woods,' he retorted, his focus fixed on Beorhtwyn.

'It was not her choosing to do so,' Hugh spoke up. 'I made the call. And I knew the risk. But I deemed it the only way. Else she would have succumbed to her wound.'

'Then you have trapped her here, boy.'

'So it would seem,' Hugh replied. He turned to Beorhtwyn. 'Forgive me.'

But Beorhtwyn seemed lost for words, contemplating the confines she now found herself in.

'You seek forgiveness?' Eoforgār snapped. 'Because of you and your master our homes lie in ruin. The forest to which we fled is no longer fit for sanctuary. Half of our folk are soon to be slain, if not already so, all for trying to spare *you* from such a fate. And now you have let loose a long-bound demon.' He turned to his fellow druids. 'We can aid this outsider no more. We must leave him to his fate, and seek out a new one for those of us who are left.'

'You mean to abandon our own?' Fugolcwēn asked.

'We cannot return to the village. And these woods are safe no longer, not with the demon now free. We must venture until we find another crossing.'

'That could take us months. Years even.'

'We have little other choice now. We are as good as dead if we return, and no better remaining here.'

'My father,' Beorhtwyn said. 'If he yet draws breath… we must help him.'

'We are outnumbered as it is, Beorhtwyn. And now you cannot cross with us,' Eoforgār's words were devoid of feeling.

'We cannot leave him to be killed!'

'It pains me to say. But your father stayed there so that you might escape. I am sorry. Now you must come with us. You must help us seek out another crossing. It is what he would want.'

'I am not leaving him,' she turned to the other druids. 'You would not forsake those we might yet save, surely?'

Not one of them spoke up. Beorhtwyn looked directly at Fugolcwēn.

'I…' Fugolcwēn began. 'If He Who is Held in the Tree walks free, then I fear Eoforgār speaks true. It is not safe for us here.'

For a moment Beorhtwyn stood in silence and Fugolcwēn was unable to meet her eye. Then she said, 'So be it.'

'Come with us,' Eoforgār said once more. 'Here there is only death. Even if you are bound to this realm, we may yet find a distant part of it, away from the threat of the demon. Another crossing, where we might build a new village by its border. A new Ealdgeat.'

'I cannot.'

'Beorhtwyn—'

'I *will* not.'

A silence followed. Eoforgār gave a single nod. 'I bid you well, then.'

He did not afford Hugh so much as a side-eye as he turned, the five other druids following him, one by one. Fugolcwēn was the last to turn her back on them. From the look on her face, it clearly pained her to do so.

'You think they will find another crossing?' Hugh asked, once they had disappeared into the thicket.

'I do hope so.'

'And what of us now?'

'I… I know not.' Beorhtwyn's words rung with resignation.

'You mean to say you have no plan?'

She shook her head.

'Yet still you chose to stay.'

'If my father lives, I must find a way to help him.'

'But we are trapped here.'

'*I* am trapped here. You may yet leave.'

'And face the folk from the village alone? I am greatly outnumbered.'

'I mean that you may leave this place altogether. I can open the passage and you can go. Leave the woods, leave Ealdgeat, or Crooklingsham. Leave and never come back. Leave your old life behind, Hugh Brombury. Begin anew in some far-off place.'

'Is that what you wish?'

'What I wish no longer matters. Guilliam would not have you stay needlessly behind on my behalf.'

Hugh sighed, and considered her words. A moment passed where neither looked the other in the eye. Then, he spoke. 'I would do Guilliam and all he has taught me a grave disservice were I to forsake you. To leave you alone in this realm. No, Beorhtwyn. I shall not abandon you now. I would instead stay, and help you find a way around this demon's deceit.'

'Hugh—'

'And if there is truly no way, then I shall endure this destiny alongside you. For it is a destiny of my doing. But until then, *we* have a plan to come up with.'

'Even with time passing slower, those left behind… they may have died fighting by now. Guilliam was battling the knight when we fled…'

'Yes,' Hugh lowered his head. 'I fear I have failed him. But there is also a chance that the others are captured, not killed. If not all of them, some, at least. Perhaps your father amongst them. They risked their lives to save me. If I am not willing to do the same for them, then I was never worthy of being a squire.'

Beorhtwyn's face softened, and the corners of her lips curled into the slightest of smiles. 'You are a good man, Hugh Brombury.'

'I had a good teacher, is all. Now, if we are to find a way to undo this creature's cunning trick, would you have any ideas where we might begin?'

They were once again cut off from the world they knew. The sky above them had about it an odd purple hue, as if in perpetual twilight, and as far as the eye could see the trees grew thick and tall, and they all now seemed to be ever so slightly different, though the precise manner of this difference was difficult to determine. They were even, perhaps, shifting. On more than one occasion Hugh could have sworn that a view from not a moment before had been replaced, had rearranged itself in some way. Subtly, mind you; perhaps leaves that were at first glance a vivid green were now an earthy brown, or what had been deeply furrowed bark now seemed to be smooth. Or perhaps not. He could not know for sure.

As they both pondered precisely which direction to venture, a rustling in a nearby shrub drew their attention. They turned and looked at the undergrowth at the same time. Something was moving towards them. They shared a knowing look.

'Do you think…' Hugh began, his voice a whisper.

'He Who is… *was* Held in the Tree,' Beorhtwyn finished his thought. 'Ready yourself to run.'

The rustling grew louder as whatever approached grew nearer. Hugh and Beorhtwyn made to turn, but before they could, something came charging out of the bushes before them. The both of them stumbled backwards due to the sheer speed at which the creature emerged, Hugh's heel snagging on a root, sending him tumbling until his arse was planted on the ground. For a second or so he thought the creature meant to pounce, but then it slowed, coming to a stop before the two of them. It was not, as they had feared, He Who was Held in the Tree.

They both recognised it, with its antlers and branch-like fur.

'Hello again,' Hugh said, brushing himself off as he stood. 'Little nipper.'

Chapter 28
The Domain of the Dam-Dwellers

Whether the creature understood him, Hugh knew not. However, it seemed, at the very least, to be *fine* with them following it, if not outright encouraging them to do so. Presently they were doing just that, with the dam-dweller leading them ever-deeper into the woodland realm. It scampered along on all fours through the dense thicket, much faster than either Hugh or Beorhtwyn were able to run, only to – on more than one occasion – stop and wait when they grew too far apart, clearly eager for them to catch up. Ever present in the air appeared to be little specks of light, floating and falling slowly, glowing all the while, like tiny petals or pieces of pollen. But they were neither of those things, they were their own thing altogether. The same could be said for much of the surroundings that Hugh and Beorhtwyn followed the dam-dweller through; a myriad of flora that exuded exoticness – whilst somehow retaining a faint familiarity

– grew every which way, and that purple-tainted sky above was ever-bleeding through the interwoven branches – themselves abundant with clusters of curiously coloured leaves – emitting a dainty gleam. Perchance, pondered Hugh, it was this lavender light that caused such peculiar plants to grow here. And peculiar they undoubtedly were. They saw trees with twisting trunks and slender yellow-leafed branches swaying gently in the whistling breeze; waded through wild gardens of tall, dark-stemmed plants with flowers formed of pale petals, so see-through they looked like they might vanish at any moment; and all the while beneath their feet, in the underbrush, untamed tendrils seemed to be ever-moving, winding their way through multicoloured moss and leaf litter as if pulled along by an invisible seamstress, pausing occasionally to cautiously coil, only to stretch out again upon deciding on their path.

But neither of them could pause to take in such sights, for the dam-dweller would run ahead, stopping to wait for them only just before vanishing entirely from their view. And so this went on, for how long they could not say (as it was with most everything in this realm). Then, at some point, both Hugh and Beorhtwyn could hear a soft melodic sound. But it was no person, or creature for that matter, that emitted this almost music.

Breaking through a barrier of brush, the source of the sound revealed itself; a stream of silvery water, weaving its way through the woodland. It flowed as far as they could see, widening into small, shallow ponds in places, narrowing into thin, shimmering stretches in others. Here, on either side of the path of slowly flowing water, the trees grew sparser, the thicket not so dense as it had been during their journey, and as such the purple sky above coated the expanse, the stream mirroring its hues in ripples of violet and lavender. The dam-dweller had stopped again, perching itself by the water's edge. As Hugh and Beorhtwyn approached it now, though, it did not scamper onwards, instead it waited for them.

'Is this your home?' Hugh asked the creature, for all the good it did. Of course, it did not respond, but it did turn its head, seemingly gesturing for the two of them to look past it. They did just that, and after a moment Beorhtwyn grabbed Hugh by the shoulder.

'Look!' she exclaimed.

He didn't see it at first. Or, at least, could not make it out. But then he spotted one. Another dam-dweller, same as the one that had led them there, its branched fur camouflaging it against the backdrop of the forest. And then another, and another. All around them were pairs of eyes of every shade of brown or green you could imagine, above which grew pointy ears and antlers. There were at least two dozen dam-dwellers looking at them, and when their bushy bodies did become clear to Hugh, he could see that they were poised to flee, their dispositions ones of timid trepidation. What prevented them from doing so was, in all likelihood, the one who'd led them here. Plentiful pairs of eyes flitted skittishly between Hugh and Beorhtwyn and their fellow dam-dweller; its lack of unease a signal to the others that they had nothing to fear from the two newcomers, that these were guests, not trespassers. And so, whilst remaining wary, several dam-dwellers slowly began to approach the two of them.

Hugh and Beorhtwyn shared a glance.

'Have you ever seen so many of them?' Hugh asked.

Beorhtwyn shook her head. As she did, it seemed that more now revealed themselves, slowly encircling the both of them.

'You are certain that they are friendly?' Hugh asked quietly.

Although they were small, they were quick, and should they, for some reason, take a sudden dislike to their visitors, the pair of them would be overwhelmed within seconds.

'So far, it would seem,' Beorhtwyn replied, her tone betraying any sense of certainty. She stepped forwards ever so slightly, and a good few dam-dwellers scurried away some paces. But what could only be termed a look of reassurance from the one who had led them there calmed the scurriers. No, it was more than just a look. It was as if he had spoken to them, but without speaking, without so much as making a sound.

'We mean you no harm,' Beorhtwyn said softly, though projected her voice so that all the surrounding dam-dwellers might hear. If they did, their unchanged, wide-eyed glares all but confirmed they understood nothing of what she said. 'Me and my friend were led here by your friend,' she continued nonetheless, gesturing to him. 'We found ourselves in a place no longer safe. And he guided us here. Might we take that as an invitation, to stay a while? At least, whilst we gather our bearings?'

There was, as to be expected, silence.

'It's no good,' Hugh said, placing a reassuring hand on Beorhtwyn's shoulder. 'They cannot comprehend what—'

'Ve-tay-shun,' came an utterance.

Both Hugh and Beorhtwyn turned to the source of the sound. It had come from the dam-dweller they had followed.

'Did it…' Hugh exclaimed, albeit under his breath. 'They possess speech after all?' Then he noticed that the surrounding dam-dwellers appeared almost as amazed as he and Beorhtwyn were by this revelation, their own attention fixed on the one that had spoken. 'At least, that nipper does.'

'Ni-per.'

Hugh and Beorhtwyn exchanged a glance, smiles on both their faces.

'Do you think… *he* understands us?' she asked.

'It may be no more than mimicry… although…' Hugh trailed off.

'What?'

'Suppose we could communicate. Perhaps it… *he*, could help us. Could help you find a way to leave, to rectify the tree-man's wicked trick. Then we can return to the village, to aid your people. To aid your father.'

Beorhtwyn pondered this for a moment. 'Teach him to speak,' she said eventually, sounding somewhat resigned. '*This* is our plan, is it?'

Hugh looked down at the wide-eyed creature, who returned his gaze, appearing ready to imitate whatever word he might like the sound of next. 'It would seem so,' he said.

Chapter 29
Lessons in Language

They started, naturally, with simple things. A rock, to be precise. Not knowing how long they would be welcome to stay in this secluded grove by the stream – if they were indeed welcome to stay at all – Hugh set about teaching this particular word to the curious dam-dweller without wasting a moment more. Beorhtwyn sat back at first, casting an apprehensive eye over the many other dam-dwellers, themselves observing the interaction with their own apparent apprehension. It had given her a good opportunity to account for their number, though tallying them accurately was no simple feat, especially once reaching the early hundreds. She found it tricky to distinguish them from one another, what with their branched fur blending into the backdrop of the forest. What's more, she struggled to tell those who held back, choosing to keep their distance from their guests, apart from actual bushes, at least at a glance, and would find herself losing count as she tried to determine whether she was counting creature or nature. After a few attempts, she settled on there most certainly being more than one-hundred twig-coated creatures in the grove, though likely less than two-hundred.

The creature that had led them there observed Hugh with continued curiosity, and was soon able to utter a sound which somewhat resembled the word *rock*.

'You hear that?' Hugh beamed, turning to Beorhtwyn as the dam-dweller did its best to mimic him. He looked back to the creature before him, whose wide green eyes blinked, 'He understands!'

'*He*,' the dam-dweller repeated.

'Yes,' Hugh nodded, pointing to him. '*He*, that's you.'

'*He*,' the dam-dweller gestured to itself now

'He thinks *He* is his name,' Beorhtwyn said.

'*He*.'

'Ah, no, *you're* not *he*,' Hugh said, 'though, you are a *he*. Just, that is not your name.'

'*He*,' clearly, He had not understood.

'Well we can't be having this,' Hugh said, looking to Beorhtwyn.

'You're the one teaching him.'

'I… true enough. Though we shall make little headway with him thinking his name is He.'

'Suppose you give him a new name, and teach him that.'

' Any suggestions?'

'A word he knows already?'

'*He*,' spoke He once more.

'He now knows the word for rock,' Hugh said, 'though that's no fit name.'

'What was it you called him earlier? The word he repeated.'

'Nipper? Why, that was only because he nipped at my leg when first we—'

'Aye,' Beorhtwyn nodded, then looked to the dam-dweller. 'Has the look of a Nipper. At least more than he does a Rock.'

Hugh, casting another glance at the dam-dweller, nodded too. He pointed once again, only this time he said, 'Nipper. You are Nipper. Nipper.'

And, after a moment, came the reply: 'Nip-er.'

Lessons continued. Days didn't feel like days, with the sky remaining a perpetual purplish, changing only in shade to mark the passing into what might be considered this realm's night, though not following any discernible pattern as it did. It was more as if the mood of the place itself determined the tone from above. Throughout this cycle of indeterminate purples, Hugh taught the newly named Nipper as many rudimentary English words as there were things he was able to point to, moving on from *rock* to any and every surrounding object. Soon Nipper had learnt to say tree and leaf and sky and river and stone and stick and after that various variations of the words. Then soon after that, when Hugh had seemingly run out of things to point to, he began drawing in the dirt, which somewhat confused Nipper at first – perhaps on account of Hugh's disputable artistic wherewithal – though after Hugh etched some of the objects they had already named into the dirt to illustrate his new technique, the dam-dweller began to grasp it.

Beorhtwyn would join in too, from time to time, though Hugh couldn't help but notice that she was, more often than not, distant.

Now that all the back and forth had stopped, the reality of her situation seemed to be settling in. She was alive thanks to the deal Hugh had made with He Who was Held in the Tree, but she was also trapped in this realm. He would spot her, on occasion, peering down her smock, examining where the arrow had struck and the now non-existent wound.

'Does it hurt?' he asked one (what may or may not have been) afternoon, having spent most of the morning teaching Nipper basic sentences; *leaves are green, stones are hard* and the like. 'Sorry,' he said a second later, as she looked slightly taken aback by the question. 'It is not my place to—'

'At times I think I can feel it still,' she said, casting her eyes down to her chest. 'It is faint, and fleeting. But it is as if the wound is still there, and that it has simply been… hidden.'

'Beorhtwyn… had I known, I…'

'You'd have let me die?' she asked, though with a kind natured, albeit slight, smile.

'No, I… I merely mean to say—'

'Fret not. You did what you thought best, and for that I am grateful.'

'Yet because of me you might never leave this realm.'

'That may be,' she looked Hugh in the eye, 'though if not for you, I would not now draw breath. No matter where I was.'

He held her gaze, as all around them seemed to fall silent, save for the whisperings of a gentle, cooling breeze that passed more often than not through the grove.

'And Nipper,' she cleared her throat, 'may yet show us a way in which I might return. That is our plan, after all.'

'Yes… indeed,' Hugh cleared his throat. 'I best be getting back to his lessons.'

'I… he's coming along. You are a fine teacher of language. Far better than me.'

'I've Guilliam to thank for that. He insisted I take up letters when I first came into his service.'

'He taught you himself?'

'No, though he saw to it I had learned tutors.' As he thought back to those times, Hugh's lips curled into a smile. It just as quickly became a frown as he thought on the fate that had likely befallen his friend. He sighed. 'Perhaps if I had focused more on swordplay than scribing during my squiring, I might have fought off Lockwood. And Guilliam and your father would have escaped, and you would not have been shot and—'

'But you did not,' Beorhtwyn cut in. 'You are not good with a sword, nor at fighting.'

Hugh did not know what to say to that, not having expected her to agree so assuredly with him.

'And if you were,' she continued, her tone softening 'then you might not be such a good teacher to our friend here,' Beorhtwyn gestured with a nod, and Hugh turned to see Nipper. He had been eavesdropping, with a look of curiosity and now – that he had been spotted – a touch of timidness.

'He-lo,' smiled the dam-dweller.

'Hello, Nipper,' Hugh smiled.

Then Nipper turned to Beorhtwyn. 'Her-t,' he pointed to her as he said the word, a touch of sadness to it.

Hugh and Beorhtwyn exchanged a glance, and he appeared just

as surprised as she that Nipper had been able to take that away from what he'd heard of their conversation, the two of them having spoken in sentences far more advanced than he should rightly understand.

'Yes,' Beorhtwyn crouched down, so that she was level with Nipper. 'That's right. I was *hurt*.'

'Tree… man,' Nipper replied.

'He… he didn't hurt me, no. But for his trickery. You know that word, *trickery*?'

Nipper's eyes narrowed, as though he was struggling to comprehend.

'We've yet to cover that one,' Hugh added. He thought to himself for a moment, and then he picked up a small pebble with his left hand. He held it clearly before Nipper, both hands outstretched with wide open palms. 'I am going to close my hand,' he spoke clearly, despite Nipper not having learnt any words from the specific sentence, save *hand*. However, during the course of their lessons Hugh had began to speak to the dam-dweller in fuller sentences of largely unlearnt words, peppered with one or two that were known, and found this to be quite an effective method, especially when it came to Nipper forming small sentences of his own, and as such he was confident Nipper would decipher the demonstration.

And so, Hugh closed his hand.

'Now tell me, in which hand is the *pebble*?' he asked, putting particular emphasis on the last word. He had to repeat the question a few times, yet Nipper couldn't seem to make sense of it. So, Hugh asked Beorhtwyn the same question, and she pointed to the hand he had clearly closed around the pebble, at which he opened it.

'Now you,' he addressed Nipper once again, repeating the steps as before. Nipper raised a short arm and pointed to the fist which held the pebble, and Hugh revealed it. 'Good,' he said. 'Again.'

They did this twice more. Then a third, only this time Hugh held his hands a little more closely together, and as he closed both fists at the same time, tilted his left ever so slightly above his right, so that the pebble slipped into it as the fingers pressed towards the palm, precisely at the point where Nipper would not see. He held out his clenched hands again, and Nipper pointed to the left. When Hugh opened it to reveal nothing there, the dam-dweller took a step back, his eyes wide with surprise. Then, Hugh slowly unpeeled the fingers of his right hand, revealing the pebble.

'Trickery,' Hugh said.

As Hugh drifted into sleep, his thoughts were of those left behind, of Beorhtwyn's people. Of how long had passed in their world, of what might have befallen them, if they really might yet be saved. And of the friend he had failed. He had dreamed strange dreams since staying at the grove, or so he thought, what with the waking world of the realm he was in being just as strange, just as vivid and at times disorientating as that of the dreaming one. Perhaps they were not dreams at all. Perhaps this realm did not allow for dreaming.

He was in the woods, *these* woods. Only alone. Lost, as he had been before first meeting He Who was Held in the Tree. But he was not scared now, not panicking. He noticed that he held the axe he had taken from the stump. He walked calmly, and he could feel the sun on his face, and he could see it in the sky. And yet there was a shadow, and it followed him, and as he glanced over his shoulder he could see that it engulfed all that was behind him.

Passing him were men and women, robed and rugged. The druids. They were walking towards the shadow, just as calmly as he himself had walked, and slowly, so slowly. They did not look at him as they passed. But they were going the wrong way. He tried to tell them, but they could not hear, or perhaps it was that he could not speak. Eotenfrēond walked by then, he was also heading for the shadow. Hugh reached out, calling his name, but still he did not hear. And Guilliam followed shortly thereafter, and now Hugh was trying to stop him, but he also did not hear. Hugh reached out to touch him. For the briefest of moments Guilliam stopped. His head turned ever so slightly. But before his eyes found Hugh he carried on, following the druids towards the shadow. Suddenly there was a vast distance between them. Still they walked slowly, barely moving but so far away, and still headed towards the shadow. 'There is still a chance—' Beorhtwyn said, her voice behind him. He turned and it was bright, so bright. A girl stood before him. Her hair was blonde. But it was not Beorhtwyn. She wore white, but her gown was unlike any Hugh had ever seen. It was a cream white and it clung to her, and her waist was drawn so very tight that her body stiffened in a strange manner, but below the gown billowed about her as if it were a cloud. It was embroidered with what might have been pearls and it shimmered; it was silken perhaps. 'Who are you?' Hugh asked. He could not see her face fully for it was veiled with a fine fabric, but what he could see was wholly unfamiliar. He then felt the need to look at his hands. He no longer held the axe. 'The trees 'ave taken it back,' the woman spoke, answering a question different to the one he had asked. Hugh looked to the druids in the distance. 'They walk slowly towards the darkness,' the woman spoke in a voice not only unknown to Hugh, but one that sounded far, far away. 'Slowly, to your eyes. But they ain't there yet.' Her accent was peculiar, unplaceable. It was a voice unlike any he had heard before. Hugh looked over his shoulder again. Guilliam and the druids inched ever closer to the all-engulfing shadow. 'Guilliam still lives?' Hugh asked, turning back to face the veiled woman. She gave a single nod. 'So we can save him?' She shook her head. '*You* can.' 'I… what of Beorhtwyn?' 'She cannot leave here.' 'Our plan… it is in vain, then? Nipper cannot help her.' 'No. Not her. But he can help Guilliam.' Her voice was even further away now and it was fading with each word. 'How?' 'Keep teaching him, Hugh Brombury. Then you'll 'ave your answer.' 'What answer?' But she did not speak anymore. And just as suddenly as she had appeared, the girl in the peculiar gown, with the peculiar voice, was gone.

Chapter 30
Gruel Before a Duel

Nearly ten full days had passed when Sir Leland Lockwood returned and demanded the prisoners be fed more than the scant scraps that had barely sustained them, a request met with much ill-temper, not least of all from Father Dobbe.

'First you would have me keep these fourteen heathens in a house of God, now you would see that they dine there too? Might I remind you, Sir Lockwood,' Father Dobbe now found himself uttering the knight's name with a modicum of malice, 'Not only are they pagans, but they attacked the good people of this village. It is a miracle they did not kill anyone during the skirmish.'

'You would make a dishonourable knight of me, should you leave Guilliam near starved to death before our duel,' Lockwood retorted, his tone just as biting as the priest's, only his words were emboldened by the fact he stood facing the holy man clad in full plate, sheathed steel hanging from hip. 'I will not fight him until he has found his strength.'

'This is—'

'Those are my conditions, Father,' he said, a finality in his tone. 'If my conditions displease you, perhaps you should not have sent those two wretched fellows the Baron saw fit for guards with your request for my aid.'

The priest stood silent, suppressing a scowl.

'Now I should break my own fast, for I have ridden through the night.'

With great reluctance, Dobbe had a meagre excuse for a meal prepared, and though the portions were certainly not generous enough to fill all fourteen bellies, the prisoners fed fervently from the bowls of over-boiled oats they were given. It was Guilliam who had been offered the fullest and largest of all the bowls. By Sir Leland himself, no less.

'Do my companions not get such generous a helping,' he said, sarcastically emphasising the word *generous*.

'It is more than you deserve,' Dobbe – who lingered behind Sir Lockwood – retorted.

'That will be all, Father,' the knight responded, without so much as turning to face the priest, his gaze fixed firmly on Guilliam, whom he stood over.

Making his disdain for the situation abundantly clear through a series of sighs, Father Dobbe turned and left his church, very much at his own pace. When the doors finally shut behind him, Sir Lockwood continued.

'It seems to me that you need this more than them. They should want you to have your strength after all, now that you fight for their freedom. For their lives.'

'I've rendered men limbless on less,' Guilliam replied. 'Do you know what it is like when supplies run dry during a siege, Sir Lockwood, only for the walls to be breached thereafter?'

'I do not,' he answered, following a drawn out pause.

'Ah, so you have been blessed with good fortune. Plenty of provisions in the sieges that you've suffered, I'm to take it?'

'I have never been part of a siege.'

'Oh, have you not?' Despite his frail state, Guilliam's lips curled into a smirk. 'My apologies, Sir. Not as seasoned a knight as I had you for, it would seem.'

Sir Lockwood dropped the bowl from where he stood, sludge splashing from it and covering the surrounding ground. 'Eat,' he said. 'Or don't. Regardless, we shall face one another the day after next.' With that, the knight turned and left the church.

'A morsel more for everyone, at least,' Guilliam said. 'So long as you don't mind feasting from the floor.'

He felt a hand on his shoulder. 'The knight speaks true,' Eotenfrēond said, his voice trembling and as weak as he now looked. 'You are our only hope of leaving this village alive. You must eat more than us.' Those who could muster *ayes* did so, and the others simply nodded.

'What good is it if you are starved before then?'

'The helpings we've had now should see us until the morrow. If Lockwood brings us another serving, even if it is no more than this, we will make it to the day of the duel. But you,' he handed Guilliam the wooden spoon he had used for his own portion, 'must do more than merely make it. You must build some strength between now and then.'

Perhaps it was simply that he hadn't wanted to give Sir Lockwood the satisfaction, but he knew it was right. And hearing it from Eotenfrēond, Guilliam did not bother to object. He had, indeed, fought more fatigued than he now found himself, but that was a very long time ago, and his rival had at least a decade on him, if not a half on top of that. So, Guilliam took the spoon and scooped a serving of slop up from the cold, damp stone floor of the back of the church where they had been shackled to one another for nearly ten days. And once he had eaten that spoonful – despite the sour tang of spoiled grain and burnt aftertaste that accompanied overcooked gruel when it had to be scraped from the bottom of the pot – he took another. And after that another. And when there was not enough left to spoon up, he licked the stone clean.

Chapter 31
Spearfishing

It was not all too long after Nipper began to converse with Hugh (that is to say in a manner not so dissimilar from how an infant might converse, though converse nonetheless) that Beorhtwyn, in an effort to distract herself from dwelling on the nature of her vanished wound, slowly started to spend time with the other dam-dwellers. She watched them at first, from a distance. Though they had clearly come to accept that both her and Hugh were there to stay for the time being, they didn't seem as keen on the learning of their guest's language as Nipper was. He had, in fact, become something of an emissary between the two of them and his kind, bringing them food – fish from the stream and fruit from the trees – twice a day. Despite the sharing of their spoils, they never feasted alongside the dam-dwellers, not to begin with. Nipper's trust in them may have quelled the creature's suspicions, but not their cautious nature.

But Beorhtwyn knew this would not do. Not if she were to remain in this realm, in *their* realm, as might very well be her fate if Nipper did not have the answer to undoing the trickster's affliction that had befallen her. If that was the case, she would have to earn their approval and their trust if she were to survive here. So, as Hugh taught Nipper how to speak their language, she took it upon herself to do her part, to learn the dam-dwellers' ways. To begin with, she would follow them, leaving a fair few strides in between, as they went about their foraging. They would venture from their settlement, out into the denser woodlands in groups of two dozen, give or take. On the first few occasions that Beorhtwyn tailed them, she was afforded regular glances, and deemed it best not to forage any berries of her own. However, by the third outing, a group of dam-dwellers appeared to pay her no heed, and she helped herself to a small handful of fruits. And so this continued, and each outing Beorhtwyn would collect a slightly larger batch of berries than she had the time before, which was useful in not only integrating herself amongst the creatures, but in learning about the unusual food that grew from this realm's branches and bushes. Much like the plant life, the produce here was not to be found in the world she knew – there were no figs or plums or pears, at least not as she remembered them, only what could perhaps pass as odd imitations. Though, as peculiar as what she assumed to be this realm's berries appeared (turquoise and teardrop shaped, blood red when bitten into) they were undeniably delicious, as sweet and rich as she imagined the finest honey might be.

There was one instance, however, in which Beorhtwyn found, growing on the branch of a tree, what appeared to be a fruit that was indeed familiar to her. An apple. A single apple, its shining scarlet skin drawing her to it from some distance away. Perhaps it was the familiarity that made the apple appear so alluring. Whatever it was, all she knew, upon catching a glimpse of it, was that she wanted it. Needed to bite into it. To hear it crunch, to savour its sweet juice in all its splendour. And then she was stood before it, reaching out to pluck it from its branch. Only, before her fingers touched it, she felt a tugging at her boot. She turned, faced now with one of the dam-dwellers. She had seen this one before; fine branches grew from its face as side whiskers might on a man. It shook its head, wearing a worried expression.

Beorhtwyn looked between the dam-dweller and the apple.

'No good?' she spoke her question aloud, despite knowing it would not take the meaning. The dam-dweller tugged at her boot some more, appearing to go against its instincts, its apprehensive nature, in doing so. All of a sudden, the apple didn't seem so appealing. It seemed alien. As if it had been left there. A lure. 'I s'pose not,' she said, backing away from the fruit.

Later she mentioned the apple to Hugh. 'I can't explain it,' she told him. 'It was as if it wanted me to take it. And then, when I saw how it unsettled the dam-dweller… I was overcome with a great unease.'

'You think it may be another trick?' Hugh asked. 'Courtesy of our friend from the tree.'

'Perhaps,' Beorhtwyn answered, gazing into the distance. Into the endless woodland. 'We shall have to keep our wits about us.'

Before long, these outings became a routine to Beorhtwyn, but they weren't only for foraging. She would follow the dam-dwellers along the stream and watch them slip in, their flat tails steering them as they swam, twigs and branches between their teeth, dragging larger logs and rocks and setting them down to slow the flow of water. They would then weave as many branches between these foundations as they could, before plugging the gaps with mud and stone, thus building the very dams for which they had been named. And it was as Beorhtwyn watched them do this that she discovered precisely why they built dams. Fish. They would fashion their constructs into enclosed areas, channelling their soon-to-be-supper into concentrated sections where the water was shallow enough for scooping. And scooped they were.

This system worked well for the dam-dwellers, affording them fistfuls of the smaller, slower, fish, though after some time spent watching them trap and grab, Beorhtwyn noticed that the larger ones were getting away. It wasn't that their dams weren't trapping them like the others – if anything the meatier fish had a harder time abiding them – it was simply that when they went to grab the fish, they wriggled and writhed so rapidly that more often than not they were able to escape. Even if a dam-dweller were able to clench one between its sharp-nailed fingers and snatch it straight out of the stream, there would be an ensuing struggle that tended to result in the fish frantically thrashing, its body too sleek to keep still, and launching itself back into the water before making a swift swim for freedom.

It was quite clear that this ongoing struggle irked the dam-dwellers, that they were trapping the bigger fish but rarely managing to actually catch them. After having watched the scene play out for the eighth time, Beorhtwyn decided to try. Only, she did not attempt to grab the fish with her hands. As the dam-dwellers approached their dam, she – having noticed a fish perhaps the length of her own forearm entrapped in the enclosure – took a nearby branch for herself. With the hunting knife that hung from her belt she began to sharpen one end of the stick, whittling away until it was so pointy that poking it with her little finger produced a spec of blood. Then, no further than two inches from the tip, she cut small, diagonal barbs in the wood, angling them backwards. Impromptu spear in hand, Beorhtwyn slowly approached the dam. There was one dam-dweller already standing near up to his neck in water, scooping smatterings of smaller fish and tossing them onto the bank, where the five surrounding dam-dwellers would collect them. All of them stopped in their efforts as she neared though, turning to her with curious looks about their vaguely people-like faces.

'May I?' Beorhtwyn asked, gesturing with her stick, hoping that whilst they might not understand the words, they would gather her intent.

The dam-dweller in the water – who kept one eye on the forearm-length fish that swam in confused circles, growing ever more agitated – paused for a moment before obliging, retreating far enough back as to afford her a clear shot, making sure his body still blocked the opening in which the fish had entered. Beorhtwyn's eyes narrowed as she leaned over the dam. She had caught fish in such a manner many times before, and in murkier waters than the stream before her. In fact, the water here was perhaps the clearest she had ever seen, and with the dam stilling it, the fish would make for an easy target. She raised her arm and steadied the spear, taking in a deep breath and holding it. She lined up her prey, then thrust the spear towards it. Seconds later it was skewered, the spike-tipped stick piercing both scale and flesh. The fish writhed violently for all of a few seconds, and then the writhing subsided, until it simply floated. The dam-dweller standing nearby looked at Beorhtwyn, as if asking her permission to pick up the fish. She nodded.

That very evening, for the first time since they had arrived at the grove, when it came time for the dam-dwellers to eat, Nipper approached Hugh and Beorhtwyn.

'Yu eet wif us,' he said to the two of them.

They glanced at one another. Beorhtwyn had not told Hugh, who appeared pleasantly surprised by the offer, about her catch yet.

'That would be our pleasure,' he replied.

As they sat amongst the many dam-dwellers, they drew more looks than usual, not least because they took to skewering their own helping of fish onto sticks and holding them over the open fire (which the dam-dwellers used only for warmth, favouring their fish raw).

'They must be starting to like us,' Hugh posited as they enjoyed modest helpings of the fish that Beorhtwyn had speared.

'So it seems,' she replied, the corner of her lip curling into a subtle smile. Once it had been shared out between themselves and the dam-dwellers, there were only a few bites worth of fish to be had. Still, it was the most delicious tasting food she had eaten in a long time.

Chapter 32
Truer Words are Spoken

It started soon after Hugh had taught Nipper about *trickery*. He began speaking the word regularly, although almost always in ways that didn't quite make sense, and more often than not he appeared to simply be reiterating what Hugh had initially told him.

'Tree man… *trik-uh-ree*… H-yoo,' he had started saying this often.

'Yes, that's right,' Hugh would reply with a nod, and then Nipper would repeat himself, or rearrange the order of the words, and Hugh would nod some more and try to make sense of it, offering suggestions in response, things he thought Nipper might be seeking to say. Though this would simply lead to more confusion.

'He is trying to tell me something,' Hugh said to Beorhtwyn after one of these interactions. 'About He Who was Held in the Tree.'

'We know we were tricked,' she replied. 'Our telling him is how he first came to learn the meaning of the word.'

'Tis why it must surely be something other he seeks to speak of. He simply does not yet possess the words to do so.'

'You think it might be… might be a way for me to break my binding to this place? Perhaps your plan is working after all.'

'Beorhtwyn, I…'

'Yes?'

'It… it might be nothing more than a trick of the mind…'

'What is it, Hugh?'

'I had a dream. Most strange.'

'*Strange* does not lessen its worth,' she replied, encouraging him to continue.

'I was here, in the woods. Then there was a woman, dressed in white. I have never seen such clothes before.

'You did not know this woman?'

'No. She spoke in an odd manner. But it sounded so real. I was holding the axe in this dream. The one I used to cut free He Who was Held in the Tree. Then it was gone, and the woman told me that the trees had taken it back… Since waking,' Hugh's voice quietened, as if he were afraid of someone listening, and leaned in. 'It is nowhere to be seen.'

Beorhtwyn pondered this. After a moment, she said, 'If the axe truly is gone, maybe this was more than a dream?'

'That is what I fear.'

'Fear?'

'They were there, too. All of those who stayed behind. Guilliam, your father, the other druids. They walked in the woods, slowly. So slowly. But they were walking towards… darkness. They couldn't hear me, nor see me. All they did was walk. Slowly, yes, but towards it nonetheless. She told me, this woman, that Guilliam is still alive. And that I can save him.'

'Then what is there to fear? This is good news,' Beorhtwyn said, her lips curling into a slight smile. 'It means we were right to stay!'

'She said *I* can save him. But…'

Beorhtwyn's smile faded.

'You cannot leave here,' Hugh said. 'She told me that, too.'

Her head lowered slowly, and neither spoke for a moment.

'So, it has been a wasted effort, then,' she said, matter-of-factly. 'Teaching Nipper to speak. He cannot help me leave this place.'

'I… if the woman in my dream is to be believed…'

'It was a fanciful idea from the start.'

'I am sorry, Beorhtwyn.'

She lifted her head again. 'But they *are* all still alive. Guilliam, my father, all who you saw.'

He nodded.

'And you can save them.'

'I… think so. But I fear the time we are afforded *here*, may be fleeting out *there*.'

'So, what will you do?'

'Teaching Nipper was not a wasted effort. This woman in white, she told me he had the answer. I didn't know what she meant then, but now I wonder if what he yearns to share might aid me in saving them.'

'Well then,' Beorhtwyn said. 'You best keep teaching him.'

This is what Hugh did. He doubled down on their lessons, spending (what felt like) hours at a time introducing the dam-dweller to new words and sentences, with a particular focus on words he thought may prove useful in enabling Nipper to say whatever it was he sought to say concerning the tree-man. Beorhtwyn helped where she could, often times sitting by and listening, aiding Hugh in demonstrations that would clarify certain phrases, much as they did when they had first taught Nipper about trickery. But, for the most part, she left Hugh to the teaching, and simply watching proved an education for her. She had, after all, grown up with wanderers, none of whom – though learned in a great many things – could read nor write particularly well, if at all. It was to be expected that the vocabulary of her people was lacking when compared to a squire, who had been raised not only reading English, but Latin.

'You must have started learning young?' she asked Hugh after he had finished another long lesson.

'Since I was a boy.'

'It shows,' she smiled.

'I excelled in reading and writing. T'was when I started swordsmanship and horsemanship that I… found myself lacking.'

Beorhtwyn laughed, and Hugh couldn't help but chuckle.

'I would not have made a squire for as long as I did, had I not proven so useful at writing. Lockwood took every opportunity to remind me that was all I was good for. He was right in that regard. If not for all his correspondence that needed attending to, he'd have surely done away with me sooner.'

'A good thing you squired for Guilliam first, then.'

'If not for Guilliam, I would have never been a squire at all. And I would certainly never have learnt to read or write.'

'You were not born into it?'

'My father worked the fields on the estate of a baron. Baron Hubert Mandeville. My mother was a servant to him – I think it is why she named me as she did.'

'Your family are peasants?'

'They were. And I would no doubt have worked the land too, if not for the fire.'

'You mean to say the land is no longer—'

'Oh, it is there still. Much of the estate had to be rebuilt. But my father and mother remained there after it was. Until their last days.'

'Hugh… I am sorry. I did not know…'

'I barely knew them, in truth. I visited only twice, after the fire. I was a child of seven years when I left. With Guilliam. He took me on at the request of my father. To repay him.'

'Your father—'

'Saved his life. The night of the fire, Sir Guilliam was a guest of the Baron. As I understand it, he and his host had enjoyed a great deal of wine that evening. The smoke and the flames woke most of the estate, but Guilliam slept right through. My father went back in and carried him out. He offered them land of their own as way of thanks, I was later told. Though my father asked that Guilliam take me as his page instead.'

'I suppose being in the service of a knight makes for a better life than working the land.'

'It was their way of giving me a better life, yes, but also… I had brothers. Four of them. James, he's the only one I remember, really. He died, the year before the fire. None of the others saw two summers. I have often wondered if it was their way of saving me. From a similar fate. Even at the cost of giving me up.'

For a moment, neither of them spoke. Then Beorhtwyn lay a hand on Hugh's shoulder. 'It can be a peculiar thing, to not know one's own mother and father,' she said.

'Aye,' he nodded. 'Do you ever ponder, what might have been? If you had…'

'Not been left in the woods?' she finished his sentence. 'No, least not for a very long while. Perhaps it is easier for me, never having known where I came from.'

'I don't suppose either of us would have wound up here if we'd have lived the lives we were born into.'

The two of them looked about the grove as he spoke those words, taking in what had now become familiar surroundings. Though neither spoke then, it was likely that they both, in that moment, let their minds wander, and perhaps even ponder just where they might now be, if things had played out differently.

It was the word *village* that led to the revelation. As it happened, Nipper hadn't been taught the word during a lesson, but much like *trickery*, had overheard it, and so asked, 'Wot is *veel-ahj*?'

'It is where the men and women come from,' Hugh explained. 'Where they live. You live here, in the woods. The men and women live in the village.'

Nipper looked to be in thought for a moment, then said, 'Man in tree… did trik-uh-ree. Did trik-uh-ree to man from *veel-lahj*.'

'The man in the tree tricked someone from the village?' Hugh reiterated what he had just heard. 'This is what you have been trying to say?'

'Yes. Man come from *veel-lahj*. Speek to tree, like H-yoo. *Bee-for* H-yoo. Ask… help. Help from tree.'

Beorhtwyn and Hugh looked at one another. 'Someone from the village struck a bargain with him too,' he said.

'We need to find out who,' she replied.

'Nipper,' Hugh turned back to the dam-dweller. 'Can you tell me more of this man from the village? How did he appear…' Hugh sighed with frustration as he spoke, knowing Nipper would not understand. 'What did he look like?' he asked, pointing to his own eyes as he said *look*, and then, with further hand gestures, 'Big? Small?'

'Big,' Nipper repeated the word along with the gesture, raising his little arms above his own head just as Hugh had done.

Hugh glanced at Beorhtwyn.

'Hardly narrows things,' she said. 'Have you taught him colours?'

'Aye.'

'What about this man's hair?' Beorhtwyn asked, holding her own up as she emphasised it. 'What colour? Yellow, like mine?' then, pointing to Hugh, 'Red, like Hugh?'

A few seconds later Nipper responded, '*Brown*. Like… me.'

'A big man with brown hair,' she said to Hugh. 'Does that help at all?'

Hugh remained silent for a moment, his brow crumpled, deep in thought. Then, his eyes grew wide. 'This man,' he said to Nipper. 'Have you seen him since? Has he returned to the woods since he spoke to the man in the tree?'

'Yes. Haf seen… *sins*,' Nipper replied, not entirely sure if he had used the word correctly.

'Yes! It makes sense,' Hugh said, though to neither Nipper nor Beorhtwyn, but to himself.

'What makes sense?' Beorhtwyn asked.

'I had thought it strange, the day I found Guilliam, near hanged by the blacksmith's boy and Ethel's father,' Hugh began. 'How it was that they managed to walk so freely through the woods, with the way open as it was then, with the effects of this realm bleeding into ours. Guilliam was used to it, but to those who aren't, it can feel like a maze. At least, 'tis what I found when first I entered.'

'Aye, to the unfamiliar these woods are not easily wandered,' Beorhtwyn nodded, eager to hear more.

'And yet those two, Hammond and Elias, were able to bring Guilliam here, and they did not appear, least not to me, the slightest bit lost. You saw Hammond, yes?'

She nodded.

'And how would you describe him?'

'Big. Brown hair, to my recollection,' Beorhtwyn answered. 'You think it is Hammond who Nipper saw? You think the blacksmith's boy struck some bargain with He Who was Held in the Tree?'

'It would explain his bringing Guilliam here. And it might just answer another question.'

'The girl's death, you mean?'

'He was betrothed to Ethel. I put it to Guilliam, when we were in gaol, that if Hammond had known about the two of them, he could have killed Ethel. Guilliam did not think he was capable, however. But if it was him that Nipper saw, then it means that he was in the woods, that likely he *did* discover them together...'

'So he struck a bargain with He Who was Held in the Tree. To have her slain, rather than do it himself?'

'He struck a bargain, yes. But Nipper says he was tricked, just as I was. Perhaps he didn't mean for her to be killed.'

'What manner of deal do you reckon he might have made?'

'I know not. She was dragged through the forest, too. How the trickster managed that remains a mystery also.'

'Whatever bargain was struck, this Hammond can't have upheld his end, or surely He Who was Held in the Tree would have walked free before your meeting him.'

'Maybe it was Ethel's death that halted Hammond's freeing him. Who is to say? But I intend to find out, for if I can prove this—'

'The priest has made up his mind. And even if you are right and could somehow compel Hammond to confess, the priest would not believe you.'

'It is not the priest I mean to persuade.'

'Who then...' Beorhtwyn asked, only for it to dawn upon her as she did. 'The other knight. Lockwood.'

'Aye.'

'And you think *he* will believe this?'

'Sir Lockwood is a hard man. He suffers no fools and certainly holds no love for me. But he will hear me, at the very least.'

Beorhtwyn did not speak for a moment. Her eyes lowered, and she gazed at the ground. Then she looked at Hugh and said, 'It is decided then. You must bring your theory to Lockwood.'

'And you—'

'I will go with you, until I can go no further. Before I begin to... before my wound returns.'

Hugh nodded. 'I'll ready myself then,' he said. 'No use in waiting any longer. We do not know how much time has passed in our realm already.'

'H-yoo... leef?' Nipper spoke up.

'I…' Hugh turned to the dam-dweller. 'I must return. To my realm. To help my friend.'

'Fr…end,' Nipper repeated, yet another word he had not learnt. 'Wot is fr-end?'

'A friend is someone who helps you. And you help them, when they are in need of it,' he gestured to Beorhtwyn. 'Like how Beorhtwyn has helped me, and I her. Like how you,' he pointed to Nipper, 'have helped us both.'

'I am… friend? H-yoo friend. Be-yor-twin friend.'

'Yes, Nipper. You are our friend,' he placed his hand on the dam-dweller's prickle-furred shoulder. 'A most worthy friend, indeed.'

Chapter 33
Polished Steel

It was the day after next. Sir Leland Lockwood had woken in The Unpleasant Pheasant – in the very same room that Baron Turbert's throat had been slit, still not a month passed (though the bloodstains had since been scrubbed from the floorboards), and was sat polishing his sword. He chose not to breakfast that morning, his preference for fighting being on an empty stomach, finding it made him sharper, more astute. He had, however, feasted until his belly was full the night before – not that the inn offered much in the way of a feast, mind you, though that was to be expected. The bread was stale and onions overpowered the stew he'd been served, but the ale was just about drinkable and the innkeep had provided him with a good amount of cheese, though it was nowhere near as aged as he would have liked. Despite adhering to his pre-fight fasting ritual, though, there was an unmistakable air of nervousness about Leland Lockwood. Not that nerves before a fight were unusual, but something felt different this time.

As the sun rose over Crooklingsham, Leland Lockwood could not shake this lingering apprehension. Whilst not an experienced duelist, he had bloodied his blade countless times on fields of battle, facing down brutes bigger than himself on more occasions than he cared to count. Needless to say, he had bested every single one of them, or he would not now be thinking of them as he ran the linen cloth along the edge of his sword. Of course, those men, as far as he knew, did not have the reputation of the man he would soon meet, which was perhaps the cause of such atypical anxiety. He had witnessed Sir Guilliam's skill with a lance first-hand in tourney's over the years, though he had only heard stories of his prowess with a blade, as had most every knight and their squire in England. In his younger days, it was said he was worth ten men on the battlefield, and was rumoured to just as easily have cut through so many with ease. Of course, now Guilliam was older and weaker, and would be tired and hungry – despite the offerings of gruel – which would only work to serve Sir Leland. Dwelling on the man's reputation would not, he reminded himself. Yet, his palms perspired as they polished his sword.

Gilbert Giffard had bothered Leland earlier than he would have liked to have been bothered, knocking on his door several hours before the duel was due to commence.

'What is it?' Sir Leland asked, after the lad had made himself known from the corridor outside the room. Taking the words for an invite to do so, Gilbert opened the door.

'Your armour is polished, Sir,' Gilbert said.

Sir Leland looked away from his blade and slowly turned to face his squire. 'So what is it brings you here?'

Gilbert opened his mouth, only for it to close again. A silence lingered.

'Pray tell,' Sir Leland continued, eyes unblinking.

'I… forgive me, Sir. I do not follow.'

'What has brought you here at this hour?'

'I… Sir?'

'I trust, Giffard, that you are not so bold as to trouble me during my morning, merely to declare that you have polished my armour?'

'I… well…. I thought you might like to know—'

'You are my squire, and thus it is your duty to polish my armour, is it not?'

'It is, Sir.'

'Therefore I take it as a given that you will polish my armour. Much as I take it as a given that when I need to shit, I shit. Should I then seek to inform you when I shit, Giffard?'

Gilbert stuttered, quite unable to respond.

'Well, should I? Should I let you know every time I take a shit, boy?'

'No, Sir,' Gilbert managed, which was followed up with, in all seriousness, 'Unless it pleases you, that is.'

Sir Leland needed not respond to this, for his expression spoke for him, an expression which Gilbert Giffard took quick note of and backed away.

'Forgive me for the disturbance, Sir,' he said with a bow of his head. 'Your armour is ready for you, I shall await your instruction.' He closed the door.

Leland sighed as the boy left, hearing him hurry away down the stairs. Had it not been for the fact that the Giffards had long served his lady wife, he would have done away with Gilbert years ago. He was capable enough in following orders, but he was quite plainly a simpleton. It occurred to Leland, as it had before, that had all his squires been rolled into one, then perhaps they would make a worthy apprentice to him. Of all those that had been in his tutelage, they might possess one, maybe two, desirable traits, though would be completely lacking in others. Take Brombury, the boy behind his summons to this village in the midst of nowhere. The lad was intelligent (not that he cared to praise him for this) with a keen understanding of the written word, but utterly useless when it came to swordsmanship and bowmanship and horsemanship, all traits required of a knight-to-be. He had only taken him on because he had come to him from the man he was about to fight. Leland was sure, at the time, that a squire of Sir Guilliam the Great would make for a worthy apprentice. How wrong he had been on that count.

There were footsteps again, heading up the stairs, along the corridor and towards Leland's door. They fell silent outside. Leland awaited a knock.

'What is it now, boy?' Leland called out when there was no knock. Presumably Giffard had more needless news to convey.

There was no answer.

'Giffard,' Leland said, rising from his chair. He lay down the cloth and gripped his freshly polished blade. 'Is that you?'

The door creaked as it slowly opened, not so much as to reveal who stood behind it.

'Who is there? Announce yourself,' Leland ordered.

Whoever it was did not announce themself. There was no time for it. Before Leland could react to the door swinging open, they were already inside the room.

Chapter 34
A Meeting of Metal

There was a disquiet as they headed back, neither quite sure just how long they had been gone. To Hugh, it felt as though a month, maybe more, might have passed in the realm of the dam-dwellers, though he didn't suppose a month mattered much as a measure of time there. What mattered was that he had used that time to teach Nipper the basics of his language. And whilst he had this disparity in time passing on his side, and the words of the white-gowned woman in his dream to go on, it was nonetheless a worry that he might well return to find Guilliam and the druids dead, their heads long – or perhaps very recently – since separated from their bodies. Though neither said as much aloud, both he and Beorhtwyn thought it, and they both knew the other thought it at that. But to speak of it was fruitless, for there was, after all, only one way of knowing for certain.

They returned again to the border between realms, and once more Beorhtwyn dug her fingers into the dirt and opened the way. Her wound did not return immediately after this, and so she accompanied Hugh a little further, perhaps testing to see how far she might make it, though not commenting on the matter. But it was not long before Beorhtwyn's gait grew strained. Her breathing, too.

'The wound,' Hugh said, stopping. 'It is returning.'

'I'll be alright, at least for a short while longer.'

'I can make my own—'

'It is fine, Hugh,' she spoke with a wince.

Hugh nodded, and continued, though at a slower pace, his eyes ever on her as they progressed. Soon, their surroundings lessened in the sense of surrealness that they had grown accustomed to, with the colour of the sky gradually fading from purple into the blue of their world, the peculiar plants growing increasingly sparse until they were all but unseeable. Beorhtwyn didn't make it much further past that point before stumbling, supporting herself with one hand resting against a tree and the other pressed against her reappearing wound.

'Beorhtwyn,' Hugh spoke her name gently.

'I know,' she replied, her head lowered. 'I thought I might at least try… You know the way from here?'

'I shall manage, I am sure.'

'I am sorry I cannot go with you.'

'You've nothing to be sorry for.'

'I would like to have been of more use.'

Hugh placed a hand on her shoulder.

'This is farewell, then?' she asked, looking at him now.

'Farewell? Why, I should think not.'

'You mean to… return?'

'I've many words to teach Nipper still,' Hugh smiled. 'And I imagine teaching the other dam-dwellers to talk will take some time.'

'You'll come back?'

'Yes.'

'And… stay here? With me?'

'If… if you wish.'

'I would like that.'

'Me too. Besides, I rather think my squiring days are over.'

They shared a gaze then. It was broken by another wince from Beorhtwyn, the pain creeping its way back in.

'You must return, now,' Hugh said.

'I should like to wait for you.'

'Then wait yonder, past the threshold, where it does not hurt you.'

Beorhtwyn nodded. She turned and began back, and as she did Hugh opened his mouth, only to close it thereafter, unable to find the words to convey exactly what he wished to say. Then, as if she had heard those unspoken words, Beorhtwyn turned her head to face him again.

'Hugh… I…' she began, seeming similarly unable to find the words that were left hanging between them.

Hugh smiled. 'I will see you soon,' he said.

She smiled back.

The sun reared its warming rays as Hugh reached the pasture. He kept low, crouching as he stuck to paths of taller grass for fear of the shepherd whose flock grazed here spotting him and alarming Father Dobbe. Though he would have to face the priest soon enough, it would be better, Hugh decided, that he remain unseen for as long as possible. Of course, as he approached the fallow land between the pasture and Crooklingsham, his cover all but vanished, and should any wanderers happen to be passing yonder, there would be little he could do to hide himself. Though presently, all seemed perfectly still and quiet. As houses in the distance came into view, it appeared to remain that way. He gave the village itself a wide berth, very much hoping he would find the man he sought on the outskirts. Heading for the stables he soon saw it. An all too familiar tent, and nearby, in the stables, an all too familiar horse.

Sir Leland Lockwood's black steed.

Hugh had helped erect the tent more times than he cared to count. If he was lucky, Lockwood would be in there now, and he could speak his piece. At the very least, hopefully Gilbert Giffard would be there, in which case he'd have to bid his former fellow squire go fetch the knight, and do so discreetly.

Presently, Hugh was crouched behind a cluster of bushes, peering at the tent, no more than a bowshot (for an archer better than himself) away. To reach it he would have to pass by three houses, though he was still yet to see or hear a soul, which bode well. He waited a moment, his eyes flitting between the windows of the three abodes. No one walked by. He made a dash for the tent.

He was halfway when the door of one of the houses began to open. His strides became near leaps, culminating in a dive towards the tent. He landed harshly and managed to scramble for cover behind the canvas as the door fully opened. A person walked out. Hugh held his breath for a moment. Then whoever had opened the door began to speak. There were two of them. Precisely what they were saying to one another, he couldn't quite determine, though he heard mention of something *commencing shortly.*

It was as he listened, laying there on the ground, that he felt the wet beneath him. He thought this strange; to his knowledge it had not recently rained. Glancing down revealed this was no ordinary wet. It was red.

Blood red.

The voices were fading now. Were they making their way to the soon-to-commence happening, whatever it was? Hugh picked himself up. The blood was seeping out of the tent, pooling outside the canvas.

'Sir Leland,' Hugh spoke quietly, a faint tremor to his words. There was no answer. 'It is Hugh Brombury… I bring news. News of Ethel's killing.'

When still there was no reply, Hugh peeled back the canvas. He froze. Before him, a bloodied body lay felled. His eyes flitted about the tent. It was all but empty, save for some satchels. Sure that the assailant was no longer inside, he looked over the corpse. It was face down, but he knew who it was.

He crouched beside the body of the boy who had priorly been his peer. It was fair to say the two had never been fond of one another. Still, he felt a deep sadness.

'Who did this to you, Gilbert?' he spoke softly. There didn't appear to be a wound on his back, so he placed a hand on his shoulder and turned him over in order to see just how he had met his end. He could barely suppress a gasp as the body rolled over.

Gilbert's eyes were still wide open, his face frozen in an expression of utter terror, and the blood running from his nose and corners of his mouth was not yet dry. But it was not his face that made for such a shock; it was his chest. Or rather the hole which whatever had ripped through it had left behind. His flesh was torn as if fabric, and the few ribs that Hugh could see were skewed and crooked. He did not linger too long in looking, though made sure to gently close poor Gilbert's eyes and then untied the cloak from the boy's back and lay it over him. Hugh stood over the covered carcass and lowered his head. It was then he heard more voices.

He could not determine anything specific, though it was certainly the sound of chatter. He peered out of the tent, catching sight of small crowds making their way towards the centre of the village. He turned and began to search through the few satchels that lay around him, finding precisely what he hoped to mere moments later. A long, dark hooded cloak. He wrapped it around his shoulders, brought the hood over his head, and made to leave the tent. Before he did, however, something else caught his eye. A sheathed shortsword. Gilbert's shortsword. He picked up the leather-bound blade and tied it to his own belt, then left the tent and began to follow the steady flow of people.

They had formed a large circle in the centre of the village, clustered together, loud and lively, despite a palpable tension in the air. Hugh kept his head low and gently weaved his way into the amassed crowd. It reminded him of The Fighting Cock, only there were more people here; the entire village seemed to be present, in fact. As he reached the innermost edge of the circle, a sigh of relief escaped him.

Guilliam was alive.

And it appeared he was who the people had come out to see. He was standing with his back to Hugh, facing the other side of the spectators, where the crowd had split partially to allow for a walkway. Beyond that, Hugh noticed now, stood a number of the druids, chained and bound, but watching just as intently as the villagers. Amongst them was Eotenfrēond.

Then the crowd began to quiet as Father Dobbe appeared, marching measuredly through the parting towards Guilliam. He held in his hand a sheathed sword. At the sight of the blade, Hugh's mouth dried up. Whatever sound there was around him seemed instantly drowned out by the increasing beating of his own heart, a sudden realisation that *this* was the execution. He should have called out, objected, demanded to speak with Sir Lockwood, but in that moment he felt quite incapable of doing anything. And then the priest had unsheathed the blade, and taken another step towards Guilliam. He held out the sword.

Guilliam took it.

It was not an execution. Hugh felt some semblance of control over his body return, though his heart still hammered at his chest as if it were shaping a breastplate. If this was not an execution, then wh—

'Good people of Crooklingsham,' Father Dobbe bellowed, silencing those who still mumbled amongst the onlookers. 'Today we stand as witnesses to God's will. For it is written: *Deus iudex iustus, fortis, et patiens; numquid irascitur per singulos dies,*' he looked around the crowd. 'Does anyone here know the meaning of that passage?'

The crowd stood silent.

Then Guilliam spoke. 'God is a righteous judge, strong and patient,' he said, swinging the sword.

Father Dobbe took a step back.

'And God is angry every day,' Guilliam finished the passage.

'Close enough,' Dobbe replied, animosity in his voice. 'And now He shall judge you.'

'He is *your* God, priest. Not mine. Tell me, when will he judge you?'

Father Dobbe did not answer. He simply scowled at Guilliam, then called aloud, 'Sir Leland. It is time.'

All was silent. Heads turned, looking past the priest, the crowd eager in their anticipation. As the moment lingered, the priest turned his head too. For a second he seemed concerned, as no knight had answered his summons.

Then came the toll of metal plate marching towards the crowd. The narrow walkway widened further as the heads of each and every onlooker turned to the source of the closening clank. In full plate Sir Leland appeared, striding with unnerving haste, longsword in hand. Hugh was not the only one amongst them to be shocked by the near-charging knight; those surrounding him let out gasps and curses of their own as Guilliam's opponent stormed towards them. But it was not simply the furious rush with which he approached that startled the crowd – causing a great many of them to retreat some way – it was the sheer size of the man. Sir Leland Lockwood was known to Hugh, more so than anyone else there, though the village had all laid eyes on him. Yet now, fully armoured and with a visor covering his face, he appeared to have grown in height, with the steel suit stretched and clinging tightly to his long body, leaving his limbs taught and rigid in their movements, the cuisses in particular warped, appearing to have been forcibly bent around thighs far thicker than the rest of an otherwise slender frame. But he was still able to careen towards Guilliam whilst swinging his blade with an untamed ferocity. So ferocious the entrance was, in fact, that a dozen or so of the crowd dived out of the knight's path as he lunged through the opening, bringing the longsword up over his head with one arm.

Guilliam lept backwards as the steel came slashing down towards him, holding his own sword with two hands, horizontally, over his own head, the edge of the blade deflecting the attack but sending him stumbling backwards in the process, resulting in a deafening clang as Sir Leland's steel bounced off his, denting it.

But it was not Sir Leland. It could not be. Hugh knew the measurements of the man, had not only seen him fully armoured many times, but armoured him himself. The immense, berserk knight before him was not the knight he had served. He found his voice then, and tried to call out to Guilliam at that moment, but the noise of the crowd had picked up again; a mixture of yells and howls and jeers. They were shoving and barging now too, those at the fore pushing their way back, looking to distance themselves from the melee as whoever it was who wore Sir Leland's armour seemed to give no heed to the crowd, swinging his blade frenziedly in an effort to strike Guilliam. It was amongst the sudden chaos and flurry of reckless flourishes that a woman let out a shrill shriek. From between the shuffling shoulders of the now skittish crowd, Hugh managed to spot the lady who had made the sound; she held desperately onto the man beside her who had slumped into her arms, he himself clutching at his cheek where the flesh had been ripped apart, caught by the end of the now bloodied blade that still swung capriciously through the air. The sight – and sound – was enough to start thinning the herd. A group of villagers helped to drag away the wounded man, and a good many more took it as a sign to flee. All the while Guilliam's eyes remained fixed firmly on his opponent, dodging and ducking and deflecting – where he could – the ceaseless slashing and swiping of the sword.

'Sir Lockwood,' Father Dobbe cried out amongst the fast-growing panic, trying his very best to suppress the dismay that his expression was fast giving in to. 'Control yourself!'

His words fell on deaf ears. More people were dispersing, distancing themselves from the indiscriminate reach of the lashing longsword. Hugh braced himself against the shoving and barging of the retreating onlookers. Guilliam was holding his own, only just, but whoever was beneath the armour possessed far superior strength. He would need help.

'Lockwood!' Dobbe shouted. He took a step towards the knight, whose back was turned to him, and placed a hand cautiously on the shoulder. 'Temper this recklessness at once—'

The knight did not acknowledge Father Dobbe by turning to face him, but simply with a sudden steel elbow, bringing it back into his face, bloodying his nose and sending him swiftly to the ground. Hugh pushed his way through the few remaining spectators, reaching the priest and dragging him back by his collar, so that he was out of what had been the middle of the now scattered circle.

'Where is Sir Lockwood lodged?' he asked, shaking the priest by the shoulders.

Dobbe mumbled something in response, his hand reaching to his clearly broken nose.

'Where did you last see him?' Hugh pressed.

'You...' the priest managed to mutter.

'Listen to me. That is not Leland Lockwood. If he is still alive, I must find him. Where did he sleep last night?'

A tremendous clang startled Hugh, his head shooting up to see Guilliam parry a lumbered blow. Although his armoured opponent had strength and size on his side, he was growing cumbersome in his movements. Guilliam, on the other hand, moved dexterously, unrestrained by plate or mail and buttressed by decades of experience.

'This…' Dobbe coughed as he spoke. 'This is your doing.'

'I am trying to help,' Hugh gripped the collar of the priest's robe and yanked his head up. 'Now if you want to do the same, if you actually wish to be of use, you will tell me where I can find Leland Lockwood.'

Perhaps it was the way in which Hugh said it, or perhaps it was the look on his face, or perhaps it was simply the chaos unfolding around them. Whatever the reason, Father Dobbe decided, in that moment, to oblige Hugh.

'He… the room. Where Turbert died.'

Hugh let go of his collar and Dobbe slumped back to the ground. He turned and ran, weaving through what wary villagers remained watching (at a greater distance) the chaotic clash before them. He was not the first to reach the door of The Unpleasant Pheasant, a fair few villagers had retreated there, though all were too busy peering through the window, pressed together, to pay Hugh much attention as he burst in. He rushed up the stairs, and found himself outside of the familiar door to the room that Baron Turbert had occupied.

He wasted no time in knocking, nor did he need to, with the door ever so slightly ajar. He stepped inside. A fist swung for him. Hugh swerved to the right, narrowly avoiding the blow.

'Sir Lockwood!' Hugh cried, his voice enough to calm the reactionary outburst of the bruised, bloodied man stood before him.

'Brombury?' Lockwood's right eye was swollen, his brow above leaking red. 'What are you—'

'You are being impersonated,' Hugh interrupted. 'Right now, someone faces Guilliam, clad in your armour.'

'I know,' the knight's words were strained, as if they hurt to speak. 'I was ambushed, beaten. I have only come to, minutes ago,' he looked around the room. 'He... he stole my sword.' He paused, as if something had suddenly occurred to him. 'Where is Giffard?'

'He is dead, Sir.'

'What is the meaning of this? Who is this man?'

'He is not a man. I do believe he is a trickster, a demon escaped from the woods.'

'Do not mock me, boy.'

'I am not, Sir. And I don't have time to explain, but Guilliam is innocent. It was this creature that killed Ethel, and Gilbert. Now it means to kill Guilliam. Please, help me stop it.'

'This is madness.'

Hugh drew the shortsword from his waist. For a moment, Sir Leland Lockwood perhaps thought that he meant to use it on him, as his expression sharpened and he took a small step backwards.

But Hugh did not mean to use the blade on his former mentor. He looked into his eyes for all of a second, meeting the gaze of the man whose face had frightened him for as long as he had known him. It frightened him no more. He turned and left the room, heading back towards the fray as fast as he had fled. Perhaps there was no point in trying to get Lockwood to understand. There was certainly no time.

Hugh barged his way through the crowd in the inn, reaching the door, and as he stepped foot outside, he came face to face with someone looking to enter. Hammond stood before him. He was completely white. The blacksmith's boy took a second to recognise Hugh, though stumbled ever so slightly backwards as he did, noticing the sword in his hand.

'Close the door, for God's sake!' came a cry from the inn.

But Hugh did not turn, nor did he close the door. He stood there, in the doorway, looking at Hammond. 'You know who is beneath that armour, don't you?' he said.

'Let me past!' Hammond demanded.

'You have seen him before,' as Hugh spoke, he could hear the sound of the folk behind him quieten slightly.

'Move out of my way,' Hammond looked past Hugh, appealing to his neighbours.

Hugh could hear them nearing, but he stood firm. 'You struck a bargain with him,' he felt a hand on his shoulder, it began to pull, but still he faced Hammond. 'You did not know it would lead to Ethel's death, did you?'

He was dragged back then, by more than one pair of hands, his sword arm grabbed and held tightly. But then came the cry of, 'Wait!'

All inside the inn turned. Elias was there. He approached the doorway. 'What does he speak of?' he asked Hammond.

'Elias… please,' Hammond stuttered.

'What does the lad speak of?' the innkeep snapped, looking between the two of them.

'You knew about Guilliam and Ethel,' Hugh shook off the hands of those that had grabbed him, their grips already loosened. Hammond did not answer at first, but now everybody in the inn was looking at the blacksmith's boy.

'I will not answer to *you*,' Hammond retorted.

'You will to me, boy,' Elias said firmly. He was staring into Hammond's eyes, unblinking. But Hammond could not meet his gaze. 'Tell me. What does he speak of?' he stepped towards the doorway, and Hugh moved aside. 'What happened to my Ethel?'

He did not answer.

'Hammond!' Elias barked.

'I… I followed her… into the woods,' he said softly. 'But I lost my way.'

'And you found the man in the tree?' Hugh asked.

Hammond's head dropped. He nodded.

'What bargain was struck?'

'I had no intention of treating with him… I meant to flee at first,' Hammond uttered. 'But he promised to help me, if I helped him….'

'What bargain?' Hugh pressed.

'He knew of Guilliam and Ethel… he said he could see to it that Guilliam pay for leading her astray… for taking her from me.'

'Guilliam's life, in return for the creature's freedom?'

He nodded again.

'But you never went back to free him?'

'I asked him how I could trust he keep his word. He told me he could do it from the tree… told me to wait. To cut him loose after Ethel next visited Guilliam. Some days passed. And then she set off again. So, I went back and sought the axe he spoke of. That's when… when I found her…' he looked up now. His eyes were filled with tears.

'What did you do?' Elias asked.

'I only wanted Guilliam gone! I did not mean for… for this.'

'He tricked you,' Hugh said to Hammond. 'You asked for him to take Guilliam's life. Only, he would do so indirectly. By making it seem as though Guilliam was a killer. I don't suppose he meant for you to find Ethel *before* cutting him free. For what it's worth, it is a small mercy that you did.'

'I did not know… oh God… God, I did not know.'

'That man out there killed… he killed my daughter?' Elias asked, looking at Hugh. All in the inn stood silent, their eyes on him too now.

'It is no man,' Hugh said. Then he stepped past Hammond.

'Where are you going?' Elias called to him as he headed away from the inn.

'To kill it.'

Dobbe had managed to drag himself even further from the duel as Hugh rushed past him, headed for it. Bent over and bloody-faced, the priest stumbled past the squire, seeking the cover of a nearby house. With blade grasped firmly, Hugh charged the armoured demon, the creature still unleashing a clumsy flurry of calamitous blows, blows that Guilliam was still managing to ward off, though the sheer force behind each one sent him stumbling, threatening to unbalance him. It was as he sidestepped another of these heavy-handed strikes that Guilliam caught sight of Hugh, taking his eyes off of his opponent for no more than half a second. As Hugh neared, Guilliam pushed forward, stabbing at the midriff of his rival. His sword did not pierce, of course, but it was enough to force the creature two steps back. And as its foot found ground, Hugh's sword found its calf, unarmoured. Steel met fur-coated flesh, tearing the skin. The creature let out an almighty cry of pain, the knee of the leg Hugh had bled buckling. It dropped to the knee, now half the height it had stood at, and half as imposing.

'Hugh!' Guilliam sounded both surprised and laudatory at once. But before either of them had the chance to exchange any further, the kneeling creature turned, sword gripped between its steel-gloved fist, and punched Hugh in the chest.

He felt his ribs break as his feet left the ground.

Guilliam called out his friend's name again, though this time his tone laden with distress.

'You,' the creature's voice was muffled behind the metal visor, though quite unmistakable to Hugh. It let out a guttural groan as it rose, standing unsteadily on its torn calf, but standing nonetheless, and standing over Hugh. It accounted for Guilliam before raising its blade, grabbing a fistful of his shirt with its free hand, dragging him off his feet before tossing him to one side. Guilliam landed far enough away that he would not be able to stop what came next, and even if he were somehow able to put himself between the creature's blade and Hugh, he had been unarmed as he was thrown, his own sword wheeling off in the other direction.

Now the creature was bringing his blade up, and in a matter of seconds it would come down, and likely impale not only Hugh but the cold, hard ground beneath him.

Swoosh.

The creature stumbled. It looked to its left shoulder. An arrow. Had its body not been too large for the armour, perhaps it would not have pierced the flesh between the spaulder and the breastplate.

Swoosh.

This one met metal, but the creature was distracted. Hugh rolled, winded by such simple a movement, feeling the broken bones in his chest grind against each other. And then he saw the archer behind the arrows.

Approaching the fray, nocking another arrow and bringing the bow up to shoot, was Sir Leland Lockwood.

The creature was unsure now, its head shifting between the approaching adversary and Hugh, who was crawling away, groaning against the pain of his fractured ribs. He didn't get far before the creature made up his mind. A long shadow spread over Hugh as he dragged himself away. Another clang as an arrow hit the armour. But the creature ignored this one. Hugh didn't turn to face it, but he heard the single heavy footstep as he desperately pulled his body. That one step was all the creature needed to close the distance. He could feel it standing over him.

He closed his eyes.

The air left his body as the sword entered it, piercing his back. His mouth opened, but couldn't make a sound, merely a choked, breathless gasp. But before the steel could fully skewer him he heard a clang and a grunt, and then he felt the steel slide out as quickly as it had stabbed in.

'No!'

He peered to see Guilliam and the creature falling, his friend's shoulders digging into its legs as he scooped them from beneath it. He watched through blurring vision as the beast stumbled, driven by Guilliam putting all his might into driving it away.

'Sword,' he heard a moment later. Though it was spoken curtly as ever, the command was a welcome one. He glanced up, Sir

Lockwood's open palm above him now. With the fast-fading strength he had left, Hugh reached for the shortsword by his side, handing it up to the knight. Then he turned himself over, so that he was facing the fray, not sure which pain belonged where anymore, to stab wound or shattered ribs.

Guilliam was still wrapped around the felled creature's legs, but as easily as it had swatted him away before, the creature kicked him off. It was half-risen when Lockwood landed his first blow, slipping the tip of his slain squire's sword into an exposed area of midriff between steel. Yet with the blade still stuck in it, the creature rose to its feet. Lockwood pulled back, withdrawing his bloodied sword, poised to strike again. But the creature blocked it, with the very sword he had stolen from the man now attacking him. Standing over him, the creature pressed down, the sharp of his steel pushing nearer and nearer to Sir Leland's throat, held at bay only by the trembling shortsword, but it wouldn't be for long. It was then that Guilliam rose and rushed the beast, diving at it barefisted, unleashing a flurry of furious punches on whatever unarmoured areas he could, for all the good it would do. It was enough to save Lockwood's neck from a slicing, with the creature once again turning its attention to Guilliam. But Hugh could see, through fading sight, that it wasn't for Lockwood that Guilliam still fought. It was for him; a righteous anger had overcome his friend. As agile as he had been whilst dodging those first swipes, Guilliam now kicked and punched in quick succession, not enough to seriously injure the creature, but enough to antagonise it. And this time he refused to be swatted away, avoiding his enemy's every attempt to do so. He was a man possessed, and all he wished to do was to hurt his opponent, with whatever means he had.

Sir Leland sought to use the welcome distraction to strike again, but the creature was still alert to him, swiping away his attempts whilst fending off Guilliam, unarming him in the process, before a blow to the temple put him on his back. But as soon as Sir Leland dropped the sword, Guilliam went for it, rolling forwards, ducking a swipe, and landing next to the blade. He grasped it, turned and the newly grabbed sword met his opponents. Guilliam's burst of vigour yet to leave him, the creature was on the back foot. As Hugh struggled to hold his head up, he pressed a trembling hand against his wound, blood spilling through his fingers. He could see before him, for those fleeting moments, the Guilliam of old; Guilliam the Great, the knight who fought with the strength of ten men.

The creature was cut, staggering, Guilliam's attacks sending it stumbling, near tripping as it deflected what strikes it could. Guilliam's fury was mighty, but it served to ignite his opponent's. Laden with cuts, the creature snarled, exposing its neck to Guilliam as it did. He plunged for what could have been a fatal blow. But it was a feign. The creature took a step back and pivoted, and brought its own blade down as it did, slicing cleanly through Guilliam's arm, inches above the elbow.

His severed limb hit the ground with a soft thud, the shortsword with a rattle.

Guilliam followed half a second after. No cry of pain left his mouth. Perhaps shock had surpassed the supposed suffering one might expect when their limb is sliced clean off. No sooner had he fallen than his skin had turned a sickly white, his eyes wide and staring at where his arm had been, now a fountain of blood, wetting the dirt. Perhaps instinctively his hand came to it, palm pressing against the spurting, suppressing of the sudden spill what it could. And now it was Hugh who was, despite his own unpluggable bleeding, overcome with a sense of desperate rage. He, Guilliam and Sir Leland lay unarmed and fallen.

But there was yet a weapon in his reach.

He began to crawl then, paying no heed to his own wounds. He took his hand away, letting the blood stain the ground beneath him as his torso was drawn across it, a trail of warm red wet marking the dirt as he neared the bow that Sir Leland had let fall moments before. Alongside it lay a single arrow. The creature didn't notice Hugh crawling. It was focused solely on Guilliam now, watching him bleed. It was then that it removed its helmet. Sure enough, it was the face Hugh had seen bound in bark; sharp and pronounced, eyes as black as pits. The creature held the sword steadily above Guilliam's neck, lining him up as an executioner might.

Hugh reached the bow.

Trembling, he grasped it. The creature, unaware, raised the sword. With what fading strength Hugh could muster, he sat himself upright. Then he took the lone arrow.

And now he was back in France, in Crécy. Gripping the bow tightly in his right hand, he brought arrow to bowstring with his left. His hand quivered as he drew back. His aim was crooked, faltering, as he pointed the bow and the arrow it held at the demon who held the sword above his friend's neck. But then it's face turned, and the creature's black eyes met Hugh's own, and it paused for all but a second. In that second Hugh's quivering hand steadied.

He released the arrow.

The tip pierced a black pupil on the right side of the creature's face. It did not fell the beast, only his sword arm, which gripped the blade still, though came lazily down, and not on Guilliam's neck. It seemed confused, at first, as if not quite sure what had happened. Then it stumbled towards Hugh.

Resigned, the bow slipped from his hand. He held the creature's gaze as it staggered nearer to him, quite unable to maintain a straight path.

'My good fellow,' it said with strained resentment, its unpierced eye blinking rapidly. 'You… you could have left. Wh… why come back? Why… interfere?'

'I could—' Hugh coughed. Blood. 'Could ask you… the same question.'

He wasn't sure if the creature smiled then, if it let out a faint cackle. 'Not all of… us,' it said, unsteady where it stood. 'Can so easily break our bargains.'

'I know what you did…' Hugh's own voice trembled, 'Hammond's bargain.'

The creature fell to its knees with a heavy thud. It was looking Hugh directly in the eyes now. 'Ah… the blacksmith's boy.'

'You made it seem as… as though Guilliam had murdered her… Ethel. You knew he'd pay with his life. That was your… trick.'

It managed a subtle smirk. 'He made it so… *easy*. When he gave her that pendant…'

'How though… you were still in the tree… how did you kill her?'

'My good fellow,' it croaked. 'I merely whispered… as she wandered the woods… lost… like you were… I took the voice of your friend, of her love… to call her to me… It was she who dragged herself through thorn and thicket to answer… She was famished, you see… so I bid her take fruit from one of my branches. Then, I simply sent her on her way…'

Hugh suddenly thought back to the apple Beorhtwyn had told him about. 'You… poisoned her?'

'I merely offered her my fruit,' it scoffed scornfully.

'You're a victim of your own wicked games then,' Hugh groaned. 'He found her… 'tis why he never cut you loose… Hammond…'

'Yet… cut loose I was, eventually…' a streak of dark green liquid leaked from its pierced eye.

'But why… steal the armour? Why fight Guilliam?'

'The woods hear *all*. These people spoke of their little duel…' it slowly turned its head, albeit ever so slightly, to where Guilliam lay, his hand still pressed over his severed arm. 'The knight was not dead. I had not kept my… end… of the bargain. Only whence I had… could I be truly… free…' as it spoke the word, the creature all of a sudden stiffened and fell sideways, becoming limp upon meeting the ground.

Hugh exhaled.

Then he fell back too.

Chapter 35
Brombury

'He will live.'

Eotenfrēond, and the other druids who had been held prisoner with him, now free of their chains, stood over the body. The eyes were shut but the chest rose slowly.

'You are sure?'

'He survived the searing iron. So yes, the worst is passed. He must rest now, and salves must be applied oft. For many days to come.'

Sir Leland looked over to the villagers. Over the past hour they had regathered, encircling the aftermath of the scene that had unfolded at the centre of their community. 'Does any of you have a bed to spare?'

At first not one of them spoke up.

Then, 'Aye,' came a voice from the crowd. The villagers parted. Elias stepped forwards. 'He can have a room in The Pheasant.'

Sir Leland nodded and two of the druids lifted the body, following the innkeep to his inn.

'And the lad?' Sir Leland asked Eotenfrēond.

The druid shook his head. 'Nothing could be done.'

They stood in silence for some time.

'The body of this… demon. What is to be done with it?'

'The sooner it is burned the better. Once your armour is stripped from it we should put it to the pyre. Some way away from this place. Lest its wicked spirit linger.'

'No need to strip it. I've no intention of wearing that armour again. Not now that demon has donned it. And let my sword go to the flames along with it.' Once again, Sir Leland, looked to the gathered villagers, and spoke aloud, 'You heard the man. Build a pyre, far away from this place. And build it fast.'

The villagers dispersed, and set about following the knight's instruction. All except for one. Father Roger Dobbe remained, staring at the unmoving body of the creature, an arrow stuck in one black eye, the other still wide open.

'Did you not hear me, priest?'

Dobbe looked at Sir Leland, dazed.

'Gather wood. Build a pyre.'

'I… yes,' Dobbe nodded.

* * *

A fortnight passed.

It took as long for Guilliam to regain strength enough to leave the bed at The Unpleasant Pheasant. Eotenfrēond had barely strayed from his side in that time, and those who had been held prisoner alongside them tended to him, applying honey and herbal ointments to the cauterised limb, keeping it clean and re-dressing it regularly. It had taken him some days after first waking to understand what Eotenfrēond had told him, though when he eventually did, he remained unspeaking and bedbound, for a further two days.

Sir Leland Lockwood was still there, too, the day Guilliam left the bed. He was waiting for him, standing outside the inn. With Eotenfrēond by his side, Guilliam approached the man he had fought both against and beside a fortnight prior.

'Your strength has found you again,' Sir Leland said.

'Just about,' Guilliam answered. The stump, freshly dressed that morning, was cradled in a cloth sling tied around his neck. 'Grown fond of the place, have you?'

'I thought it wise to remain until you were able to leave. The villagers are still wary of you people,' he looked at Eotenfrēond. 'And I do not think it likely that the innkeep meant his offer of board to be indefinite.'

'I mean to rejoin my folk soon enough,' Eotenfrēond assured.

'They have taken again to the border of the woodlands, I hear. There is talk of them rebuilding.'

Eotenfrēond nodded. 'Is this agreeable?'

Lockwood pondered for a moment. 'You kept to yourselves, before the girl's death?'

'Aye.'

'And those who rebuild will do so, still?'

'They will. Their number is much smaller now, too.'

'Then I see no reason why not,' Lockwood stated.

'Not so long ago,' Guilliam cut in, curtly, 'you were happy to watch us be burned alive.'

'That was the priest's call. And that was before the demon came. The villagers witnessed you battle him, just as I did. You may no longer take yourself for a knight, Guilliam, but you defended the innocent, even after they condemned you to die.'

'I was defending myself.'

'Maybe so. Regardless, I should think those who rebuild, will, in time, be left in peace. Your most vocal opposer left three nights gone.'

'Dobbe fled?' Guilliam asked.

'Aye. And the blacksmith's boy is up and left too. That day, Brombury spoke of his hand in this matter, before a tavern full of witnesses. I should think that has also lessened the villagers' animosity towards you and your friends. The lad had this Hammond admit his part in the girl's death, unintentional though it was. Had him admit to a bargain he made with that demon.'

Guilliam's head lowered at the mention of his friend.

'I… I shall give you a moment,' Eotenfrēond said, leaving the two men alone.

'I had him buried here,' Sir Leland said. 'As he had no family to speak of. And I can't imagine he would have wanted to be laid to rest on my estate.'

'He did find you to be a bastard.'

Sir Leland appeared to accept the affront, not responding.

'I remember nothing after my arm was taken,' Guilliam continued. 'They say Hugh shot an arrow into the creature's eye?' he glanced over the ground on which the duel was fought.

Sir Leland nodded.

Guilliam chuckled faintly. 'He was a woeful shot.'

'He was no marksman,' Sir Leland agreed, albeit humourlessly.

'Despite my efforts.'

Guilliam sighed. 'You were proven right, I suppose.'

'To what end?'

'Hugh told me you warned him that his quest would be ill-fated.'

'I did. But you are mistaken.'

Guilliam turned to Leland, curiosity curling his brow.

'It was he who proved *me* wrong,' the knight said.

'He did?'

'He saved your life, did he not?'

A hint of a curve took shape at the corner of Guilliam's lips, though he could not quite bring himself to smile.

'There is another matter I must mention,' Sir Leland spoke after a moment. 'It would seem the priest swept the church of its meager metals before he fled – a pewter chalice, brass candlesticks, some bronze bells, so the locals say. I suppose he means to sell them. Yet he left this behind,' from a purse tied to his belt, he removed a golden oval engraved with three geese, wings spread, and a long faded Latin inscription around its edge. It was smeared with a stained shade of faded crimson. 'Curious that he chose not to take it. Arguably the only metal of any true worth.'

Sir Leland held it out for Guilliam to take. He glanced at the medallion. He did not take it.

'You do not want it back?'

'The druids are rebuilding, you say?'

'A small few of them, yes.'

'Then let its worth aid in that.'

* * *

Beorhtwyn waited by the border of the crossing.

'He will come with us, then?' she asked her father.

'Aye,' Eotenfrēond nodded. 'There is nothing left for him on the other side.'

'And those who wish to stay?'

'A handful. They have started to rebuild Ealdgeat.'

'For it to be torn down again?'

'The knight, Lockwood, has assured me he will make it plain to the villagers 'tis their lot to live there, and that they shall live side-by-side those who choose to remain. And that this border will be sealed after we have crossed, so that naught they deem unholy shall come near their kin or hearth.'

'You think they will listen?'

'I know not,' Eotenfrēond sighed. 'But I do hope so.'

Yonder, Guilliam bundled his few belongings – food mostly; dried meats and a few days worth of boiled eggs – into a coarse cloth cutting and bound it with cord. Then he walked to where Beorhtwyn waited. The border between worlds.

'We are set, then,' he said.

'He would have come, too,' Beorhtwyn replied. 'He meant to return. To roam this realm with me. To teach the dam-dwellers in speaking.'

Behind her, there was a rustling. A pair of wide green eyes neared, as towards the three of them wandered Nipper. He gazed up at Guilliam.

'Heh-low, *friends.*'

'Hello,' Guilliam smiled at the dam-dweller, and then, to Beorhtwyn said, 'It would appear he made a fine start.'

***

Before riding for Ragstone, Sir Leland Lockwood called the villagers to gather, along with those rebuilding druids, and once again reiterated that they were to live side-by-side in peace. There were, of course, mutterings and utterings and begrudged grumblings, predominantly from the villagers, but Sir Leland insisted that every man and woman agree to these terms with an "Aye", which he took to be their solemn oath to him, and after each man and woman had said their "Aye" the knight made it quite clear that if any person broke their oath, and saw fit to disturb this new peace, they would have him to answer to. It was only when a boy no older than nine, known to the villagers as Benjamin the bellringer, raised his hand and asked a question that all utterings and mutterings and begrudged grumblings ceased, as the gathered villagers and druids alike, fell silent, each of them pondering the boy's question, which had been: 'What name shall we give the village now, Sir Knight?'

'I beg your pardon?' Sir Leland answered, sat atop his black steed.

'Their name?' Benjamin replied. 'Or our name?'

Sir Leland raised a brow.

'Pardon, M'lord,' a man stepped forward. Elias. 'I believe what the boy is trying to ask is, those folk there have *their* name for the village, and we have *ours*.'

'Yes,' Sir Leland nodded. 'I recall the priest saying as much.'

'Then are we still to call it Crooklingsham?' asked Elias. 'Or their name?'

'Ealdgeat,' replied one of the druids, which reignited the chorus of disgruntlement.

'Can you not decide amongst yourselves?' Sir Leland spoke above the discontent, to which most of the villagers nodded.

'They have the greater say, though,' the same druid spoke up.

'Their voices outnumber ours.'

'Then it is settled!' cried a villager.

And then a druid spoke up against this, and all of a sudden insults and curses were being traded between the groups. Sir Leland sighed.

'Quiet!' he demanded, which indeed shortly followed. 'If you are so quick to bicker over a matter as simple as the name for this village, how can I trust you all to honour your oaths?'

The crowd stayed quiet, save for subtle, stubborn stirrings.

'Perhaps *you* should choose a name, Sir Knight,' Benjamin the bellringer spoke. The words of the boy seemed to quell all stirrings. The crowd fell utterly silent. Then there were mumblings again, but different from before. Soon, heads on both sides of the divide were nodding, Ealdgeatian and Crooklinshamian alike. The suggestion, it appeared, was well-received.

'If it would serve to settle the matter?' Sir Leland asked aloud, his question met with more nodding and cries of Aye. 'So be it.'

Atop his horse, he pondered for a moment. He could see, from where he sat, the spot in which Hugh had fired the arrow that brought down the demon. He thought on what he had said to his then squire, when he had left his service to set off and save his friend.

Just know that when you fail, and you will fail, the name Brombury will be forgotten.

Harsh words. Though likely true words. Yet perhaps they need not be.

'From this day hence,' Sir Leland Lockwood declared for all to hear. 'This is the village of Brombury.'

THE END

Return to *The Woods Beyond* in

The Bride of Bygone Gifts

Coming Soon

Acknowledgements

When I decided to publish *The Briarmen*, I had no idea just how many people, outside of my family, would read it, nor if anyone would think it was any good. Fortunately, most of the early reviewers did think it was pretty good (some even thought it was *really* good) and far more people ended up reading it than I imagined would. So, I'd firstly like to thank all those who read my first novel, and especially those who have reviewed it and posted about how much they enjoyed it, for letting me know that writing a story about strange little bush-creatures wasn't, as I once feared, a waste of time. Secondly, I'd like to once again thank Alex Smith, whose editing has bettered my writing for over a decade now. Here's hoping that continues to be the case in decades to come. And finally, I would not have been able to start this novel, let alone finish it, without the support of Clara Landgren, who not only gave me feedback on my first draft, but encouragement to write it long before I had typed the first word.

About the Author

Joseph A. Chadwick studied History at the University of Hertfordshire, where he took a Creative Writing class to fill out his timetable. After graduating, he wrote a short, darkly comic stage play called *No Proof, No Pudding*, which went on to be produced and performed in 2016. *The Briarmen* was his first novel, which he released in 2021, setting up Crescent Swan Publishing to do so after he was unable to secure an agent for his manuscript. The novel went on to become a #1 Amazon UK best seller. He then tried his hand at publishing other writers through Crescent Swan, and in 2024 he published Tim Franks' speculative crime novel, *Days of Long Shadows*. In 2025 he released *Brombury*, a prequel to *The Briarmen*, and at the time of writing this is working on the third book in The Woods Beyond series.

A note from the Publisher

Thank you for reading this book, we hope you enjoyed it! If so, we'd really appreciate you leaving a review on Amazon and Goodreads, to help others find and enjoy this story.

Also, if you'd like to keep informed about our latest releases, please sign up to our mailing list at: www.crescentswan.com/news